the realm of last chances

the realm of
last chances

STEVE YARBROUGH

ALFRED A. KNOPF · NEW YORK · 2013

THIS IS A BORZOI BOOK
PUBLISHED BY ALFRED A. KNOPF

Copyright © 2013 by Steve Yarbrough
All rights reserved. Published in the United States by Alfred A. Knopf,
a division of Random House, Inc., New York, and in Canada
by Random House of Canada Limited, Toronto.
www.aaknopf.com

Knopf, Borzoi Books, and the colophon are
registered trademarks of Random House, Inc.

Grateful acknowledgment is made to Hal Leonard Corporation for
permission to reprint an excerpt from "Blue Moon of Kentucky," words and
music by Bill Monroe. Copyright © 1947 by Bill Monroe Music, Inc. (BMI),
renewed 1975. Bill Monroe Music, Inc. administered by BMG Rights
Management (US) LLC for United States only. All rights reserved.
Reprinted by permission of Hal Leonard Corporation.

Library of Congress Cataloging-in-Publication Data
Yarbrough, Steve, [date]
The realm of last chances / Steve Yarbrough.
pages   cm
ISBN 978-0-385-34950-5
1. Married people—Fiction.   2. City and town life.
3. New England—Fiction.   4. Domestic fiction.   I. Title.
PS3575.A717R43 2013
813'.54—dc23   2012050904

Jacket design by Jason Booher

Manufactured in the United States of America
First Edition

For Ewa

Now that this danger has passed I can see that nothing is as it was, and that such danger was in fact the one true meaning of life.

—Sándor Márai

kundera rocks

they were both fifty when they moved to Massachusetts, settling in a small town a few miles north of Boston. Like a lot of people around the country over the last few years, they'd recently experienced a run of bad luck.

Due to the state budget crisis, she'd lost her job as vice president for academic personnel at a large University of California campus in the Sacramento Valley. The year before her layoff, everyone, even the football coaches, had been subjected to mandatory furloughs, and things had turned ugly as the union blamed the shortfall on "managerial bloat." She'd had a hand in denying tenure to a number of professors, and many faculty members rejoiced when the administration was reorganized and she received her pink slip.

His business was construction. He was the man you engaged if you needed to have something small and delicate done and could pay for fine work. You had to accept certain things about him, though. He'd come and go on his own terms, and he would bring a small Bose along and listen to music throughout the day. He wouldn't have much to say. The fact that he was working for you didn't necessarily mean he'd return every phone call. People who'd put up with such idiosyncrasies when the economy was healthy proved a lot less understanding after the downturn. By the time they left the valley, he hadn't had a job for close to six months.

Her friends had always considered them an odd pair. He was from someplace down around Bakersfield, a tall, angular man who'd attended college only a semester before dropping out. His great passion was stringed instruments, and he could play the guitar, mandolin, banjo and Dobro well enough to earn money doing it if he'd chosen to, but the only audience he ever performed for was the other amateur musicians and assorted hangers-on who gathered at a crossroads grocery outside Sacramento on Friday nights. That was where they'd met, when she went there with a friend a year or so after the demise of her first marriage.

Of medium height, trim and fit, she'd earned a Ph.D. in comp lit and published a handful of articles on writers like Kafka, Broch and Svevo before moving into administration. With a laugh, she sometimes referred to her days in the classroom as "my previous life." She didn't think she'd been a very good teacher, perhaps because she had trouble reaching out to those she taught, who were often first-generation college students from migrant families. She loved cooking and sometimes wondered if she'd missed her calling and should've owned a restaurant.

She had what she always described as bad hair. Blond, it had always been thin, and as she aged it grew even thinner. The valley's arid climate didn't help. When she attended a conference in the Deep South or went back home to Pennsylvania, the moisture in the air lent it a bit more body. But it is what it is, she liked to say. She'd watched a couple middle-aged women—friends of her mother—quietly go crazy in the small town where she'd grown up, doing all sorts of bizarre things that caused others pain and kept the local gossips entertained, and she'd promised herself that when her time came to grow older she would accept it with grace.

Moving to Massachusetts was itself an act of acceptance. She got another job in academic personnel, this time at a state college, where she'd earn barely half her former salary, and they sold their house in the valley for barely half of what it had once been worth and bought a three-story colonial that needed lots of work. They wouldn't hire anyone to fix it up. Cal could do whatever needed doing to any house, anywhere.

. . .

The couple owned a dog, a ten-year-old black Lab named Suzy that they'd given themselves for their fifth anniversary. The first evening in the new house, with most of their things still in Bekins cartons, they decided to take her out for a walk. She'd had a rough trip across the country, mostly riding in the cab of Cal's pickup, though a few times they switched and let her get in the car with Kristin.

It was August and hotter than either of them had expected. "This feels like New Orleans," she said as they stepped off the porch. "I don't know if we can make it here without AC."

He gestured at the house directly across the street, where a pair of window units droned on the second floor. "I'll go look for one of those as soon as we get unpacked. We can put it in the bedroom. From what I read online, the most we'll ever get's three or four weeks of heat and humidity. Some years even less."

The neighborhood, according to the Realtor who'd helped them find the house, was a good one, on the dividing line between two distinctly different North Shore towns. The one to the east, Cedar Park, was a little more upscale, with a fine seafood restaurant and a Mexican place the lady claimed would pass muster even with Californians. It also had a bakery where you could buy real Irish soda bread, a couple of nice cafés, several antique stores and an antiquarian bookshop. They never bothered to remove the Christmas lights on Main Street, she told them, so even a balmy summer night seemed to hint of nutmeg and cider, and you almost expected to hear sleigh bells. An early Temperance Movement stronghold, it was still legally dry, though you could get a drink in both restaurants, provided you first ordered food. Montvale—the town to the west in which they technically resided, though its center was farther away—had a grittier, blue-collar air. According to Wikipedia, back in the seventies it had earned an entry in the *Guinness*

Book of World Records for the highest number of gas stations in a one-mile stretch. Most of those were gone now, apparently displaced by liquor stores: the day they made the offer on the house, Cal had counted seven. Chains like CVS, Walgreens, Stop & Shop and Shaw's were driving out the mom-and-pops, but he'd noted two independent hardware stores within a few hundred yards of each other. He hoped to scope them out over the next few days.

"A lot of things seem strange here," she said as they turned down the sidewalk.

"Like what?"

She nodded at the house they were passing. Like almost all the other Victorians and colonials in the neighborhood, it must have been built well over a hundred years ago. Through the window she could see a couple sitting there watching TV. Dropping her voice, she said, "Their car has an Obama sticker on it."

"Well, it's Massachusetts."

"But they're watching Bill O'Reilly, and that means Fox News."

"Maybe they're disillusioned. Aren't you?"

She knew how he voted—the same ticket she did—but sometimes didn't have a clue what he was thinking. He was prone to silence. It was a matter of aesthetics, she supposed, like his disdain for musicians who played too many notes. "Not with Obama," she answered.

He laughed. "With me?"

"Not you, either," she said, refusing to consider whether she was telling the whole truth.

He jiggled Suzy's chain. "Guess that means it's you, pooch."

They walked around the neighborhood for thirty or forty minutes, both of them wearing shorts and T-shirts, and in no time his were soaked. He'd always perspired a lot, but unlike her he relished being sweaty. In California, she'd often return home to discover that he'd switched off the AC, even on days when the temperature soared above a hundred. They had a black-bottomed pool overhung by tall pines, and she frequently found him there reclining on the steps at the shallow end, a visor pulled low over his eyes, three or four empty beer bottles on the poolside, his ever-present Bose providing string-band music from the nearby picnic table.

When Suzy paused to relieve herself, he handed Kristin the leash, pulled a plastic bag from his pocket and bent to collect the waste. They were in Cedar Park proper, at an intersection maybe three hundred yards downhill from their new house. While knotting the bag, he asked if she'd noticed how many streets were unmarked.

From here she could see two other intersections—but not a single street sign. "You're right," she said. "That's funny, isn't it? Do you think kids are stealing the signs?"

He stuck the first bag into a second one, then tied it up and put it in his pocket. He'd always done that, and it had always troubled her to know that he was walking along beside her with dog shit in his pocket. She'd objected once, but he said he'd rather have it there than dangling from his hand where everyone could see it. And for reasons she couldn't specify, that troubled her even more.

"I doubt kids are stealing their signs," he said. "They just don't put 'em up to begin with. They probably figure if you don't know where you're going, you most likely don't belong here. Who knows? They may be right."

She lay awake a long time that first night, drenched in perspiration and thinking about that observation until she gave up on sleep and got out of bed. In the bathroom she took a quick shower, toweled herself dry, slipped into the thin robe she'd worn in motels from one side of the continent to the other and went downstairs. In the darkened hallway Suzy lay twitching, no doubt lost in a troublesome dream, so she stroked her neck until she woke, and together they went outside. Kristin sat on the porch steps with Suzy perched beside her. "We'll get used to it here," she whispered, realizing that she really didn't have much more choice than the dog.

their first full day was spent unpacking boxes—more than two hundred, all told. Before beginning to arrange their contents, he insisted on breaking down the cardboard and stacking it neatly in the backyard. Once he learned where a recycling center was, he said, he'd haul it away.

Toting out all that cardboard required more than forty trips, many of which started on the upper floors. He got so hot he pulled off his T-shirt and hung it from the railing of their rear deck, but he enjoyed the exercise. Sitting behind the wheel in his pickup for five straight days, he'd had too much time to think, and most of his thoughts were dark. Every time Kristin's car disappeared from the rearview mirror, he whipped out his cell phone to call and make sure she hadn't gotten lost or had an accident or turned around and headed back. Certainly, what awaited them on the opposite side of the country was anybody's guess.

After depositing the last boxes on the shoulder-high stack, he surveyed the houses on either side as well as the ones behind them over a flimsy fence. He could be seen, he knew, from any number of windows, just as he'd been able to see into any number of backyards when he looked out of his own third-story window at dusk the previous evening and observed a woman—early fifties, reddish hair, chunky build, khaki knee shorts and a blue Red Sox T-shirt—walking around the corner of the house directly behind theirs. She looked over her shoulder as if fearful somebody might be following. Apparently satisfied that no one was, she pulled a pack of cigarettes from her pocket and, while he watched, stuck one between her teeth. She withdrew a lighter, and the flame flicked on and off. Then she squatted with her back against the wall and enjoyed the cigarette, her eyes closed the whole time. He knew he ought to quit watching—it made him feel dirty—but couldn't tear himself away.

On a trip to Shaw's to buy coffee and paper towels, he spotted some window units sandwiched into the seasonal section between marshmallows and charcoal. Their second evening in the house, he installed one in their bedroom.

Finally cool, she slept a full nine hours, waking shortly before seven. At some point during the night she'd heard him climb out of bed, the door then opening and closing. They were back to normal, she guessed: her asleep, him awake. That had been the routine for years. She never knew what he did after he left, but sometimes in the morning she'd find a guitar or mandolin lying on the living room couch, a couple of picks on the coffee table beside an empty whiskey bottle.

On the first trip they'd ever taken together, to a bluegrass festival in Napa Valley, she'd loved watching him move from one group of parking-lot pickers to another, joining in on whatever tune they were playing, never at a loss. He didn't even ask what key the song was in, just slid a little clamping device up or down the guitar neck and started strumming. He told her it was called a capo. "When you've got one, all you need to do's play in G or D. Put the capo at the second fret and G becomes A. D becomes E, and so on." That night they ate dinner at a country inn and drank two bottles of wine, and though they'd reserved a pair of rooms they needed only one. Opening her eyes the next morning, she found him propped on his elbow, studying her face as if he hoped to memorize her features. His guitar was standing beside the bed. "Play something for me," she said.

Now, however, his instruments were thousands of miles away in the home of a former colleague of hers who soon would FedEx them, and he was beside her on his back, his mouth wide open and an arm thrown over her chest. She lay there looking at his long, thin fingers, cupped as if in supplication. Having been with him for more than fifteen years, she thought she knew how large his hand was, but for an instant it looked as garish as a flesh-colored fielder's glove. That it could once have been the source of pleasure seemed impossible. She gently shifted his arm aside—*Unnh,* he muttered—and slid out of bed.

In the room next door, which would eventually serve as her study, she flipped on the light. Books were piled against the wall, on top of her desk, even underneath it. When she stepped into this room for the first time a few weeks ago on their home-hunting expedition, a pair of bunk beds came together in one corner, and the floor was littered with the kind of junk only boys could own: two or three baseballs, an aluminum bat, several pairs of smelly, mud-encrusted sneakers of various sizes, a surprisingly realistic replica of an AK-47, a desktop computer with a keyboard that had a huge wad of chewing gum stuck to the space bar. A milk crate was full of video games, and some of the titles made her shudder: *Resident Evil 4, World of Warcraft, Killer 7.* On the wall hung a Tom Brady poster. Somebody had used a black Magic Marker to render the famous quarterback toothless.

She'd been afraid to look at Cal that day. During the previous week they'd seen so many homes she'd lost count, and he'd detected major flaws in most of them before they even got inside. But when they entered this one he kept silent until he was standing in the opening between the living room and dining room, where he thumped the white facing. "These belly casings," he observed, "most likely have pocket doors behind them. They were common in houses like this. They look real nice and can help preserve warmth." He pointed at the fireplace in the corner: "That's unusual in a dining room." Examining it, he said, "Looks like the original firebox. Carved brass." In the basement he ran his hand over one of the beams. "Hemlock," he told her. "It's good strong timber, resistant to rot. They ran single spans in here, too." By then, she knew that after they told the Realtor good-bye and returned to their hotel, he'd sigh and say they might as well do it. They'd make an offer on this house, and it would be accepted, and in five or six weeks she'd be standing right where she was now, trying to find the new beginning she wanted to believe must be inherent in each ending except the last one.

She drew her nightgown over her head and put on the shorts and T-shirt she'd tossed on her desk. She went downstairs and fed Suzy, then laced up her tennis shoes and hooked the leash to the dog's collar. In California, especially in spring and summer, the days often got hot before she really got going. While "resolve" was a word she'd never had much use for—generally, people who employed it as a verb lacked it as a quality—she'd resolved to begin her mornings earlier in this new place. She'd become uncomfortably aware that fewer of them remained.

They started off, Suzy dropping her nose to sniff the ground every few feet. Newspapers lay on a couple of porches, reminding her they ought to subscribe to the *Globe*. A couple of houses down, on her side of the street, an elderly woman sat in a porch rocker sipping her coffee, and despite the reputation of New Englanders for being unfriendly she raised her hand and waved. Such a simple gesture shouldn't have meant all that much, but right then it did. Kristin lifted her hand and smiled but kept on moving, because her throat had tightened and she wasn't sure she could speak.

In summers when she was a child and out of school, her father would have been sitting in a porch rocker, too, drinking his coffee and reading the Harrisburg paper. But he never would've seen anybody out walking a dog; back then they roamed the neighborhood at will, and nobody saw anything wrong with that. Her family lived on a narrow strip of land between Penns Creek and the Susquehanna, and dogs didn't run away or get lost because the bridge over the creek was an open-grate construction they couldn't cross. Sometimes you'd see the Airedale that belonged to their next-door neighbors, the Connultys, standing there looking as if he might try it, but eventually whatever reason he possessed would take over, forcing him to turn around and head for home.

Sooner or later on those mornings in the late sixties her mother would get up, go outside and join her father, and through her window she would hear them exchange pleasantries.

"How are you, dear?"

"Fine. And you?"

"Perfectly wonderful. I don't think I ever rested better."

"Want part of the paper?"

"No, thank you. I believe I'll just sit for a while and listen to the morning."

Whatever sounds the morning made, her own ear wasn't attuned to them. Sometimes she'd fall asleep again, but more often than not she'd pad downstairs, and before long her father would come back inside and begin making breakfast.

At the time it hadn't occurred to her that her family was living the kind of life that many people around the country were starting to question. As far as she knew, it was just normal, and if it was normal for them, she figured, it must be for everyone else. But once or twice she'd wandered into the living room, where her father was watching the evening news, and seen footage of young people lying around in the mud up in Woodstock with glazed expressions on their faces, or wielding bullhorns on the steps of some building in Berkeley or Madison, or burning a flag on the National Mall.

"Why are they doing that?" she once asked.

Her dad was having his evening drink, a double shot of Tullamore Dew. A copy of *Look* lay spread open on his knee. The sound on the Zenith was turned down so low you could barely hear it. "Doing what?"

She pointed at the screen. "Burning the flag."

He squinted at the TV. "They're against the war."

"Will setting the flag on fire make the war stop?"

"No."

"Then why do they do it?"

"It's a symbol."

"Of what?"

"Everything they don't like about America. Or at least a lot of what they don't like."

"What else don't they like?"

He drained his glass of whiskey, closed the magazine and laid it on the floor by his easy chair. Then, moving with the stealthy grace of a big man who'd once played football at the small college on the other side of town, he leaped out of the chair, gathered her in his arms and pretended he was rocking her in a cradle, even though she must have been seven or eight years old. "They don't like *this*," he said.

She was looking right up into his rosy face. When the high school where he and her mother taught held its Christmas parties, he always played Santa, so deeply had he impressed himself on everyone as a man of good cheer. "This *what*?"

"Family bliss," he said, faint fumes on his breath. "They hate it worse than cancer."

As if his statement were the moral equivalent of a dollar bill, she accepted it at face value, leaving aside any question she might have had as to why anybody, anywhere, at any time, could hate the sight of a happy family. She was in her father's arms, and he was holding her so high above the Zenith that she no longer could see those people burning the flag and within seconds had forgotten they even existed.

She walked around for more than an hour, familiarizing herself with Cedar Park. There was an elementary school five or six blocks from their house, and a little beyond that, on the other side of the commuter rail line that she'd been told had its terminus in Haverhill, she passed Cedar Park High, deserted now except for a couple pickups she assumed must belong to the janitorial staff. Otherwise Tremont Street was lined with body shops, auto-parts stores, lube centers. She saw a car wash, too, and decided that either today or tomorrow she'd ask Cal to run her Volvo through. A thick layer of road scum covered the car, and some of it had probably attached itself before they even left the valley. It was odd to think that a speck of dirt picked up on one end of the continent could have made it to the other, but she supposed it wasn't out of the question.

When she trudged back up the hill into Montvale, she was bone-tired. Suzy was doing even worse, panting like her heart was about to burst, her loose tongue sprinkling the sidewalk. At one point Kristin thought she was going to lie down and refuse to walk any farther. If that happened, she'd have to sit there beside her until Suzy made up her mind to get moving. She couldn't carry an eighty-pound Lab.

But they finally reached her street, where a fair amount of activity seemed to be in progress. In one yard, two boys were tossing a baseball back and forth, their father backing out in a black pickup that said KELLY'S HEATING AND PLUMBING on the door, and in the next yard another boy was laying out balls and mallets, getting ready for a game of croquet. The old woman who'd been sitting in the rocker the last time she walked by was now down on her knees beneath a lush hydrangea, wielding a small spade.

Across the street, on the porch of a blue Queen Anne with bay windows on all three floors and badly chipped shingles, a man leaned over to pick up his paper. He had salt-and-pepper hair, looked to be about forty and wore a beige terry-cloth bathrobe. He opened the paper, glanced at the front page, then stood up straight, and his gaze met hers before traveling downward in a manner she found vaguely insolent. "Hey," he called, "where'd you get that T-shirt?"

Uncertain what she was wearing, she looked down to see. It was one she'd bought years ago in San Francisco, at a Clean Well Lighted Place for Books. There was a drawing of Milan Kundera on it and, beneath his image, the legend KUNDERA ROCKS. "I got it in California," she said. "We just moved here."

"I saw the plates on the car and truck." He stepped off the porch and into the street. "I'm Matt. Welcome to the neighborhood."

As she and Suzy moved toward him, it occurred to her that, in a manner of speaking, she might soon become his boss, that he could easily be a professor at North Shore State College, which was only a few miles away. Even in the most educated part of the country, how many nonacademics would you meet on the street who'd respond like this to Kundera? "I'm Kristin," she said.

"Pleased to meet you." He pointed at the dog. "And who's that?"

"Suzy."

He bent and patted her head. "Looks like a real sweetheart."

"I think we walked too long. She's not used to hills and humidity."

"Plenty of both around here," he said, once more glancing at her chest. "You like Kundera?"

The question wasn't complicated, but an honest answer would be. She didn't read nearly as much as she used to, and she hadn't read the Czech writer's last three or four books. She didn't even know the titles. Once she left the faculty and moved into administration, she began spending a lot of time in meetings and even more time poring over personnel files, checking people's credentials and publications. When she did read a novel, it usually had short chapters and a linear plot. "I liked his early work a lot," she said.

"Me too. What's the cutoff for you?"

She tried to recall the name of the last one she'd read. "*Immortality*, maybe?"

"It's even further back for me. I thought the work thinned out badly when he began writing in French. But then, you know, he lost his fictional universe, just like le Carré."

He was making her feel stupid and, since she knew she wasn't, she wanted to end the conversation. "Well, you may have a point," she said.

"Sure. Because of the pyrotechnics, people don't think of Kundera as a Cold War novelist, but that was his landscape. When he lost it—well, it's about like taking Mississippi away from Faulkner. You've got to know where you are to write about it well. Don't you think?"

What she thought was that she'd better find out whether or not they'd be working at the same place. One lesson she'd absorbed in California was that you needed to keep your distance from the faculty. When the time came to make a tough decision, you shouldn't let sentiment intrude. So many good people were looking for jobs that you couldn't justify rewarding the unaccomplished or inept. "You sound like you've got a serious interest in literature," she said. "Are you a professor, by any chance?"

This provoked the most curious response; she'd think about it off and on for the remainder of the day and would even wake up the next morning with it still on her mind. He looked up the street and then down at his feet as his facial muscles lost all semblance of tone. He tucked the paper under his arm and said he worked at an Italian deli on Main Street in Montvale and that sometime she ought to try their lobster salad. Then he climbed the porch steps and went inside.

the drinnans had taken up residence on Essex Street in 1961. The husband—Terrance, though everybody called him Terry—had opened an independent insurance agency two years earlier, when he and his wife were still living in an apartment in Cedar Park. They chose the Queen Anne on Essex because it straddled the border between the two towns in which almost all of his customers lived. Terry knew ahead of time that it was going to be sold—he carried the fire insurance on it—and this information allowed him to make an offer and have it accepted before the house actually appeared in the real-estate listings.

His office was just three blocks away, on East Border Road, the main link between the two towns. The proximity of his business allowed him to walk to and from work and to return home most days for lunch. He did so even in winter, no matter how deep the snow was, persisting in his habit even though this involved descending a treacherous hill—a task that became more arduous as the sixties turned into the seventies and then the eighties and he entered what would, in his own case, be a foreshortened middle age. He liked to joke that the majority of auto accidents he was forced to make payouts on occurred on the same street where his agency stood. Cedar Park residents gave East Border Road a workout every Friday and Saturday night, traveling between their homes and the liquor stores in Montvale.

Almost everybody in both towns knew and respected Terry Drinnan, but when most people thought of the family it was his wife who came to mind. Whereas he'd moved to the North Shore only after graduating from Holy Cross, Elizabeth's relatives had lived in Montvale for close to a hundred years: she'd grown up in an octagonal house on Pond Street that had once been owned by Colonel Elbridge Gerry, who, though a citizen of some distinction, was unrelated to the famous statesman of the same name.

No one ever called Elizabeth Drinnan "Liz" or "Betsy." She wouldn't have minded if they did, and in fact she often wondered why they didn't, though she never voiced her puzzlement to another living soul. She thought maybe there was something off-putting about her, some quirk in her makeup that made her seem distant, even when surrounded by friends, of which she had many. The baby shower given in her honor following the birth of her son was the largest anyone could recall, cars lining Essex for two or three blocks and a few parked all the way back on East Border.

Like her mother and both of her sisters, Elizabeth became a mainstay of the Fortnightly Club of Montvale, a women's group "devoted to the preservation of natural resources, the promotion of the arts, education, civic involvement and world peace." She served twice as president of the local chapter and, in the midnineties, after the death of her husband, was elected for a term to the same office in the General Federation of Women's Clubs of Massachusetts. Plenty of evidence proved that people liked her, and if she'd never achieved best-friend status with anybody, neither had she ever made an enemy.

That was what she told herself when she learned of her son's troubles: Thank God I've never made enemies. By then she'd been a widow for thirteen years, living on a fixed income that seemed to shrink daily. Paint was peeling off the house in great swathes, the front steps were half eaten by Ice Melt, the furnace had entered its third decade and she was still driving the last car Terry had bought, a 1991 Skylark, but she continued to dress well and take proper care of herself. People kept inviting her to social events just as they always had, and every few months one friend or another would attempt to introduce her to a man her age or slightly older who'd recently lost his wife. She declined those offers but was unfailingly polite.

It was a good thing, she decided, that she'd never asked favors for herself and that she'd lived within her means, constrained as they might be. She entertained this thought as she waited in the lobby of Cedar Park Savings and Loan one day in late January 2005. Outside, big soft snowflakes were disappearing as soon as they hit the pavement. The temperature was due to fall, though, and by tomorrow morning, according to what she'd heard on the radio, the North Shore could expect somewhere between ten and fourteen inches. The grayness of the afternoon matched her mood exactly. The previous day, George W. Bush had been inaugurated for the second time, and she'd sat alone in her living room watching TV with the sound turned off, knowing as surely as she'd ever known anything that she wouldn't live long enough to see the country choose a better leader. She was seventy-one years old, and it hadn't been quite twenty-four hours since her son asked if there was any chance that she could possibly help him raise thirty-five thousand dollars.

"I pissed, shit and came, all at the same time," Dushay said while he, Matt and Frankie worked on a trio of four-foot subs for a retirement party at Fellsway Fence Company. Frankie always insisted they finish the special orders before the lunch crowd arrived. Selling sandwiches was 70 percent of his business and working people didn't have all day to stand in line.

"See, I'd gotten banged up the previous night in the big game against Reading," Dushay continued, "and to kill the pain I went to sleep on a heating pad. Damn thing burned a hole in my hip, and then all my fucking effluvia got in the wound and created a septic situation, and next thing I know I'm in the hospital dying. Which is tragic—right?—because at the time I'm just sixteen. My old man told me later that the doctors said I was a goner. And I'll tell you something, Ziz. I'm not one of those people who questions the existence of God. I know He's up there, because while I was dying I *saw* Him. His Son, anyways—Him and the Virgin Mary. Only thing was, Jesus looked older than she did. I don't know how to explain that. Some shit's just plain mysterious."

"Douche, I got limited interest right now in theology," Frankie Zizza said, dropping black olives down the middle of a sub in a perfect row. His wife, though raised Catholic, had recently converted to some off-brand Protestant denomination with a high percentage of Tea Party members. Frankie himself had been proclaiming his atheism ever since high school. "You ask me, religion's ruining the goddamn country."

"It's not religion I'm talking about, Ziz. It's mystery. It's the mystery at the fucking heart of things."

"The mystery at the middle of my fucking heart," Frankie said, "is what made me hire this douche bag in the first place. If somebody could answer *that* one, I'd say he was positively Socratic."

The previous afternoon, a customer had ordered a pound of roast beef. Since the tray in the display case had only a few strands left, Dushay strolled into the back room, pushed aside the better part of a sixteen-pound hunk that Matt had opened just that morning and took out a new one. Frankie bought them from a high-end wholesaler who used no preservatives or caramel coating, so they didn't last long, and each one cost close to eighty dollars.

Lawrence Dushay was in his late twenties and a dead ringer for the actor Steve Buscemi, which helped the Saugus police identify him a couple years ago when he tried to fence a bunch of laptops stolen from Best Buy. He was one of several guys Frankie had hired after they got out of jail; most of them had worked out well, as he liked to note, and two owned businesses themselves now. Dushay, however, was proving peculiarly inept. His first day on the job, ogling a female customer while slicing pastrami, he caught his sleeve in the Berkel and might've lost a finger or two if Matt hadn't reached over and shut off the machine. He overcharged some and undercharged others. He cut thick slices when people asked for thin and vice versa. One day he showed up in flip-flops.

"You're not still pissed about that roast beef, are you?" he asked now.

"Pissed?" Frankie said. "No, Douche, of course not. Why would I be pissed? I'm really happy about it. I'm especially pleased for Eddie and Wolf."

"Who're they?"

"Eddie and Wolf are my fucking mutts, Douche. They'll be the ultimate beneficiaries of your generosity. Day after tomorrow they'll chow down on eight or ten pounds of rotten roast beef."

They finished the subs, and Dushay was dispatched to deliver them. As soon as the door closed behind him, Zizza shook his head. "That guy," he said, "is a walking oil spill."

Matt pulled off the gloves they had to wear when handling food. They were made of powder-free polyethylene and supposedly could not cause an allergy, but lately he'd developed red patches on both hands, around the base of each knuckle. As he'd learned some time ago, every profession has its hazards. "He might've been better off if they'd kept him in jail," he said, then instantly wished he hadn't offered that opinion.

Frankie had been his best friend from first grade through high school, though nobody could figure out what drew them together: Matt Drinnan, bookish, upper middle class, college bound, and Frankie Zizza, a working-class Italian who did so badly in school that his father finally persuaded the principal to release him each day at lunchtime, so he could hustle down to the deli and learn to make the sandwiches he'd spend the rest of his life selling. Each of them had always been able to tell when he'd aroused the other's displeasure, and Matt knew he'd incurred Frankie's just now.

"You really think," Zizza asked, "that Dushay would be better off someplace like Shirley, where a couple of BGs could hold him down every night while a third one banged him in the ass?"

"No."

"Then we've achieved rare concord, MD. Because guess what?"

"What?"

"I don't think so either." Frankie pulled his own gloves off and walked around in front of the display case to the table where the coffee dispensers stood. He filled a Styrofoam cup and took a swallow, then promptly leaned over and spat it into the trash can. "Fucking Douche Bag!" he cried, slapping his forehead. "Again he makes the coffee out of yesterday's grounds."

Around eleven, the lunch crowd began to stream in, the motion detector above the door emitting one beep after another, a line starting to form. Day in and day out, you saw the same people, usually at the same time, and one thing that surprised Matt when he started working here was that they tended to order the same stuff on each visit. At eleven fifteen, Ryan Kelly, who owned Kelly's Heating and Plumbing, would come in with mud on his knees and ask for the chicken cutlet sandwich with provolone and prosciutto. Billy Sutherland, the branch manager at the Main Street B of A, would appear at twelve sharp and request a boneless buffalo chicken sub on a braided sesame roll and a seafood salad on focaccia. While waiting for his sandwiches, he always grabbed two bags of Utz sour cream and onion chips and two bottles of root beer.

Matt observed their predictability with something akin to horror, but after a while he became their accomplice: he quit asking what they wanted, instead saying, "The usual?"

Like robots they nodded and, as if he'd been programmed, he slapped the same meat on the same bread, along with the same condiments. Once, when he and Frankie were cleaning up at the end of the day, he explained why he found such repetition appalling. "I mean, if you're going to buy your lunch at the same place every day, at exactly the same time, why not at least try something different? Would it really upset Ryan's equilibrium if for once in his life he ate pastrami with spicy mustard on a bulkie?"

Frankie was sponging off the counter, just as he had at closing time every day since he was thirteen years old. " 'The mass of men lead lives of quiet desperation.' You know who said that, don't you?"

"Of course. But I'm surprised you do."

"My kid told me about it. But Thoreau was full of shit, and so are you." He stepped over to the sink and wrung out the sponge, twisting it a little harder than necessary. "Most people just don't crave as much stimulation as you do, MD. They know there's a lot they haven't experienced and never will, but they're okay with that. Because some of what they don't know might flip their lives upside down if they *did*. You know what I mean?"

Matt didn't bother to reply. It was always there between them: unspoken condemnation liberally seasoned by thirty-five years of unbroken devotion.

Today he made Ryan Kelly "the usual" and watched him leave to eat lunch in peace before replacing yet another leaky faucet or clearing one more blocked drain. He prepared Billy's regular order, and when the three drunks who daily came in together appeared, he served them their baloney sandwiches and undercharged them like Frankie had instructed, tossing a free bag of chips into each sack. Then, as things were just beginning to taper off, he looked up and got the first genuine surprise of the day when the door opened and Paul Nowicki stepped through it.

A lifelong resident of Montvale whose wire-rims might have made him look scholarly had he not been so big, Nowicki owned one of two hardware stores on Main Street. He was four or five years older than Matt and, like Frankie, had taken over the family business when his father retired. When people used the term "solid citizen," they generally had someone like Paul in mind. For years he'd looked after his sister, who'd been born with some type of rare heart disease. You'd see him helping her into and out of the car, walking her to church, waiting for her at the doctor's office. He never had a family of his own until she died, and everyone figured it was because of his devotion. If he refused to care for her, who would? "That's just the kind of guy he is," they'd say. He was an usher at Saint Patrick's and a member of the board of selectmen. Because he'd always loved dogs, he helped establish the local chapter of PAWS, the Pets and Animal Welfare Society.

As far back as Matt could recall, he'd been unable to think of Paul without also picturing the team of Clydesdales that pulled the Budweiser beer wagon in TV commercials. He was big, he was reliable; he did nothing purely for show. All right, hell: he was *noble*. The only problem was that a little over four years ago, he'd married Matt's ex-wife and become stepfather to both of his daughters.

Whether or not all activity ceased the moment Paul walked in, Matt would never know. He just knew that it seemed to. Later on, he couldn't remember which customers were still present or if they appeared to be taking note, though he hoped not. "Hey, Paul," he said, relieved that the words actually came out. "What can I do for you?"

To his amazement Nowicki blushed, even the tip of his nose turning red. "I was wondering," he said, "if I could speak to you in private? Would that be all right?"

Matt turned to Frankie, who was taking a record amount of time to rewrap a chunk of hot ham, giving the task his full attention. He acted as if he hadn't heard the request, though he must have. Rather than ask him if it would be all right to step away, Matt pulled off his gloves, lifted the counter leaf and led Paul into the back room.

The space was small and, with a man Nowicki's size in there, crowded. Matt stood with his back to the counter where the char broiler rested. It felt like a defensive position.

Paul pointed at the grill. "I didn't know you guys cooked in here."

"Every now and then somebody'll come in wanting a breakfast sandwich. That's about the only thing we sell that needs to be cooked."

"Is it on the menu?"

"No. But if you want one, Frankie'll make it."

"That's good to know. But of course that's not what I came to talk about."

"I never thought it was."

Paul stuffed his hands into his pockets. "Look, Matt," he said, "I try to stay out of here. You know that, don't you? Before you went to work for Frankie, I probably came by three or four times a week. There's not a better Italian sub anywhere."

Matt shrugged. "You can come in whenever you choose. It's a free country, and Frankie could always use the business."

"I know that. But I think you and I have both been operating under the assumption that you've got your sphere and I've got mine. You used to come in the hardware from time to time, but not anymore."

"I haven't been undertaking any home-improvement projects lately."

"You're being ironic, I guess," Nowicki said, "but that's actually what I came to talk to you about." He said that the previous weekend, when the girls returned home after their regular sleepover, they made a few remarks that got Carla upset. "Understand, they weren't complaining, they were just laughing about stuff and having a good time, but their mom sees things differently."

The "stuff" in question was the decay they'd observed in the house that had formerly belonged to their grandmother. The hot-water faucet was gone from the second-floor bathtub, and the only way you could turn it on was to twist the stem with the pliers that lay on the windowsill. The toilet handle in the half bath was broken, though you could flush it manually by pulling the top off the tank, sticking your hand in and lifting the stopper. Two boards on the back porch had rotted clean through, the drain in the kitchen sink kept backing up and disgorging some kind of soupy substance that stank to high heaven, all the light fixtures were so full of dead insects you could sometimes hear their bodies frying. Angie and Lexa had evidently painted quite a picture, making the house sound like the one Herman Munster's family occupied.

In the far corner of the deli's back room, there was an enormous reach-in freezer that had three doors and could have held a huge amount of frozen food, except for one thing: it didn't work. It hadn't for at least twenty years, according to Frankie, but he'd never gotten rid of it because it wouldn't fit through the opening into the front room; it had been there in 1984 when his father renovated, and nobody considered the possibility that it might ever quit and need to be removed. Matt focused on that freezer now as a means of keeping himself anchored. Lately, he felt insubstantial, weightless, as if he were merely the idea of a person rather than the real thing. People weren't just a past or a present or a set of extinguished expectations. They had to have a future, too, and for himself he failed to see one. He felt as if he could readily be brushed off, as if right now, should he choose to, Nowicki could swat him aside as if he were no more momentous than a fly or a gnat.

"Matt?" Paul said. "You know I don't mean to offend you, right? I'm just trying to call attention to the problem because . . .

well, it really bothers Carla. So, look, if you'd like to come over after closing time and get some stuff for the place—some faucets, maybe, and a handle for that toilet, a few cans of outdoor latex, some drain opener, insecticide, whatever—I've got 'em, and they're yours. Hell, I even have lumber. I could help you do whatever needs doing to that back porch."

There had been a time when Matt Drinnan could talk his way out of almost any jam, when explanations and justifications and complex and simple evasions came to him so easily it got boring. Then one morning, in the basement of the Harvard Book Emporium, surrounded by millions upon millions of words, he tapped his own verbal reservoir and found it empty. He couldn't think of a single thing to say that day, and he couldn't think of a single thing to say now.

The silence took as much of a toll on the other man as it did on him. Finally, Nowicki reached out and wrapped a massive arm around him, whispering, "Jesus, Matt, I'm sorry."

their first few years together, Kristin knew nothing about Cal's father. Then she learned enough not to want to find out more.

While his father had never served in the military, he used the word "ground" like a real soldier. Cal had reached this conclusion in a Sacramento metroplex in the fall of 1993. He was there to watch the movie *Gettysburg,* and his moment of revelation came when Major General George G. Meade, played by Richard Anderson, arrived at a gathering of Union officers on the evening of the battle's first day. Addressing Brian Mallon, who played Winfield S. Hancock, Meade asked, "Is this good ground, General?" To which Hancock raised an eyebrow and replied, "*Very* good ground." They saw it as a place where their side could slaughter the opponents rather than suffering it themselves, and that was how his father must have viewed any number of properties as he drove around the northeastern edges of Bakersfield in the midseventies, gazing out the truck window at one tract or another barren but for the occasional manzanita. "That's good ground," he'd say. "*Damn* good ground."

What he saw that others missed was anybody's guess. All Cal himself saw was the kind of vacant space where you and your friends, if you had them, could pull off the road, drive a hundred yards or so into what should have been the desert and drink a little beer or get high. On an exceptionally good night, he guessed, you might even get laid, but back then he'd never had any nights like that.

His father had known quite a few of them when he was Cal's age, a fact he didn't ever bother to hide. He'd grown up on a farm in Oklahoma, but to hear him tell it he'd spent most of his time harvesting something besides corn. "In high school," he said on one of the evenings when he forced his son to sit with him in the wood-paneled room he called the bar, underneath the head of an elk he'd shot in Montana, "my best friend was a guy named Walter. He played tailback, I played fullback. He was number twenty-one, I was twenty-two. About halfway through our sophomore season, we made a bet on who could get to his number fastest. You know what I mean?" He didn't wait to find out if his son knew this. "I'm not talking about touchdowns," he said, poking him in the ribs so hard he gasped. "I made my number after the third game my junior year. Poor old Walter didn't hit twenty-one till just before Christmas."

At the time they were living in a mission-style house with smooth stucco siding, a red-tile roof, clover-shaped windows, a covered archway and dark interiors. His mother referred to it as "the dungeon." She hadn't liked the design and didn't want his father to build it, but what she wanted never mattered much. It was big, it was showy, it had all the right coordinates. It was a good place to entertain the people his father had decided to buy.

Every member of the Bakersfield City Council eventually showed up there—sometimes singly, sometimes in the company of two or three other councilmen as well as several young women who worked at his dad's company. The head coach of the Bakersfield State football team was a frequent visitor as well. On one memorable occasion he brought four of his players along—huge, beefy guys—and the high point of the raucous evening came when he ordered each of them onto the enormous dining table to perform push-ups for the pleasure of the other guests. His father accompanied these "friends" on trips to places like San Juan, Cabo and Puerto Vallarta, all of which he paid for, and while he never took Cal's mother on those junkets, he did sometimes invite one or more of his female employees. He also financed hunting trips to Alaska and once took the mayor to Belize.

The whole time he was doing those things, he was also buying cheap land north and east of the city, and all of it was quickly rezoned. "Time'll come," he'd predict, "when Bakersfield'll run clean into Sequoia. You'll be seeing strip malls in Bearpaw Meadow."

That never happened, but over the next twenty years his father's firm built a third of all the new homes in town. Most of them, unlike his own, were poorly constructed, but they looked good on the day the new owners moved in and offered a lot of space for the dollar. "Coat a turd in chocolate," he liked to say, "and folks'll smack their lips." If occasionally some irate homeowner filed a lawsuit because seams had developed in the stucco, or the foundation was cracked, or the sewers failed to drain, or the ventilation system was circulating mold through the house and making the kids sick, his father could always hire the best lawyers. And if by chance they failed to prevail—well, judges liked to go to Cabo, too.

The indictment didn't come until 1998, by which time Cal was living hundreds of miles away and had already been married for almost three years. In 1985 he'd legally changed his last name, so when the story broke nobody who knew him could have associated him with the man at the center of the FBI sting dubbed Operation End-Zone. Yet he told Kristin the truth, laying the Sacramento paper on the table as she was eating her breakfast. He tapped the headline with his finger. "I haven't been straight with you," he said. "I told you my father was dead. He's not. That's him, right there."

She swallowed her oatmeal and looked at the photo, in which three men stood before a bank of microphones. The one in the middle, flanked by two attorneys, bore an unmistakable resemblance to her husband. He had angular cheekbones, and his eyes were deeply set. He was grinning, which didn't make a lot of sense, given the headline:

BAKERSFIELD DEVELOPER INDICTED
Charges Include Bribery, Mail Fraud, Witness Tampering

Then she noticed the name of the accused: Stegall, not Stevens. Immediately she experienced the same light-headed sensation she'd felt the previous summer when they rode the cog railway to the top of Pikes Peak, except that this had nothing to do with altitude. "If that's your father," she said, "why does he have a different name?"

"I changed mine," he said. "Before we met."

"You changed yours."

"Yes."

"Why?"

"That isn't easy to answer."

"Try."

To his credit, he did. Still standing over her, he said he wanted to become everything his father wasn't. He sought only small jobs, never big ones, and wanted to perform all the work himself. He used the best materials. If something went wrong, he endeavored to make it right. He never pursued money just to have it. The only possessions he loved were his musical instruments, and though some of them would have been valuable to others, much like a Sheraton satinwood table might be, he valued them solely because of the sounds they could make. He never coveted anything for ownership's sake.

She heard him out. And then she said, "A lot of people want to be everything their fathers weren't. But they don't go out and change their names. And they don't lie to their wives about their past."

"A lot of them lie to their wives about their present," he said. "Which is something I've never done and won't ever do."

She hadn't always been straight with him, either. She'd claimed to be relieved when her first husband left, that she was ready for the marriage to end. He had no idea that she'd lost thirty pounds in six months, that her doctor thought she might have cancer of the adrenal gland or that the university granted her a paid leave in an effort to help her recover from a disease for which there was no treatment. You had to cure yourself, and she did.

"My first husband lied to me about an affair," she said now. "He didn't lie about who he was."

He walked over to the coffeemaker and poured himself a cup. "Who he was," he said, "was the kind of guy that goes out and has an affair. My dad was that kind of guy, too. Only my mom always knew. And couldn't do shit about it."

"Couldn't? Or didn't want to?"

"Didn't know how to," he said. He set the mug on the counter, and a little coffee sloshed out that he didn't bother to wipe up. "She was just a small-town girl from Chouteau, Oklahoma, who moved to California with an asshole. Then the asshole got rich. And that was the end of her."

"Where is she now?"

"I'd like to think she's in heaven, since she spent her earthly life in hell. But she's actually in a hole in the ground."

"A real hole?" she asked. "Or one you've made up?"

"This hole's as real as any hole's ever been. I'll take you there to see it if you'd like."

She rose, carried her bowl to the sink and ran it full of warm water. Then she pulled a paper towel off the rack and wiped up the coffee. "Is there anything else I don't know?" she asked. While she waited for an answer, they heard a tremendous crash, and she looked up to see the glass vibrating in the sliding door that led to the patio.

She ran over and shoved it open and saw an oriole lying on the ground beside her lilac bush, and the poor thing wasn't even moving. "Cal?" she called.

He was already there. He bent over and lifted it up—something she'd never been able to bring herself to do, because birds were so *different*—and gently stroked its feathers before resting a forefinger on its breast. He closed his eyes like he always did when playing a solo on the mandolin or guitar. Then he opened them again and set the bird on the picnic table. "Its heart's still beating," he said, his voice tinged with doubt, as though a beating heart, in and of itself, provided evidence of nothing at all.

Is there anything else I don't know?

On the day Kristin reported for work at her new job, he again considered the question that the unfortunate oriole had saved him from having to answer. Wasn't there always something else you didn't know, even about the one you knew best? To think otherwise was either downright stupid or willfully naïve, and his wife was neither. If she'd never posed the question again, it was by design. Her willingness to drop the topic, to accept the fact that her husband of three years wasn't who she thought he was, came back to him from time to time like one of those pop-up ads for malware removal, assuring him he ought to be worried. And from time to time he did worry.

In the two weeks they'd lived in the house on Essex Street, he hadn't been inside by himself for more than two or three hours. They'd spent their days moving methodically from the first floor to the second and then to the third, putting their household items in order, hanging pictures on the walls, positioning the Bose close by so he could listen to music. Always, though, there had been the sound of her voice, as soothing now as it had occasionally been annoying back in California. The notes not played, he'd always believed, were at least as important as the ones you did play, and the same was true with words: some things didn't need to be said, but sometimes she couldn't stop saying them. He never felt an urge to know what she'd done at work on any given day, which dean or vice president she'd had lunch with, which faculty member she'd had to call into her office because she'd been caught falsifying student evaluations. He hated everything he knew about colleges and universities, how they packed too many people into too small a space and called on them at any moment to ask for the answer to a question that didn't interest anybody. He distrusted the notion that there was a finite body of knowledge worth communicating to others. Professors, he thought, were mostly con artists who'd been captured and confined to campus, where they could inflict the least damage, since almost no one paid them any attention. As for administrators, they were glorified jailors with a string of initials after their names: Ed.D., Ph.D., SOB—what did it matter? Yet he listened to everything she said. That was what he did best, since listening was the best thing you could do for someone you loved.

This morning, he'd waved good-bye to her when she set off on foot for the train station, and once he turned back into the house and pulled the door shut behind him, black silence descended. Alone like that, he could easily have stretched out on the couch and given in to the sinking sensation, but he knew that if he did he wouldn't get up all day. She'd find him right there when she came home. So he went down into the basement and opened the drawer in the workbench where he'd left his pills. He took a double dose of the sertraline that he'd stocked up on last spring in Mexicali, then forced himself to tromp the stairs to the third-floor room where he planned to keep his instruments as soon as they arrived. He stared at the worn Berber carpet, which in addition to being ugly as sin would soak up too much sound.

He hunkered down in one corner and used a utility knife to loosen the fabric, pulled the edge up and peeled it back two or three feet. A tag on the underside of the carpet, right where he'd grabbed it, informed him that it had been installed by the Lechmere Rug Company, of Cambridge, Massachusetts, on April 23, 1977. He pinned it with his knee and leaned over to get a better look at the flooring.

It was in poor condition with lots of gaps that needed to be filled, a tricky task in a climate where you'd have to allow for expansion and shrinkage. He put his hand in his pocket, took out a quarter and scratched it against one of the boards. The finish flecked off easily, so it was either varnish or shellac, which meant it would require a full sanding. Though the floor had probably once been beautiful, it must have already been in terrible shape when somebody—the owner of this house in 1977—decided to cover it up, thinking the times called for something better. Whoever it was couldn't have foreseen that thirty-three years later, his specially installed carpet would be peeled up and disposed of, once again revealing what was under-neath. You couldn't hide anything forever.

the school that became North Shore State College had begun its existence in the middle of the nineteenth century. Known at the outset as Bradbury Normal School, after the town in which it stood, it welcomed its inaugural class in September 1854, admitting some sixty-six young women hoping for careers in the teaching profession. The student body grew steadily in subsequent decades and exploded in the years following the close of the Second World War, as returning soldiers took advantage of the GI Bill and programs in the liberal arts, nursing and business administration were added to the curriculum.

The enrollment was now around ten thousand, including students from twenty-eight states and more than thirty foreign countries. "We've got a brand-new ice-hockey arena," the president proudly informed Kristin during a walk around campus when she visited for her interview, "as well as a new eighty-seat black-box-style theater. Due to budget constraints, the library renovations had to be pushed back, but they should still be completed in the next few years. And as of this past fall, *all* of the residence halls are green and sustainable."

In a purely academic sense—and almost every other sense as well—NSSC was undistinguished, its deficiencies rendered all the more glaring by its close proximity to Harvard, MIT, Tufts, Brandeis, even UMass Lowell. It was just a third-rate state school, where the students often worked full-time and took seven or eight years to graduate, but this was where she'd ended up. The day President Randall finally called to offer her the job, he said, "We think you can help us make the big leap," and for an instant she saw herself dressed in a bulky suit, complete with boots and a helmet and an oxygen tank, a female Neil Armstrong bounding across the moon like some lost kangaroo.

Her assistant, Donna, was on the phone when she arrived. In her late fifties or early sixties, she kept her mouth permanently pursed, as if she'd assessed the world in all its particulars and found it disagreeable. She must have recognized Kristin— they'd met during her interview—but did nothing to acknowledge her presence, just let her stand there with her bag in hand while she listened impassively to the person on the other end. Finally, after what felt like five minutes but was probably less, she said, "Okay, that's enough. I'll have to call you back. Someone's here."

She laid the receiver down and observed Kristin for a few seconds before rising to offer her hand. "So you made it," she said, then glanced at the wall clock.

It was a quarter past ten. When they spoke the previous Friday, Kristin had told her she'd be in by nine thirty. "I know I'm late," she said, shaking hands, "but I took the wrong bus in Andover."

"Andover? What in the world were you doing there?"

"I live close to the Haverhill Line, and they said I could ride it north to Andover and then grab a bus. Somehow I ended up on one to Lynn."

"*Lynn?* It's a wonder you made it out alive. For God's sake, don't you own a car?"

She'd had two assistants in California, and neither of them would have talked to her that way. "I *own* one," Kristin said, "but I'm not the best driver, and I'm not sure yet about some of the local traffic laws."

"If you're a bad driver, you'll fit right in. The main traffic law you need to know is never to use your turn signals."

"No?"

"Of course not." A smile flickered across her face, then fled. "Why share information with the enemy?"

Kristin spent the remainder of the morning running from one office to another, having her ID made, picking up keys, filling out payroll forms. In so doing, she learned a lot more about the school than she had on her previous visit. Most of the offices she stepped into had decrepit Dell computers, frayed carpeting and furniture that looked like it came from a Reagan-era flood sale. She heard one payroll assistant complaining about a paper shortage, while another said paper wouldn't do them any good since the copiers were out of toner. At the parking office, where she went to pick up a permit she wasn't sure she'd ever use, she saw a fuming young woman write a check to cover fines. "They're just issuing tickets to raise revenue," she said, ripping the check out and shoving it at the cashier. "Tell the fucking football team to buy their own jocks."

At one o'clock, she attended a luncheon in the faculty dining hall with the president, the provost and the four academic deans. They'd absorbed an 8 percent cut this year, she learned, and while so far they'd avoided layoffs of tenure-track faculty, between seventy and eighty adjuncts had not been rehired. In addition, fifty-five staff positions had been cut by HR, with Mail Services and Purchasing taking the hardest hits. Furthermore, the formerly freestanding Schools of Education, Nursing and Social Work had been turned into "divisions" and rolled into a single School of Human Services. No one alluded to it, but she knew this had sent two former deans back to the classroom. Unlike her, they'd been wise enough to secure a fallback position.

When the conversation flagged, the provost, a heavyset woman named Joanne Bedard, who had an Iowa State doctorate in family and consumer services, looked across the table at Kristin. "You and I," she said, "will *earn* our salaries this year."

"Oh, now," said Norm Vance, the dean of liberal arts, whose bushy black mustache called G. Gordon Liddy to mind, "must we drop the *t* word here in the middle of August?"

"The *t* word?" Kristin said.

"Tenure, dear," Bedard replied.

At her interview, Kristin had understood, as one sometimes grasps certain things without being told, that the provost opposed her candidacy. She didn't know why that was, but she'd decided not to let it hurt her feelings. She used to conduct orientation sessions for new faculty, and she always urged them not to take peer reviews and student evaluations personally—or tenure decisions, either—to remember that people were judging their performance, not their worth as individuals. "The fact that you might not be a perfect fit here," she'd say, "doesn't mean you won't be exactly that somewhere else." It was good advice, and she'd tried her best to follow it when told she was losing her job. She hadn't cried or thrown a tantrum or filed a lawsuit. She'd brushed off her résumé, reactivated her placement file and put her house on the market.

"Are there some dubious cases coming up?" she asked her new colleagues.

Everybody except President Randall laughed.

"Aren't there always?" said the provost. "The stakes are just unusually high now. In times like these, with budgets crumbling everywhere, you get the heave-ho at a place like this, what's next? A job teaching ESL at the University of Bangladesh?"

As if suddenly realizing that Kristin herself had just been canned, everyone grew quiet. The same thing could happen to any one of them, the president included, and all of them must have known it. This was the new reality in higher education, which was sinking lower day by day.

Norm Vance said, "Hey, at least it's not as rough as it is in California, right? That state's in deep trouble."

Kristin swallowed one last bite of overbaked seafood quiche before agreeing that no, nothing could be as rough as that.

Her office adjoined Donna's, so no one could get to her without first passing scrutiny. "Your predecessor," her assistant told her later that afternoon when she started unpacking the cardboard boxes she'd shipped ahead from California, "was pretty grateful for this arrangement the day Stuart Simms came after him with a rolling pin."

Kristin slit the tape on the first box. She was eager to reclaim her possessions and make the office her own. It would just take time, she told herself, but it would surely happen. It had to. "Who was Stuart Simms?" she asked.

"An English professor that got fired. I keep my cell phone set to speed-dial the campus police. The whole time I was arguing with him, telling him Dr. Reichardt was busy, that he couldn't just barge in on a vice president whenever he felt like it, I had it in my hand, and the dispatcher could hear me. A couple of cops rushed in and put him in a headlock."

"A rolling pin was his weapon of choice?"

"Apparently he did a lot of baking, and that was the most lethal thing he owned."

"Why did he get fired?"

"He wasn't who he said he was."

Few sentences could make her heart race like that one. Were any of us who we said we were? Was she who she used to be? For most of her life she'd thought her identity was stable and fixed, but she wasn't so sure anymore. "In what sense?" she asked.

"By claiming he had a Ph.D. when he didn't."

"He faked his doctoral degree?"

"Sure did. The B.A., too. But the M.A.—now, that was bona fide." Donna walked over to the window and looked out onto the quad, where two bare-chested male students were tossing a Frisbee. "If you could earn one real degree, why not three? That's what gets me. But maybe some people enjoy gaming the system. If they weren't doing that, they might be dropping a pile of money at the casinos."

Kristin opened the box she'd just slit the tape on and pulled out several photos: her and her dissertation director years ago in Chapel Hill; Cal sitting on a rustic bench, eyes clamped shut while he picked the mandolin; Suzy at poolside, basking in the sunlight. She scanned the walls for hooks but didn't see any; tomorrow she'd bring a hammer and some nails.

"There's no reason for anybody with a bogus degree to get hired here," she told Donna. "From now on, we'll make candidates submit to a complete background check before offering them a campus interview. Sometimes it's surprising what turns up."

"I guess there's not much of anything that you can't find out anymore, is there?"

"Not if you really want to."

Donna turned away from the window, then looked directly at her. Off and on all day, Kristin had been trying to determine precisely what it was about her assistant that made her uncomfortable. Now she believed she knew: her gaze was too openly analytic, as if she were gauging how any stimulus, small or large, affected Kristin.

"We're on summer hours until next week," the older woman said, "so I'm going home. See you later."

After she left, Kristin opened another carton, and there was her teapot. Her father had given it to her the day she left for college. She'd probably owned it longer than anything else and always placed it on a windowsill, first in her dorm room at Case Western and then in various offices, even though she'd long ago quit drinking tea in favor of coffee. To have kept it all these years suddenly seemed odd to her, as if it were an attempt to hold on to some part of herself that, in the natural course of things, should have been left behind. Tucking it under her arm, she walked through the outer office, then opened the door and stepped outside.

Down the long hallway, past the provost's office and a conference room, stood a large green trash can with the school logo on the side. She pushed the slot open and dropped the teapot in. The receptacle must have been empty, because her father's gift hit the bottom and smashed to pieces.

in the afternoon, when Matt got off work, he was often at loose ends. Before his mother died, he usually headed home and spent time with her; she was always good company, liked to have a glass of wine and talk books or listen to classical music, recalling when she and his father heard Charles Munch or Seiji Ozawa conduct a particular piece at the BSO. But once she was gone he hated returning to the big, empty house. Though he'd never been athletic, he decided to join a gym.

He chose a new LA Fitness right off Main Street in Montvale. What he liked about it was that he almost never saw anyone he knew. Montvalians, as you could tell by the sight of them strolling the aisles at Shaw's or Stop & Shop, filling their carts with Ruffles and Chips Ahoy, were not especially health conscious, and the few who did belong to a gym tended to prefer the Cedar Park YMCA, which had occupied the same spot for fifty years. At LA Fitness you saw people from Winchester, Woburn, Reading, Wakefield, even Burlington, all of them strangers, just as he preferred it. A year ago, when he first started, it was almost empty at four thirty, but a series of membership drives had attracted more and more people, and now he sometimes had trouble finding a locker.

Today he got there before the rush started, so he quickly changed into his workout clothes. He spent thirty minutes on the treadmill, starting at four miles an hour and working up to five, raising the incline several times. When he finished, both he and the machine were dripping with sweat, so he grabbed a handful of paper towels and the spray bottle and wiped it down. After a quick stint on the StairMaster and a few chin-ups, he told himself he'd done enough. Since the gym was starting to fill up, he went back to the locker room and put on his swim trunks. He enjoyed ending his session with a soak in the Jacuzzi, then a trip to the sauna.

This afternoon, the Jacuzzi looked like somebody had dumped bubble bath in it, though he knew the foam resulted from body oil and chlorine. Two guys were in there now, both about his age, neither familiar. As Matt lowered himself into the water, one of them was saying, "You know how much I'm out to my lawyer?"

"Ten, fifteen thousand?"

"I wish." The guy sloshed some foam away from himself, into the middle, and it floated toward Matt. "I owe that bastard sixty fucking grand."

"*Sixty?* What's he doing for you?"

"He files motions. I'm getting sick of that word. You know how some words make you think of something that's got nothing to do with them?"

"Give me an example."

"Okay: 'motion.' When I was a kid and I heard 'motion,' it made me think of a milk shake. God knows why."

"Maybe because it rhymes with 'lotion.' Lotion's a thick liquid, like a milk shake. See what I mean?"

"I guess."

"Sure. Your tendrils are at work."

"What the fuck's a tendril?"

"A little thread in your brain that connects the cells together. You got a motion cell and a lotion cell."

"Yeah, well, what I started to say is that when I hear the word 'motion' anymore, I don't think of a milk shake. Because I *like* a fucking milk shake. I hear the word now, I think of all the dollars floating through the air from my pocket into his."

His philological analysis was followed by a rant against the Massachusetts courts, whose judges ignored the rights of fathers in favor of the mothers who'd divorced them. This, in turn, led to several increasingly maudlin confessions: that for the first thirty-nine years of his life, the guy who owed sixty thousand always had a woman to answer to—first his mom, then his wife—whereas now he had only his attorney. That the other guy, who'd been divorced for nearly five years, had only recently moved out of "the mourning phase." They began tossing around terms like "speed-dating" and "availability index" and discussing such services as Singles in the Suburbs, Good Genes, Telemates and Lavalife.

Fearing it was only a matter of time before they tried to include him in the conversation, Matt vaulted out of the Jacuzzi and took off for the showers. No sauna for him today.

Needing to do a little grocery shopping, he decided to drive up Route 28 to the nearest Whole Foods. He'd let a lot of things go since Carla left him, but he couldn't be accused of eating badly. Most days there was only one mouth to feed, and he fed it well, preferring organic fruits and vegetables, free-range chicken, grass-fed beef.

The store was in Andover, a town he otherwise tried to stay out of. It boasted the second-oldest continually functioning bookstore in the country, and until a few years ago his secret aspiration had been to buy it. He saw himself working on his own stuff in the morning, then going in midafternoon to sell the books of others. He knew he'd never make much money— harboring few illusions, if any, about the future of bookselling, and everyone knew the Andover shop wasn't profitable—but he thought it would be a marvelous thing to do. And it would've been, if only he hadn't fucked up.

At Whole Foods he gathered his items slowly, caressing the navel oranges so carefully that he drew strange looks from other shoppers, though he failed to notice. For a time, before moving out to Montvale to manage the local Stop & Shop, Carla's father had been in charge of produce at the DeLuca's on Beacon Hill, and he'd taught his daughter how to tell good oranges from bad ones, and in turn she'd instructed Matt, who used to drive her half mad with his rush to get out of grocery stores as quickly as possible. "You're looking for smooth skin," she'd tell him, holding one up for him to examine. "You want it to be shiny, small pored and firm—but *not* hard." What he wanted was to go home, finish the galleys he was reading so he could decide how many copies the Book Emporium would order, put the girls to sleep, drink some wine, snort a line in the bathroom and make serious love to his wife. In order for that to happen, he first had to master oranges.

He put five nice ones into his shopping cart, then picked out a couple tomatoes and some butterhead lettuce before moving on to the butcher shop, where he splurged on a New York strip. When there was no need to save because there was nothing to save for, small, easily purchased pleasures assumed inordinate importance. For that reason, it occurred to him that he probably had a lot more in common with the countless people around the country standing in line and waiting for their Double Quarter Pounder with cheese and a half gallon of soda than he did with anyone here. These people probably had investments, IRAs, season tickets to the BSO, vacation homes in Vermont, New Hampshire or the south of France, and they probably regarded a trip to Whole Foods as, at best, a necessary nuisance. They'd have better ways of spending their time. Who, besides him, went to Whole Paycheck for fun?

He grabbed a loaf of French bread, a pound of coffee beans and some other things, then went through the checkout line. The parking lot was full when he got back to his car, and a few drivers were circling, looking impatiently for a space. He quickly stuck the sacks in the backseat, climbed in and pulled out.

You couldn't make a left and go uphill to Route 28. You had to make a right on Railroad Street and pass the train station, then hang a left and drive back through downtown. Today, due to the hour, traffic was slow, so he was just inching along when he noticed his new neighbor—Kristin, was it?—plodding toward the station, on the opposite side of the street. She had on a very sensible beige dress and businesslike shoes. Her hair was askew.

There were too many cars for him to make a U-turn and wheel in behind her, so he pulled onto the shoulder, hopped out and jogged a few steps toward her. "Kristin?" he called. "Hey!"

She stopped and turned, shading her eyes. At first, she appeared not to recognize him. He was wearing sunglasses and, after all, they'd met only once, though he'd seen her many other times as she walked her dog, sometimes alone, more frequently with her husband. "Yes?"

He looked in both directions, caught a break and made it to the other side. "It's me, Matt. Your neighbor?"

"Oh . . . well, hello," she said. It was clear she hadn't the faintest idea why he'd run across the street to talk to her.

Neither did he. He didn't find her particularly attractive; she had a nice figure, but she was probably close to fifty, her complexion was pale and he'd never been drawn to blondes. Carla's hair was thick and as close to pitch-black as you could get without opening a bottle. She had long, dark lashes, butternut skin, a majestic heaviness in hip and thigh. And there was nothing tentative about her—her own mother used to call her Hurricane Carla. Whereas Kristin, even when walking her dog down the sidewalk, moved with her head down as if in retreat from some catastrophic defeat, with the expectation of further losses ahead. "What are you doing in Andover?" he asked.

Her lips formed a skirmish line. "Is there something horribly *wrong* with this town? This is the second time today someone's wondered what I was doing in Andover. It looks like a really nice place, but there must be something bad about it that I'm not aware of, so I'd love to find out what it is."

He grinned and shook his head, and she recalled a boy in her hometown who, even in the dead of winter, would ride his bicycle up and down South Market Street clad only in shorts and a T-shirt. She and her friend Patty Connulty once asked him if he'd lost his mind, and he'd grinned and shook his head in a similar manner and said he'd never had one. When she was in college, they found his body in Penns Creek. He'd run a nylon rope through the hole in a fifty-pound barbell, then knotted it around his waist and jumped off the bridge.

"Why are you grinning like that?" she asked Matt. "Won't you say something?"

"I just had a funny thought."

"Care to share it?"

"A second ago," he said, "I realized that you might be the only grown woman I've spoken to in almost two years who wasn't ordering a sandwich."

His car was a garbage dump. Climbing in, she surveyed the backseat. Along with two grocery sacks from Whole Foods, there were several balled-up towels, a few empty Gatorade bottles, a green gym bag from which a grimy sneaker protruded, two or three issues of *The New Yorker* that looked like they'd been left out in the rain, a plastic container of 10W-30 Castrol, a yellow raincoat, a leather boot with no laces, some orange peels and a dog-eared paperback entitled *Kaputt*. When she leaned back in the passenger seat, a spring poked her spine.

"Sorry about the mess," he said, sliding behind the wheel. "I take comfort in it, though. Some of what's back there's been with me a long time."

"Whatever *Kaputt* is?"

"No, that's fairly new. Gave it to myself for Christmas."

"That looks like something from graduate school."

"You went, huh? Where?"

"Chapel Hill."

"English?"

"Comp lit."

He put the car in gear, looked over his shoulder at the line of cars behind them, then told her to hold on and floored it. His tires shrieked, and somebody laid on the horn.

"Jesus," she said.

"Sorry. Can't be too polite if you want to get anywhere in a car around here. Thought you'd be used to that, though, coming from California."

"Not really. Californians drive fast, but in some sense they're old-fashioned."

"Yeah? How so?"

"They pay attention to things like traffic lights and stop signs."

They merged onto Main Street and headed south toward Montvale. When he offered her the ride, she'd accepted because the next train wouldn't come for half an hour, and she felt like getting home sooner rather than later. She could use a glass of wine. She'd called Cal before leaving work. He was going to grill steaks.

"To answer your snarky question about Andover," Matt said while he drove, "there are a few splotches on its character." He explained that during the Salem Witch Trials, around forty people from here, primarily women and children, were accused of entering into a pact with the devil, and three were executed. The rapacious mill owners who'd tried to break Lawrence's 1912 Bread and Roses strike had lived here to keep their distance from the masses, and while you couldn't blame it on anyone, Franklin Pierce's son was killed here in a train wreck not long before his father's presidential inauguration. "On the other hand," he said, "it has a few things to be proud of. Harriet Beecher Stowe called it home for several years, and it was a center of abolitionist sentiment and a stop on the Underground Railroad." As they passed Phillips Academy, which looked a lot more like a college than the place she now worked, he tipped up his sunglasses to glance at her. "Who else asked you what you were doing here?"

She told him her administrative assistant at North Shore State had, and while she now understood she'd gone out of her way by taking the Haverhill Line and then complicated matters by getting on the wrong bus, she hadn't liked the tone of the exchange.

He laughed and lowered his sunglasses. "In New England it helps to be tone-deaf. People here tend to speak their minds."

"Speaking your mind's just fine. Since I'm going to be her boss, though, I thought more politeness was called for. Especially since I work in administration, which is pretty serious. But who knows, maybe I got a little touchy-feely during my years in California."

He asked where she was originally from, so she told him, and then he wanted to know how she'd become an administrator. She fielded that question all the time and usually responded with platitudes about wanting to help faculty members maximize themselves, but today she didn't feel like fudging the truth. "I wasn't much of a teacher," she said, "and I'd lost interest in what I was doing. So when something up the food chain opened up, I applied. And it turned out I was good at it."

"It's great to be good at something," he said, his tone suggesting he might be the rare exception who was good at nothing. But since he'd told her not to pay too much attention to tone, she went ahead and asked, "What do you excel at?"

"That's a tough one. But all things considered? I'd have to say pastrami on rye."

He was posturing, and nothing put her off quite as much as a man who could fluently marshal a line. Her first husband had been able to, and he'd done it so well, for so long, that she couldn't distinguish between a spiel and the truth. He wrote about the poetry of high modernism—his first book was *T. S. Eliot and the Shifting Persona*—so perhaps she shouldn't have been surprised when he informed her that the trip he'd taken to Ann Arbor was for a job interview, not a conference, or that he'd just accepted a position there, or that his thesis advisee, the twenty-three-year-old daughter of a Visalia dairy farmer, would be going with him in the fall. The primary attraction to Cal, if she wanted to be honest, was that he initially appeared incapable of delivering any lines at all. When asked why he alone, of the many musicians who gathered at the crossroads grocery, never tried to sing, he smiled shyly and said he couldn't remember lyrics. It took her a few years to discover that while he might be no good with poetry, even he could tell a story.

"You asked me two serious questions," she told Matt, "and I gave you two serious answers. I asked you one, and you gave me nothing."

They were out of Andover now. On this stretch Route 28 had only two lanes, and they'd fallen in behind a large truck with the Salvation Army logo on its rear door and were doing all of thirty miles an hour. The train might have been faster and less taxing.

"Well," he replied, "it's complicated."

"Isn't that what people put under 'Relationship Status' on Facebook when they're seeing somebody who's seeing somebody else?"

"Maybe. I don't know the first thing about Facebook."

"I don't either. But I live in the world in the year 2010, and I have some idea of what other people are up to."

"I used to be good at books."

"Reading them? Writing them? Stealing them?"

He drummed his fingers on the steering wheel. "I never stole a book in my life. You don't steal what you love."

Rather than take issue with an assertion she considered suspect, she said, "So what did you *do* with books?"

"I bought them."

"For yourself?"

"No, for the Harvard Book Emporium. For years I ordered every work of fiction that came through the door."

Ahead of them, a traffic light was just turning red. Knowing he'd shoot right through it, she braced herself against the dash, and he didn't disappoint her. "And?"

"And then the complications started. I lost my job."

"I lost mine, too. That's why I'm here."

"I'll be damned. Really? What did *you* do?"

"I didn't do anything," she said. "You might not have heard, but the country's going through a recession? As always, California got ahead of the curve. We had cutbacks. My position was combined with someone else's." She should've held her tongue then, and might have if she hadn't started her day by climbing aboard a bus to Lynn that sat in a spot marked BRADBURY. And ever since, people had been acting as if the signs and signals that were supposed to govern behavior had no meaning. "So what," she asked, "did you do?"

He didn't answer right away, and she knew he was trying to decide whether to lie, tell the truth or change the subject.

He finally said, "I didn't have to work the cash registers, but I made a point of doing it for an hour or so every day. The staff loved it. You've got a very leftist workforce there, and for me to do something as lowly as ringing up sales . . . well, that created a kind of egalitarian atmosphere.

"What I'd do once or twice a week was engage somebody in a lot of book chat while checking them out—usually, customers who were getting on in years, very often women, and only when they were buying a number of big hardcovers—and then I'd immediately hit the RETURNS button and zero out the entire sale. Toward the end of the day, I'd take exactly that sum in cash.

"I eventually made the mistake of canceling out a sale on the same customer twice. She was one of those Cambridge types we referred to as 'the wives of dead professors.' In her seventies, reasonably well off, not too much to do anymore except read. When she got interested in something, she'd research the topic and then come in with a list of titles. When she decided to bone up on LBJ, she wanted all the Caro books, Doris Kearns Goodwin, the Dallek stuff, *Lyndon Johnson and the Great Society*, *The Best and the Brightest*—even Lady Bird's *White House Diary*, which to my surprise we had with the used books in the basement. We'd follow her around with two or three hand baskets. She gave us a pretty good workout.

"When she went in to see the manager, she told him that the first time it happened, she assumed it was a mistake. Said I was the nicest, most helpful person she'd come across in ages, which was why she always asked for me. Most people never look at a receipt as long as the total sounds right, but she wasn't most people. The second time, I didn't even remember having done it before—close to three years had passed—but she never threw away sales slips and she still had the old one and handed both of them over to my boss.

"When they got through auditing my receipts, it was stunning how much I'd stolen. I had no idea. I could've gone to prison, but my boss was a softhearted guy, and he let my mom pay him back and didn't press charges."

He quit talking, which she took as indication that the time had come to move beyond narrative into analysis and perhaps even criticism. "Why did you do it?" she asked.

"For the most predictable of reasons. I was snorting a ton of coke, and that's not cheap. Plus, a lot of writers come through that store, including some huge names, and quite a few of them were willing to hang out late and get blasted. I tried too hard to impress them. I wanted to be what they were."

"To be a writer?"

"Sure. Didn't you?"

"No. Never."

He shook his head as if he didn't believe her. "I thought almost everybody doing a Ph.D. in literature wanted to be one, that you all had two or three novels or a stack of poems secreted away in your desks."

"I don't have anything like that in my desk."

"Amazing," he said. "No secrets."

"I didn't say I don't have *secrets*," she said, then immediately regretted it, since this was an invitation for him to ask what they were.

It surprised her when he didn't, and even more so that she felt offended by his failure to ask, as if he considered it a given that her secrets, whatever they might be, were less worthy of discussion than his own.

When Matt stopped in front of her house, he saw her husband sitting in a lawn chair on the patio, having a drink while the black Lab snoozed at his feet. A charcoal grill stood nearby, smoke rising from the grate.

"Here," she said, "let me introduce you to Cal."

He protested that they could do it some other time, since she'd had a long day and her husband was enjoying himself.

"Don't be silly. Come on, we're neighbors."

So he climbed out of the car, and they started across the yard. At first the other man just stared at them, his long jaw slackening into an expression of puzzlement. As they came closer, he set the drink on the ground—straight whiskey, it looked like—and unfolded himself from his chair, all his angles straightening simultaneously. He was even taller than Matt had thought. At least six four, if not more. "Hi, there," he said.

"Cal, this is our new neighbor. Matt Drinnan. He happened to be in Andover, and when he saw me marching glumly toward the train station, he was kind enough to offer me a ride." She pointed across the street. "He lives up there, in the blue Queen Anne."

As Matt's hand was enveloped by one twice as large as his own, Cal sighed. "Oh, thank God."

"For what?" she said.

Before offering Matt a drink and demanding that he stay for dinner, Cal said, "When I saw you get out of someone else's car, my first thought was that you'd had a wreck. Then I realized you didn't drive to work."

Though each of them, in the months ahead, would recall the exact remark differently, all three noted that his initial reaction, upon seeing them together, was to assume disaster had struck.

in the morning, *the old general spent a considerable amount of time in the wine cellars with his winegrower inspecting two casks of wine that had begun to ferment. He had gone there at first light, and it was past eleven o'clock before he had finished drawing off the wine and returned home. Between the columns of the veranda, which exuded a musty smell from its damp flagstones, his gamekeeper was standing waiting for him, holding a letter.*

"What do you want?" the General demanded brusquely, pushing back his broad-brimmed straw hat to reveal a flushed face. For years now, he had neither opened nor read a single letter. The mail went to the estate manager's office, to be sorted and dealt with by one of the stewards.

She stuck her finger in the book and closed it, unable at the moment to progress beyond the first page. The other night, after Cal grilled steaks and they sat outside with their neighbor and consumed two bottles of Cabernet, Matt had insisted they walk over to his place so he could loan her his copy of the best novel he'd read in the last two or three years. He hadn't invited them inside, just let them wait on the porch while he pulled it off the shelf. When he mentioned the book at dinner, she hadn't recognized the author's name—Sándor Márai—but kept that to herself because she could tell Matt thought surely she would've known his work. Later, this failure to admit her ignorance troubled her and was the main reason *Embers* had lain untouched on her bedside table until this morning. She'd been spending her daily commute familiarizing herself with work-related documents like the faculty handbook, which listed the school's policies on tenure, promotion, professional leaves and sexual harassment.

Holding the novel in her lap, she looked out the window at the houses the train was passing, each right next to the other, and even at this relatively low speed they all blurred together. Perhaps because she was finally back on the East Coast after so many years, she'd been thinking a lot lately about the house she grew up in, the neighborhood where it stood, her mother and father and the people who lived next door.

At one time she'd felt as much at home in the Connultys' house as her own, and the couple's daughter had been her best friend. Her initial bond with Patty was their mutual fondness for something almost everyone else in her circle would have deemed disgusting. They became aware of it a couple of weeks after the Connultys moved in. Until then, they'd studied each other warily through the line of mountain laurel that formed a porous barrier between their backyards. They were ten or eleven at the time and, since it was summer, hadn't yet met in school. But Mrs. Connulty came by one morning and invited them all to dinner, and though Kristin begged her parents to let her stay home since it was Thursday and her favorite *Bewitched* episode would rerun that night, they told her she needed to make friends with the girl next door. "Just imagine," her mother said, "how you'd feel if you didn't know a soul in the world." She said the family had moved from Allentown and that Mr. Connulty was the new manager of the Pennsylvania Power & Light plant at Shamokin Dam.

Afterward, Kristin couldn't remember what they'd eaten for dinner, though Patty always maintained they had middle-of-the-road fare: roast beef with mashed potatoes, stewed carrots, Brussels sprouts. Dessert, she said, was strawberry shortcake. While the adults sat in the spacious living room and enjoyed an after-dinner drink, the girls were told to go upstairs. A tall, large-boned woman with thick auburn-colored hair, a soft voice and an unusual accent, Mrs. Connulty said, "On your way, look in the pantry. You might find you some treats."

The kitchen closet was the kind you walked into, big enough for two girls their age to stand side by side. "I Icr idea of a treat," Patty said, "might seem a little bit weird." She'd barely spoken all night, and Kristin had already decided that she didn't want to be her friend. Unlike most people, whose expressions were constantly changing, whether happy or sad, puzzled or mad, Patty's expression remained fixed, as if she'd been captured by a photographer in a moment of bored composure—at church, say, or the funeral of a distant relative.

"What's so weird about her idea of a treat?" Kristin asked.

The other girl flicked on a light. The shelves were stocked as neatly as those at Food Giant, and they were almost as full. Most of what she saw was pretty basic: cans of Le Sueur green peas, boxes of Kraft macaroni and cheese.

But then Patty reached up and pulled down a round tin like the ones fruit cakes came in at Christmas. "Ever eaten hoop-cheese wafers?" she asked.

"I don't think so."

Patty pulled the top off, and the tin was filled with crumbly orange things that emitted a pungent smell. "My mother makes stuff like this," she said. "Want to try one?"

"What's in them?"

"Margarine, flour, red pepper, Rice Krispies and hoop cheese."

"What's hoop cheese?"

"Something they sell in country stores down south."

"That's where your mother's from?"

The other girl nodded. "Prices Fork, Virginia." She started to replace the lid.

"Wait," Kristin said, because she sensed that she'd behaved exactly as Patty expected, showing revulsion at something unfamiliar; if that was what she expected, it must have happened before. "Let me try one." As though it were a slimy creature she'd found beneath a rock, she seized a wafer between thumb and forefinger and, despite the awful odor, popped it into her mouth, where it instantly dissolved. A moment or two passed before she realized how wonderful it tasted. "I like it," she said.

"Are you joking?"

"No. Really." She took another one.

"Well," Patty said, choosing a couple for herself, "I actually like them, too."

They carried the tin upstairs to Patty's room and finished off the wafers while watching *Bewitched*. During the show they reached agreement on a number of crucial points: though her character was obnoxious, Agnes Moorehead had attractive features; Dick Sargent was a better Darrin than Dick York; and Esmeralda was a poor substitute for Aunt Clara. By the time Kristin's parents got ready to go home, she'd made arrangements to spend the night.

Over that long summer they became closer and closer, roving South Market Street after pooling change to buy candy and sodas, wading in the shallows of Penns Creek, tossing a Frisbee on the banks of the Susquehanna so George, the Connultys' clumsy Airedale, could chase it down and bring it back rimed with slobber. Three or four times a week, they took turns sleeping over at each other's house, where they fell asleep side by side after midnight, often with library books open on their chests. Both of them, it turned out, loved to read. In Kristin's case, that made sense because her parents taught English and her mother had named her after the heroine of her favorite novel, *Kristin Lavransdatter*. Mr. Connulty, on the other hand, had an engineering degree, and you never saw his wife open a book.

The Connultys had met at Virginia Tech. Or, to be more accurate, in the waiting room at the Montgomery Regional Hospital, where he was waiting for them to revive a fraternity brother whose pulse had all but disappeared after he emptied a fifth of Four Roses. Patty's mother, who was only nineteen then and worked at something called the Dixie Sweet Shop, was waiting for them to release her father, who'd lost a finger in a pulp-mill accident. "She took one look at me," Kristin had heard Mr. Connulty say, "and thought she knew all there was to know. I was a drunken frat boy, pure and simple. Probably from Northern Virginia, with parents who had plenty of money but not enough vision to send him to William and Mary, Washington and Lee or even UVA." That his background was different from what she'd imagined evidently weighed in his favor. His father had died at Saint-Mère-Église on D-day, when his parachute deposited him into a house set on fire by a pathfinder's flare. He and his two brothers were raised by their mother, who taught first grade in Fairfax. He attended Tech on an academic scholarship and, while not at the top of his class, did well there. He earned the money for his frat fees by performing brake jobs three afternoons a week at Firestone. "I convinced her I was worth a second look. Took a lot of hard work, plenty of elbow grease, but it was the best thing I ever did. And though I hate to admit it, I've always been glad her father lost that finger."

A self-made man: that was what Kristin's dad said Mr. Connulty was, on one of the rare evenings that summer when neither girl visited the other, the Connultys having gone to Virginia to see their relatives.

"What other kind of man is there?" her mother asked.

Her father was drinking his whiskey, and the television was on, the sound turned low as it so often was in those days. On the screen, President Nixon was finishing a speech, his lapels bunched up under his chin because he'd raised his hands above his head to flash the victory sign.

"There are plenty of other kinds," her father said, reaching for his Tullamore Dew.

"So just name one." Her mother had a book in her lap and

continued to look at it as if she were reading, though Kristin knew she wasn't. When she was reading, she didn't talk or even listen to what anyone else was saying.

Her father also had a book in his lap, Leon Uris's *QB VII*. He closed it and laid it on the floor. "Take me, for instance," he said. "I'm not a self-made man."

"So what kind are you?"

"Well, I'm the kind who follows a well-trod path."

"Really?"

"Or maybe I should say a worn path. Aren't you always trying to make your students enjoy that Welty story?"

"I don't try to make them. I try to help them."

"Whatever. Anyhow," her dad said, "*my* father taught school. And what do I do?" Rather than wait for her answer, he said, "And look at you. I married a beautiful, brilliant woman who also teaches school, just like my own mother did. In other words, I didn't wander off the path into the forest."

He drained his glass, got up, walked over to the sideboard and poured himself a second drink, bigger than the first. Kristin had never seen him do that before. He turned his back to her and her mother, pulled aside the curtain and gazed at the Connultys' house, though no one was there, not even the dog. They'd taken George with them to Virginia.

"If Tom Connulty had followed in his father's footsteps, he would've joined the army about five years ago, and probably would've died in some rice paddy." He let the curtain fall, went back to his chair and sat down, the cushions sighing beneath his weight. "And he wouldn't have married a woman like Sarah."

Her father didn't say why he wouldn't have married Mrs. Connulty, and her mother didn't ask. Instead, she looked at her wristwatch, set her book aside and announced dinner would be ready soon.

Whenever Kristin spent the night over there, Patty's mother made them special treats: homemade potato chips with green turnip dip, fried pickles with blue cheese dressing, buttermilk pies, pecan cakes with praline glaze, pear fritters. She'd sit at the table with them, always saying she'd try just one of whatever they were having. Then she'd leave them alone. The next morning she'd fix elaborate breakfasts of chicken and waffles, cheese grits or sweet potato pancakes. After they finished eating, she'd ask what their plans were, or if they wanted her to take them anywhere, and if the answer was no she'd wash the dishes and do some cleaning and then turn on the soaps.

At first Mrs. Connulty didn't talk a lot when the two families convened for one of their frequent dinners, but as that first year turned into the second and she and Kristin's mother began to do their grocery shopping together and even took a trip to New York City to see *Jesus Christ Superstar,* she became a lot more verbal. Occasionally, though neither of Kristin's parents ever commented on it, at least not in her presence, Mrs. Connulty messed up her grammar. "They gave it to Tom and I," she might remark, instead of "Tom and me." Or she might ask, "Where was you?" She sometimes slipped and put an *r* on the end of a word like "Alabama." During Kristin's grad school days in North Carolina, she frequently noted similar verbal mannerisms in shops and convenience stores, and each time she remembered Sarah Connulty.

In perhaps the first adult-level assessment she'd ever offered of another person, she told Patty, "Your mother is the kindest, most *decent* person I know."

Assessment—the drawing of distinctions between the acceptable and the unacceptable, the accomplished and the inept, the useful and the expendable—was the main thing on her mind when she walked into the office that morning to find Donna waiting, her laptop bagged for the Power Point presentation, her gaze flitting toward the wall clock. They had a tenure and promotion workshop scheduled for nine a.m., and it was already three minutes past. "We'd better hurry," her assistant said. "It's a good five-minute walk to the Olsen Center."

"They can't start without us, can they?"

"No. But there's such a thing as punctuality."

"I know there is. There's also such a thing as traffic, and my bus proved it this morning."

Heading across campus she made an effort, as she had each day, to engage the older woman in small talk. "How'd your husband's checkup go?"

"Fine."

"Was his blood pressure lower?"

"A little."

"And the problem with your grandson's teacher—did that get resolved?"

"They moved him to another class."

Finally, she gave up, and they covered the last hundred yards in silence.

The auditorium was an institutionally grim bowl with tiered seating for around eighty people. They walked in to find no more than eighteen or twenty faculty members there, most of them sitting by themselves, as if in implicit acknowledgment that going up for tenure was like dying. It could only be done alone.

While Donna connected her laptop, Kristin welcomed everyone and reminded them that she'd just arrived and was still learning the ropes. "I'm sure I'll make some mistakes along the way," she said, "but I'll do my best to correct them. If at any point you have a problem with that, I hope you'll first discuss it with me rather than someone else. I promise to do the same." Then she introduced her assistant, and judging from the looks on the faces of those assembled Donna hadn't made many friends in this crowd.

Kristin began her presentation with a list of dates on which probationary files were due to departments and deans. For ten or fifteen minutes she covered the role of mentors, stressing the importance of maintaining constant communication with them, and then she went over the three areas in which tenure-seeking faculty would be evaluated, pointing out that accomplishments in teaching, research and service must be properly documented. "A good file is thorough," she said. "At the same time, padding obscures real achievement. If you attend a conference in D.C., you don't need to include a napkin from the Mayflower Hotel to prove you were really there. A program listing your subject or topic will do nicely." She enumerated recent changes to the tenure and promotion guidelines, noting that the publication requirement had been raised from two juried articles to three and that the service requirement had also been raised from one committee to two.

When she'd finished, she asked if there were any questions. People fidgeted as they looked around the room to see if anyone else was going to speak first, but eventually a hand went up.

"Yes?"

The guy was around forty, with copper-toned skin and the trace of a British accent. "How does the administration justify requiring more of faculty," he asked, "at a time when it's cutting support for research and travel?"

The question was neither unreasonable nor unexpected. But the truth—that the administration believed it could raise standards because there were fewer jobs, and professors were desperate—could not be plainly stated. Nor could the inconvenient fact that while the publication requirements were still absurdly low for any institution claiming university status, the administration had raised them largely to contain costs, on the assumption that more than a few would fail to meet them and would quickly be replaced by cheaper junior faculty. "We're hoping that increased productivity," she said, "will bring increased external support to all the departments. Right now, as a result of the stimulus package, there are already more funds in some areas."

"So the recession," he said, "is a positive development if one views it in the proper light?"

A titter passed through the room. Rather than becoming angry, she was starting to feel at home. She'd been here before. "It depends on what we make of it," she said. "After all, one of the most productive periods this country ever experienced followed on the heels of the Great Depression. At this particular school, the enrollment jumped dramatically, new positions were created and the campus expanded to twice its former size."

"In other words, this is really an exciting time to be alive?"

"It's always better to be alive than not."

He didn't respond, so she took a couple more questions and, seeing no other hands raised, thanked everyone for coming and said good-bye.

While she waited for Donna to disconnect the laptop, the man who'd engaged her walked down the aisle in the company of a slim blonde who'd been sitting beside him. He offered his hand and, as she reached out to take it, introduced himself: "Robert Dilson-Alvarez," he said. "Hyphenated. And this is Gwendolyn Conley."

She shook hands with Conley, who nodded and mumbled hello without quite making eye contact. Though Kristin hadn't recognized either of them, she knew their names. Assistant professors in the history department, they'd be coming up for tenure in the next few months. She'd read through all the probationary files, flagging the ones she thought looked troublesome, and neither Dilson-Alvarez nor Conley seemed anything less than a sure bet. He'd published a book and several articles, and she already had two articles out and a third accepted. His teaching evaluations were some of the strongest in the school, hers spotty but acceptable. They'd each done plenty of service.

"Nice to meet both of you," she said. Then, looking directly at Dilson-Alvarez: "Did I answer your questions satisfactorily?"

He laughed. He was a handsome man, tall, with a chiseled chin and cheekbones and wavy black hair that seemed as if it parted naturally. "You answered them like an administrator," he said.

"Well, that's what I am."

"But not what you started out to be."

"No, I altered course midstream. It happens."

"About twenty years ago you wrote quite an interesting article on V. S. Naipaul."

It wasn't an article but a lengthy and largely negative review of Naipaul's travel book *A Turn in the South,* published in a now-defunct journal. The editor asked her to do it because he knew she'd lived in Chapel Hill, one of the places Naipaul wrote about. "How'd you come across that?" she asked.

He laughed again, his perfect teeth flashing. "The way one comes across everything. I looked for it."

"You would've had to look pretty hard. Back then, I had a different last name."

He spread his hands, palms up. "I'm a researcher, so I know where to look. And that's ninety percent of the game."

Sensing Donna was impatient to leave, she told Dilson-Alvarez and Conley she needed to excuse herself, then gathered up her materials, and they started back to their office.

"Both of them give me the creeps," Donna said once they were outside.

"Really? Why?"

A shiver rippled through the older woman's shoulders. "I don't know. They just do."

Kristin didn't say a word but knew exactly what she meant.

"It was brought by a messenger," said the gamekeeper, standing stiffly at attention.

The General recognized the handwriting. Taking the letter and putting it in his pocket, he stepped into the cool of the entrance hall and, without uttering a word, handed the gamekeeper both his stick and his hat. He removed a pair of spectacles from his cigar case, went over to the window where light insinuated itself through the slats of the blinds, and began to read.

She stayed with the novel as she rode the Haverhill Line home, even though it moved slowly and she felt no more than mild interest. Having scanned the jacket copy, she already knew the story line was one of the oldest in literature. Some force or figure from the distant past unexpectedly returns to upset a hard-won sense of acceptance. Passions long dormant are reignited. Yesterday lurches into today and in the process obliterates tomorrow.

though kristin might have preferred that he reverse the order, Cal had decided to address the exterior problems first, since it wouldn't be very long before working outside became at best unpleasant, at worst impossible. So on the Tuesday after Labor Day he set about assembling the scaffolding he'd rented over the weekend from a company on the South Shore.

He'd driven all the way down to Braintree because the place he tried to rent from in Montvale didn't seem to want his business. The guy out front demanded a huge security deposit, and when Cal asked why the figure was so high he leaned over and rested his elbows on the countertop. "No offense," he said in a voice that suggested he wouldn't care if any were taken, "but most people we deal with have been coming in for fifteen or twenty years. You been here for what, fifteen minutes? I haven't traveled much and don't know a lot of geography, but you just wrote down a cell number with an area code I don't recognize—530. Where in the hell is that?" He was a smallish man with thinning hair, a weak chin and pale blue eyes, and for a moment Cal allowed himself to imagine how he might react if a stranger reached out, twisted him by the shirt collar and told him he ought to learn some fucking manners.

He connected the units in a methodical fashion, laying out all the pieces in neat groups, snapping the casters into place on the outriggers and attaching them to the stage poles. The morning was warm—it had hit ninety-six on Labor Day—and once he worked up a good sweat he began to relax. By ten o'clock the three units were locked together. He propped an aluminum extension ladder against the house next to the chimney, cut himself a short piece from a fifty-foot nylon rope, hooked the rest of it over his shoulder and stuck a stainless-steel pulley in his pocket. Then he climbed the ladder and, when he was high enough, looped the short rope around the chimney and tied a square knot. After that, he hooked the pulley onto the loop, passed the remaining rope through it and, before climbing back down, took a good look around.

He could see all or parts of more houses than he could count, and none looked as if it had been built within the last seventy-five years. One was a small Cape Cod on the next street over, and he knew from having passed it the other day while walking Suzy that a plaque affixed to the clapboard siding said 1836. Having nothing better to do, he'd come back home, typed in the address on Google and discovered an entry for the house in the National Register of Historic Places. The original owner was someone named Ward G. Osgood, whose profession was listed as "cordwainer," a term Cal had never heard before. In Kristin's *OED,* he discovered that a cordwainer was someone who made shoes and boots from the finest leather, as distinct from a cobbler, who only repaired them.

In all likelihood, things being what they were in 1836, Osgood would have built the house himself, perhaps with help from a friend or two. Cal had often wanted to do that but not like his father had. He wanted to build it for himself and his wife, without help from anyone, starting from the ground up. Back in California he once broached this possibility as they were returning from a party at the university president's, where he'd spent the evening lurking behind a potted plant, emerging only to accept another drink from one of the waiters.

"But we've got a house," Kristin protested.

"It's someone else's."

"No, it's not."

"Yes, it is."

"Whose?"

"Whoever built it. It's the house *they* wanted. We just live in it."

She was driving because he'd consumed seven or eight glasses of wine as well as a few slugs of bourbon. "Well," she said, "that's what people do in a house. They live in it."

"Like pigs in a pen."

"You're drunk," she observed.

"Like chickens in a coop."

"We'll be home soon. You better take some Tums."

"Like rats in a sewer."

After that evening and the unpleasant morning that followed, he kept his thoughts on the subject to himself and didn't point out that their house, as nice as it looked, might not be around in another thirty years. It had gone up in the seventies when a developer with a mind-set similar to his father's bought some almond groves and started building showy homes out of drywall and stucco. Pulling the white wool carpet off the floor to replace it with tile, he'd discovered that the concrete on which the house stood looked like a roadmap. To save a few dollars, the builder had skimped on the rebar that should have gone into the chain wall and slab, and as more and more cracks developed there you'd start to see them in the walls and ceiling, too. Every time it rained, the ants turned those cracks into miniature freeways. One day they'd finally take over.

Now, standing on the ladder and looking down on so many solidly built structures that had lasted so long, he experienced a degree of wonder that he supposed must be akin to what a religious person feels upon visiting a holy site. With his own hands, he'd never made anything that would last as long as these houses. And when he was gone, he'd leave nothing behind.

He hoisted the scaffolding flush against the wall, stabilized it, then set the Bose on the picnic table, popped in a few of his favorite discs and climbed up onto the platform. Starting at the ridge line, he began scraping down the scaling paint and used a wire brush on all the rough spots. Here and there the wood looked as if it had been sandblasted. If he had to speculate, he would've guessed that in this climate, with so much wind and ice and an ocean nearby, a house probably needed repainting every three or four years, if you wanted to keep it looking good, and he did. It was as fine a way to spend your time as any, and better than most.

When he'd done everything he could reach, he climbed down and ate lunch, then turned off the music, took up his palm sander and ascended the scaffold. He worked through the afternoon, pleasantly lulled by the drone of the small motor. If it didn't rain, he'd finish preparing the surface by Thursday or Friday and be ready to prime come the weekend.

He knocked off around five, then drank a beer and took a shower. He and Kristin had decided to dine out for the first time since moving in. He was just toweling off when the doorbell rang, and Suzy started barking.

By the time he'd shrugged his robe on and gotten downstairs, the FedEx guy was in the process of printing him a notice on a bar-code scanner. "Thought nobody was home," he said, tearing off the printout and sticking it in his pocket.

"No, I'm here."

"Great. I'll get your stuff."

Cal watched while he returned to the van, opened the rear door, lifted out a guitar box and hefted it onto the porch. "There's more," he said.

"Yeah, I know." Cal carried it inside, and when he stepped outside again all three of the mandolin boxes were there, too. He took them in, then waited near the door while the driver brought those containing three more guitars, the mandola, banjo and Dobro. The cases inside the boxes were fiberglass and heavy, and the deliveryman was sweating badly. "If these are all instruments," he said, punching keys on the scanner, "you must be a musician."

"No. I just play them."

The young man, who was African American and probably no older than twenty-eight or thirty, looked up in confusion. "Well, if you play 'em," he said, "in my book that means you're a musician."

Cal had learned a long time ago that there were some conversations you should walk away from, because the words you had to use often meant different things to different people. Each ten-penny nail was pretty much the same as every other, but the woods you drove them into varied greatly; some resisted, others splintered. Nevertheless, he couldn't stop himself from pointing at the delivery van. "If you had to," he said, "could you change the oil in that rig?"

The FedEx guy shrugged. "Sure. I mean . . . Yeah, I *guess* I could."

"Would you say that makes you a mechanic?"

The young man sighed and looked down at his feet, then turned the scanner around so Cal could see the screen. "I need you to sign right here," he said. Walking back to the van, he shook his head. He was still shaking it as he drove away.

Cal had been feeling some anxiety about shipping the instruments, which he'd packed up himself and labeled FRAGILE. So even though he knew he ought to get dressed—Kristin would be home soon, and their reservation was for seven—he couldn't resist the urge to check on the one he loved most.

He cut the tape on the first box and freed the case, spilling Styrofoam peanuts all over the floor. FedEx had made him ship it unlocked, so he only had to pop the snaps open to the first nice guitar he'd ever owned, a 1953 Martin D-18 with a sunburst finish that he'd bought in Modesto when he was twenty years old. The guy who sold it to him, a drywall hanger he'd met on a construction job, couldn't play it anyway. It had belonged to a brother who'd died in a West Virginia mine.

Cal pulled it out, surprised once again that it weighed next to nothing. Resting it on his knee, he tuned it to pitch. When he strummed the first chord, he forgot where he was as well as where he'd been, not to mention what he'd done and whom he'd known. He lost sight of the room in which he was sitting—his eyes had closed—but it gave a lot back, the walls and floor returning crisp sound.

He picked through "Man of Constant Sorrow," then segued into "The Wabash Cannonball," which somehow became "The Great Speckled Bird." As always, when he heard the sound the Martin made, he felt as if he had little or nothing to do with it, that he was the instrument and it was the artist, that it would tell his hands what to do and save him the trouble of making any choices.

He didn't even notice when Kristin entered the house. She stood there and listened, watching him with envy, trying to remember how it felt when you surrendered so thoroughly to love.

the reason for the party was ostensibly Frankie's birthday—his forty-first—but that couldn't even come close to explaining the guest list. In addition to Matt, he'd invited three or four couples who lived on his block, Dushay and his mother, plus Paul Nowicki and Matt's ex-wife. When Matt asked why he'd included the Nowickis, his friend said that just the other day he'd been elected to the board of the local PAWS chapter, which of course Paul headed. Since they both belonged to the same civic organization, it would be awkward to exclude him.

Neatness counts, Frankie liked to say, and Matt couldn't deny he'd fashioned a neat argument. "When did you sign up?" he asked.

They were having this conversation shortly after closing time. Through the window they could see Dushay standing beside his old Accord, parked directly across the street in front of Felicia's Bistro. He was searching his pockets, one after another, looking for his car keys, which dangled from the door lock where they had probably spent the day.

"I joined awhile back," Frankie said.

"How far back?"

"Maybe three or four weeks ago. Not long after he came in to see you."

"Just like that."

"Well, he called me and asked. He's trying to get more merchants to participate. You know Paul's got a thing about pets." Frankie pulled his apron off, laid it on the counter, walked over and opened the front door. "Douche?" he hollered. "They're in the frickin' *lock.*"

Dushay looked down, saw the keys, then turned around and grinned.

"Look how you're living," Zizza said, his back to Matt as though he couldn't bear to say this to his face. "You never see anybody except me and the fucking Douche Bag and whoever comes in here to buy a sandwich. And ninety percent of those people you don't even notice. There aren't a lot of single women around, but there're a few, and whenever one of 'em comes in and tries to talk to you, what do you do? Same thing you do with everybody else. Slap the shit on the shingle, bag it and take their money. 'What's wrong with Drinnan?' people ask. 'Used to be the life of the party. Now he thinks he's too good to work here?'"

Matt pulled his apron off and hung it on a wall peg. If this had been a scene in one of his three aborted novels, he probably would've made the character based on himself say something about how, if he was so bad for business, he'd gladly bow out and find work elsewhere. But this wasn't a novel, and nobody would knowingly hire someone who'd embezzled thirty-five thousand dollars from his former employer. Only a special kind of fool did that.

He walked up to the front and stood beside Frankie. "Therefore you intend to administer shock therapy. Throw me in a pot with my ex-wife and my replacement, in front of an audience, and for good measure you'll have Dushay standing by with his mother, to remind me I don't even have a shoulder left to cry on and had better start trying to find one. You're really something, you know that?"

The Zizzas lived just off Montvale Avenue, about halfway between Main Street and I-93. When Matt parked at the curb and got out, it was raining as hard as it had been all day. A hurricane, supposedly too far out at sea to cause major damage, was lashing the Cape right now with sixty-mile-an-hour winds and torrential rain. Locally, the meteorologists were forecasting evening downpours and flash flooding.

He reached into the backseat and pulled out a sack that contained a bottle of wine, some petunias he'd brought for Andrea and an envelope with Frankie's birthday gift: two tickets to see the Pats' home opener against Rex Ryan and the hated New York Jets. He walked across the yard to the door and rang the bell.

Andrea opened it. A tall redhead who'd always worn far too much makeup, she had a hard face with deep worry lines departing from both corners of her mouth and long red fingernails too thick to be real. Matt knew she didn't like him. He wasn't crazy about her either, which made it all the more puzzling that suddenly—at the exact moment he heard his ex-wife say, "Frankie, you are absolutely outrageous"—he wished Andrea Zizza would pull him close and kiss him.

He lifted the petunias out of the bag and offered them to her. She didn't take the bouquet, just stared at it. "Who's that for?"

"You."

"Oh. Well, thanks." She held the flowers at arm's length, as if she thought they might be poisonous. "I'll get a vase for these," she said, then nodded toward the dining room. "All the hoopla's in there."

Despite never having been a dog lover, he understood their use as props. Zizza's mutts, Eddie and Wolf, were smelly, flea-addled creatures who barked too much and stole food, but when he walked into the dining room he dropped to a knee, grabbed Wolf around the neck and whispered, "Hey, boy, how you doing?" The dog's long pink tongue, smelling suspiciously of mortadella, mopped his chin. He wiped it off, then stood to face the jury.

As odd as it might sound given the town's size, he'd never seen Carla and Nowicki side by side until now. Yet there they were, at the far end of a table loaded down with cold cuts, salads, chips and dips. Paul had his arm around her shoulder, his fingertips gently massaging her rotator cuff.

As a literary construct, love at first sight had always seemed problematic, the fallback position of bourgeois nineteenth-century writers whose characters were prohibited by social mores from doing anything except sitting in drawing rooms, sneaking peeks and sighing. But Matt had loved Carla since the moment he first saw her in the hallway between classes at Montvale High. She was wearing a pair of Jordache jeans and a *Flashdance* shirt, and her hair was pinned with banana clips. She came toward him, hugging a copy of a magazine. *Wine Spectator,* he saw when she got closer.

She was pretty, but so were others. She was smart, but back then she didn't read anything serious and listened to awful music by people like Teena Marie and Cyndi Lauper. Her standard grade was B minus, and when he finally asked her out he discovered she had no plans to attend college, that she hoped to open a wine-and-cheese shop someday in Arlington or Belmont or some other tony suburb. While none of this made her more interesting to him, that didn't matter when he was sixteen, just as it wouldn't matter when he was twenty-six or thirty-six.

Now her eyes—big and round, accentuated with just the right amount of eyeliner—were again meeting his. And when they did, several things happened. Nowicki's face colored and he removed his hand from her shoulder. Carla's mouth dropped open, and Dushay's mother put her hands over her ears and said, "Oh, my!" Dushay lost his grip on the broccoli sprig he was about to scoop up dip with and dropped it in the bowl. One of Frankie's neighbors whispered, "Jesus H."

Zizza grabbed a wad of napkins and ran toward Matt, who was puzzled until he felt the liquid trickling out of his nostrils, over his lips and down his chin. He didn't bother looking at the front of his white polo shirt, because he knew what he'd see there. He'd seen it before. And so had Carla.

Despite having catered countless parties over the years, the Zizzas didn't seem to know how to throw one. There was no music, and conversation had started to lag. Everybody was just standing around, Matt holding a Kleenex to his nose now and wearing an aloha shirt that Frankie'd bought last year in Hawaii. It was an awful sight—yellow, with brownish-green palm trees in the foreground and behind them, in silhouette, a bunch of surfers hoisting boards on their shoulders as they trooped toward the ocean. Inside it, he felt like a scarecrow.

The Zizzas, the Nowickis and Mrs. Dushay had gone into the kitchen, where they stood looking out at the backyard. The wind had picked up and was whipping the trees, the windows of the old Victorian coming alive with sighs and groans. The rain was falling hard now, blown across the yard in silver waves.

"I know two different guys," Matt heard Dushay tell another guest, "that got personally killed by Whitey Bulger."

"Really?"

"Absolutely. And I'm even related to one of them. He was just my uncle by marriage. But still."

Carla emerged from the kitchen and walked over to the end of the table, where Matt was using his left hand to spoon potato salad onto a small plate. He didn't want to risk taking the Kleenex away from his nose; he thought he'd finished bleeding, but you never could tell.

"How have you been?" she asked. She pulled the spoon from his hand, stuck it into the potato salad, lifted out a big clump and deposited it on his plate. "Want any more?"

"This isn't what you think," he told her.

"What's not?"

"The nosebleed. God knows how that happened. I'm clean, Carla."

"I know you are."

He didn't see how she could, since she'd barely been close enough to even wave at him for at least a couple of years, and he said so.

She pursed her lips like she always did when someone said something stupid. He'd always called it making a duck face, or just making a duck. "You've never understood what it means to really know somebody," she said.

It occurred to him that this might well be true and could account for his failure to get very far with his writing. How could you write about people if you didn't know them? But what he said was, "I'd like to think I know you."

"I know you would." She glanced at the kitchen, then reached up and, as if it were something precious and fragile, took the Kleenex from his hand. She looked at the three or four gobs of blood on it for a moment, then stuck the tissue in her breast pocket and fastened the button.

The critical point at which he would turn from a solid to a permeable substance seemed at hand. He was losing viscosity. Everybody's body betrays them in the end, and his had gotten the jump on him tonight. "I'm sorry," he said. "I'm horribly sorry about what happened to us. What I did to us."

"I know you are," she said. "But you're not dead yet, Matt. You know what I mean? There's still this thing ahead of you called life." She picked his plate up and handed it to him. How many times had she done that before? He used to go a day or two without eating anything at all while she tried her best to force-feed him. And what dishes he'd passed up then: braised rabbit cacciatore, potato gnocchi with chanterelles and pancetta, veal piccata, braciole.

Loss was a sickening sensation. And no matter what he gorged on nowadays, he'd never make it go away. That might be the one important thing that he knew and she didn't.

He set the plate back down just as Andrea came out of the kitchen carrying a chocolate layer cake with flaming candles forming the numbers 4 and 1. "Okay," she announced. "Time to sing. Gather around."

So everybody assembled around the table and sang "Happy Birthday," and the most surprising thing about it was Dushay's beautiful tenor voice, which soared operatically above their grating chorus. He sang with his head held high, arms at his sides, as if he were onstage someplace like Jordan Hall and perfectly at peace in such surroundings.

When they finished, Frankie closed his eyes for a moment, then opened them and looked straight at Matt, and in that instant his old friend knew what he'd wished for, that massed hopes were headed toward him, whooshing out over the cake and mixing with a few flecks of spit to extinguish the candles while everyone cheered.

During the opening of gifts, as Frankie feigned outrage at Dushay for giving him a ridiculous male thong with the Pats' logo on the crotch, Matt slipped away. Broken branches littered the Zizzas' yard, now more of a marsh, the water two or three inches deep in many places. He picked a path through the downpour to his car. Soggy leaves covered the windshield, so he had to stand there getting drenched while he cleared it.

A light pole, snapped in half, was down in the middle of Montvale Avenue, a team of guys from NSTAR hovering around it, shouting instructions at one another. He backed up, wheeled into a side street and wove up the hill to Main, dodging a couple of trash cans rolling across the pavement. The center of town was dark, but when he turned onto East Border Road, he again saw lights.

The house was humid and miserable—his mother had never installed central air, and he couldn't afford to either—so he left the front door open while he went upstairs and pulled off his wet clothes, tossing Frankie's awful shirt into the washer. He climbed into the tub, lifted the diverter, then grabbed his pliers and twisted the exposed stem to turn on the hot water. While showering, he kept thinking of that instant when Carla put the bloodstained Kleenex in her pocket. Turning his back to the spray, he pressed his face to the wall, nearly overcome by an urge to pound his forehead to pulp on the tile.

When the water grew lukewarm, he turned off both faucets, stepped out and toweled dry. He had no idea how to spend the rest of the evening. He hadn't finished the last two books he'd started reading, and he'd forgotten to put any movies in the Netflix queue. The most exciting possibility was probably the Weather Channel.

He put on a pair of shorts and a T-shirt and went back downstairs. He was in the kitchen, rummaging through the refrigerator for a beer, when someone rapped hard at the front door. The rain was still pounding down, and the only person he knew who might be nuts enough to go out in it was Frankie. He hoped to God his friend hadn't come to fetch him. After a while it became annoying, not to mention humiliating, for someone else to remain so focused on your well-being when you had done your best to destroy it.

Through the screen door, he saw his neighbor Kristin. Her soaked hair fell over her eyes, and her mascara had started to run, leaving squiggly lines on both cheeks. The wind had worked over her umbrella pretty good, inverting it and breaking a couple spokes.

"Hey," he said and unlatched the door. "Come in. Everything okay?"

"Not exactly."

She told him she'd gotten home late. They'd had meetings all day, and then her bus flooded out, and after that, on the Haverhill Line, a fallen tree blocked the tracks. "To make matters worse," she said, "my husband's down in Providence tonight. He went to hear the Tony Rice Unit."

"Who?"

"They play bluegrass," she said, waving off further questions. "So I got home, and when I walked into the kitchen I heard running water. I checked the half bath, but it wasn't there. So I went upstairs and looked around and everything seemed fine. I couldn't even hear the sound anymore. And so then I—"

To save her the trouble, he said, "It's your basement."

"It's filling up. There must be half a foot in there already. I don't know where it's coming from—I didn't want to wade down into it—but it sounds like there's a broken pipe."

"I doubt that." He opened the door to the hallway closet, though he hated for her to see inside it. Whatever he lacked a hanger for, he'd thrown on the floor. He had to paw through a pile of coats and rain gear to find his winter boots.

As he took a seat on the bottom stair and began tugging them on, she examined the hallway. "That's a nice antique," she said, gesturing at the grandfather clock that stood at the far end, near the kitchen door. "Where did you get it?"

He was lacing one of the boots. "Belonged to my folks," he said. "It's been there as long as I remember."

"So your parents lived here?"

"Yeah. This is the house I grew up in."

"And you moved back after . . ."

"That's right—I moved back after. You ready?"

She nodded, so he grabbed a big umbrella and a flashlight, and they went outside. Crossing the street, he held the umbrella over their heads at an angle to prevent the wind from destroying it.

"You never think about hurricanes hitting Massachusetts," she said.

"If you live here, you do. One of them flattened a good bit of the North Shore back in 1938. Tore the roof off my mother's house."

"That house back there?"

"No. It's over on Pond Street. My uncle lives in it now."

While they walked, she held his right elbow. He noticed she wasn't wearing boots, just a pair of black leather pumps. If she intended to stay here, she'd need some new clothes. He bet she didn't even own a good coat. In California, she probably never needed one.

When they got to her driveway, he remarked that her husband's paint job looked great: the exterior of the house was now ocher, with gleaming white trim. He'd noticed him up there on the scaffold, working all day long for nearly a week. In late afternoon he always pulled his shirt off, and he didn't look nearly as gaunt then. He packed some serious muscle. "Must be nice," Matt observed, "being married to a guy who knows how to do stuff like that."

"Sometimes," she said, pulling a key from her pocket and unlocking the door. He wiped his boots on the mat, laid down the umbrella and followed her inside.

He'd been in the house before but not for more than thirty years. When he was young, he and Frankie had a friend, Kyle, who lived here with his brother, sister and their parents. The father was a cop, in Malden, if memory served, and his wife worked for a government agency in Boston, either the Registry or the MBTA, something to do with transportation. One Saturday night they went to dinner; it was a special occasion, an anniversary, so the kids stayed home alone. His and Frankie's friend was the oldest, ten or eleven, and Matt remembered Kyle's mother coming over and telling his mom that she'd instructed the kids to call her if anything went wrong. .

This was in winter, snow everywhere, big icicles hanging off the roofs. Though he couldn't say for sure anymore, it might have been right after the blizzard of '78. He recalled that just a day or two earlier, he and his parents had been jolted awake in the middle of the night by a popping noise that sounded like a shotgun blast and seemed to have come from the house next door. While Matt and his mother waited at the top of the stairs, his father grabbed a flashlight and stepped outside. Moments later, he returned grinning. "Remember how mad I got," he asked, "when Steve Aaron switched to Vermont Mutual? Well, I don't hold it against him now. The snow just caved in the roof of his Coronet."

The night Kyle's parents went out, the first indication they had that anything was wrong came when they heard his sister beating on their front door and screaming. Her little brother had gotten into a closet on the second floor, where their father kept his service weapon, and while playing with it he'd shot Kyle in the chest. Terry Drinnan ran down the street. When he came back, an hour or so later, he had blood all over his clothes. The next morning you could see a trail of it leading from the steps of Kyle's house across the snowy yard to the street. An ambulance had carried him to the Cedar Park hospital, though he was probably already dead.

The family moved away within six months, and since then the house had been sold three times. Kristin wouldn't know any of this history, because in Massachusetts, unlike some states, sellers don't have to inform potential buyers that a violent death has occurred on the property. And Matt wasn't about to tell her.

He trailed her down the hallway, glancing into the living room where he and Frankie and Kyle used to lie on the floor watching *Sanford and Son* or *Happy Days*. Back then it had a carpet on it, so it was easy to roll around and wrestle if you wanted to, but now the boards were exposed. They looked great, which surprised him, since the previous occupants hadn't seemed like the kind of people who cared much about appearances. The guy drove a panel truck and sometimes came home with his shirtfront unbuttoned, the woman favored baggy skirts that concealed a lumpy figure, and the kids—four boys—left their stuff all over the yard. Last winter one of their bikes got buried in the snow, a single handgrip poking out of a drift for three or four weeks.

"Did your husband redo the floors?" he asked as they moved into what used to be the dining room but was now lined with bookcases and CD cabinets.

"Yes, but only on the first floor. He just finished yesterday—and now the house is filling up with water." She opened the door to the basement. "Watch your head."

The light was on, but descending the narrow staircase made him nervous. Kyle used to keep a ball python down there in a fifty-five-gallon aquarium, and nobody—not even Frankie, who loved spiders and lizards and all kinds of creepy things—had much interest in going down to see it.

The water was lapping at the bottom step, and a Narragansett can bobbed by. "Is there a sump pump?" he asked.

"I remember Cal saying something about one, but I don't know where it is. I've only been down here two or three times."

She was somewhere behind him on the stairs. He caught a whiff of fragrance, faint but pleasant. "Can you call him?"

"I tried. His phone went straight to voice mail, and he hasn't called back. I think maybe the concert already started."

Having no other choice, he stepped into the flood. Against the far wall stood a long workbench, with all kinds of tools stacked on it: power drills, sanders, circular saws, things he could name but not use. Beyond it was an opening into a second room, where the sound of falling water seemed to be coming from. He waded over and, stooping to keep from cracking his head, got inside and played his flashlight around until he fixed it on one of the side walls. A couple feet above the concrete floor, there was a hole about the size of a silver dollar, and water was spewing through it. "Found your problem," he called. "One of them, anyway. There's a small hole in the wall, and my guess is a storm drain's right on top of it."

"Are there more problems?"

Rather than answer, he sloshed across the flooded chamber. He could see a hose like one on a vacuum cleaner coming up from the floor and disappearing through a hatch. That had to be the outflow from the sump pump. In seconds he followed the power cord over to the outlet, where it had gotten dislodged. His boots were made of rubber, so he applied a little pressure to the plug, and the pump kicked on. Immediately he heard water surging through the hose.

"Found your second problem," he hollered. "Sump pump was unplugged. It's working now, and it ought to empty this place out over the next few hours. You'll need to tell your husband about this hole, though."

"Is there a third problem?"

"I don't know yet." He moved toward the water heater carefully, doing his best not to make waves. Fortunately, it stood on a cinder-block platform. The insulation at the bottom of the tank was dry. Stooping, he slipped through a second passageway and saw that the furnace was also on a raised platform, and its bottom was dry, too.

Just ahead, on the stairway, where she'd remained standing, her legs protruded from her skirt. Seeing them like that— pale but shapely and separate from the person they belonged to—sent a shock wave through his groin. For a good while now, his sex life had consisted of several pitiful thrusts into his own hand late at night as he imagined his ex-wife beneath him, all that thick hair spread out on a pillow. While making love, Carla always kept her eyes open to observe the visual effect of her whispered obscenities, words she used nowhere except in bed. Now, he supposed, she was using them on Nowicki.

When he reached the foot of the stairs, Kristin said, "I should thank you."

He'd gone out in a hurricane and slogged around in a flooded basement where a five-foot-long ball python used to live, and now she was telling him that she *ought* to say thank you, which indicated that for whatever reason she didn't plan to? "Yes," he said, "you really should. That's exactly what you should do."

She stood there looking down on him, making no effort to move, leaving him no choice but to remain right where he was, since the stairs were too narrow to climb past her. She'd put her hands together, the left one clutching the right and squeezing it rhythmically. "That book?" she said. "The one you loaned me?"

"*Embers?*"

"Yes."

"What about it?"

"I read it."

"Well, that's what people usually do with books, isn't it?"

"No, it's not. They're much more likely to use them for doorstops. But I didn't—though I wish I had."

Not being an aquatic creature, he didn't intend to remain in the water one second longer and mounted the bottom step. He assumed she'd turn to climb up the stairs and he'd follow, and when they got to the top she'd bring him an old towel so he could dry his boots to keep from trekking water all over her nice floors. Maybe she'd offer him a cup of coffee or a glass of wine, but he'd decline. And then he'd go back home, turn on the TV and see where the eye of the hurricane was. Sooner or later the storm would blow itself out. They all do.

To his surprise, she didn't move, just continued to stand there, and when the moment grew too long for her, as it had for him, she laid a hand on his shoulder. "Would you hold me?" she said, though there really was no need to ask.

an age of expansion

in california, Cal had kept his distance from the neighbors. He knew the names of only two: Ann and Alex Neal, mortgage bankers in their sixties who lived right next door, on the other side of a redwood fence that he took it upon himself to maintain, replacing rotten boards and bearing all the costs. Because the Neals kept insisting they come over for a drink and get acquainted, Kristin finally prevailed on him to accompany her one Sunday afternoon a year or so after they moved in. The two couples sat together in the living room, which displayed all the worst traits of seventies interior design: green shag carpet, plaid wallpaper, a monstrous chandelier with transparent glass drops.

Alex, it turned out, held strong views about "Mexicans," a category that for him included everyone whose native language was Spanish, no matter their country of origin. "The ones I hire to do my yard?" he said. "Only the head honcho speaks a word of English, and he can't understand half of what you tell him. He'll just stand there shuffling his feet and saying *Sí, sí.* Problem is, he doesn't see. Last January I dragged my Christmas tree outside, intending to pull it out of the stand. But the phone rang, so I ran in to answer it and got embroiled in a long conversation with a golfing buddy, and in the meantime they showed up and lugged the whole thing off, stand and all. There's just something missing in the Mexican mind." By rights, he maintained, they'd rebuild Manzanar, where they'd penned up "the Nips" during World War II, and incarcerate all "the wetbacks" there prior to deportation. Ann reached over, tousled his thick silver hair and urged her new neighbors not to think too badly of him. "He's been a fine husband and father," she said. "He doesn't have a lot of ideas, but almost every one he *does* have is wrong."

To withstand the ordeal, Cal had three or four drinks. When they got back home, he poured himself another. Kristin watched him from the sofa, sipping wine while he strode around the living room with his free hand slashing air. "I'll never set foot in their house again," he seethed, "so don't you try to make me. Who in his right mind would choose to waste the better part of an afternoon with assholes like that? There are better ways to kill time. You could listen to the Grateful Dead. You could oil the door hinges or take a fucking nap."

As far as Kristin knew, he never spoke to Alex again, though she sometimes saw him talking to Ann near the mailbox. But when their neighbor was diagnosed with pancreatic cancer and drugged senseless, Cal went to the hospice in Sacramento every day for a week to sit at his bedside. Ann told Kristin she walked in one time and found him holding her husband's hand.

Now, here he was on the far side of the continent and once again thinking of fences. He'd spent the last few minutes hoisting sacks of sand, gravel and cement onto his shoulder and carrying them from the truck to the yard, where he propped them against a stack of rails and posts, and he had his garden hose hooked up and had grabbed the posthole digger when the guy who lived next door stuck his head over the rickety, knee-high fence that would soon be replaced. "Hey," he said, "looks like you're getting ready to build something."

Cal sighed. Later, thinking back on it, he guessed maybe he rolled his eyes. He'd been dreading the day when this guy would try to engage him. He was probably about sixty-five, maybe a little older, a short, tanned man who wore glasses and had a carefully trimmed mustache. He drove a small white BMW SUV that looked like it had become what it was against its better judgment, but he rarely left home. His house had plenty of windows and, since he never closed the shutters, Cal couldn't help but notice that there were enormous flat screen TVs in at least three rooms. Sometimes all of them would be going simultaneously—the Red Sox on one, the Patriots on another, Sean Hannity on the third. He kept the volume so loud that you could often even hear them over the noise made by his window units, which still droned day and night, though it wasn't hot anymore.

"Yeah," Cal said, "I'm getting ready to fence off the rest of our yard. We've got a dog who's tired of being cooped up inside."

The neighbor stuck his hand out. "Vincenzo," he said. "But my friends, which I hope you're gonna join the ranks of, call me Vico."

Cal laid down the posthole digger, walked over to the fence and shook his hand. Up close like that, he could see something white protruding from the man's ear. At first he thought it was cotton, then realized it was a hearing aid. "My name's Cal," he said loudly.

"Cal. That's perfect. I noticed you came here from California."

"Yeah, we did. But Cal's not for California. It's short for Calvin."

"Like the guy that started the Methodist Church?"

"I believe that was someone named Wesley."

"I'm Catholic. What do I know?" Vico spread his arms wide, palms out, as if to acknowledge his ignorance. "You like football?"

"Not really."

"Baseball?"

"Not especially."

"Food and wine?"

He could see where this was going. "Yeah. If they're good."

"Well, over at my house, if I do say so, they will be. I've been divorced for thirty years and cooked for myself every single day. I probably would've made a better wife than husband, except I'm one hundred percent heterosexual. Or I was, anyhow, back when I had the necessary tools." He pointed at the BMW in the driveway. "In there, I've got two cases of Barbera. Among some, it's got a bad name. But I buy good stuff. There's this little group of guys that get together every week or two, usually at my place, to watch a game and eat and drink. They're coming tomorrow evening. Sox versus Yankees. I'll make a big pot of pasta. We'd love to have you join us. We could use some new blood. Any day now, one of us could bite the dust. It happens."

Cal tried to think of a good excuse but couldn't come up with one. "Well," he said, "the truth is, I'm not real sociable."

For an instant, Vico's face froze as if in a fit of palsy. Then he laughed. "None of us are socialists either," he said. "That's just a mistaken notion a lot of people around the country hold about this state. Myself, I tend to vote Republican, but my buddies, they go the other way. Got an ex-cop in our group and a retired coach from Montvale High, and both of them used to be in a union. I give 'em a little hell about that from time to time, and they give me hell right back. See, I'm a retired CPA, did their taxes year after year, so they know *I* know the score. Our cop buddy routinely—*routinely*—took home a hundred forty, hundred fifty. Pulled so much overtime you wonder when he had a minute to eat or take a crap. Ever notice when there's road work, maybe a couple of public-works guys patching a pothole, you got a pair of cops standing around in those slime-green vests, slurping Dunkin' D and pretending to direct traffic? That generates overtime, and state law says you've got to have 'em. But I don't call it socialism. I just call it two cops standing around getting paid for drinking coffee."

Panic was starting to set in, a feeling of claustrophobia, of being caught out and observed and bent to the will of another.

"Listen," Cal told him, "I need to dig some holes. It's supposed to rain tonight."

"See you tomorrow," Vico said, turning toward the BMW, which he'd spend the next few minutes unloading, toting boxes of wine, bags of groceries and a pot of daffodils into his house.

that evening Kristin arrived home late again, at half past seven. He could tell from how she sank onto the couch, leaning back against the cushions while rubbing her eyes, that something was bothering her. A different sort of husband might have asked what it was, but he didn't. If she needed to tell him, she would; if she chose not to, that was her business.

"I finished the fence," he said.

"I noticed," she replied, though he knew that was untrue. If she had, she would've said so right away. She'd always been appreciative of his efforts to keep everything in good shape, properly maintained. Her first husband hadn't been able to do anything around the house. If the toilet was stopped up, they had to call a plumber. And he usually left the call to her.

"It looks great, Cal," she said. "Really." She asked then if he'd made anything for dinner, and he apologized, asking if maybe they could eat out. He'd only completed the fence about half an hour earlier and barely had time to take a shower.

"That's fine," she said. "Why don't we try that Mexican restaurant down on Main Street in Cedar Park? The one the Realtor told us about?"

"I don't know about eating Mexican food in Massachusetts. I doubt it'd measure up."

She mentioned some vice president—of communications? Finance? Cal couldn't keep them all straight, didn't care to. "He says it's really excellent, and he knows good Mexican food. He grew up in the Imperial Valley."

He acquiesced, in part because he wasn't hungry. The conversation with the retired accountant had been troubling him all day. The longer he worked on the fence, the angrier he became. His worst fear about living here was coming true. The houses stood too close together. You couldn't escape scrutiny. Pass gas and somebody'd hear it. The thought made him so mad he hit a picket too hard with his hammer and split it right down the middle.

El Gallo Fino stood on the corner, in a building that wasn't quite orange and wasn't quite pink. It might've been a dress shop at some point, since there were two display windows large enough to accommodate seven or eight full-sized mannequins. Fortunately, the tables nearest those windows were occupied. If asked, Cal would never have agreed to sit there.

The hostess, who at least appeared to be a Latina, wore a braided chignon, a Puebla dress and a gauzy shawl with floss embroidery. She led them past the bar, where several drinkers sat sipping margaritas, and through the crowded restaurant to a corner table. Handing them each a menu, she told them to enjoy their dinner.

Kristin watched him cast an eye around the room. Except for one Asian family, everyone there was white and well dressed, lots of guys with loosened ties, as if they'd just arrived back in the suburbs from whatever Boston brokerage or law firm they worked for. The Mexican murals would strike him as stereotypical. Too many cacti on display, along with one sombrero-wearing peasant leading a donkey loaded down with mangoes. Ordinarily, she would have filled the silence by explaining how perfectly awful her day had been, that her stomach was churning so badly that she'd bought a packet of Rolaids in Andover and chewed them on the platform, not noticing the milky film at the corners of her mouth until Matt, who'd appeared unannounced, pointed it out. She'd told him about her day when they stopped for a couple martinis in North Reading. That made it hard for her to tell Cal anything at all, as did the fact that she'd insisted Matt drop her three blocks from the house, so it would look like she'd walked from the station if her husband happened to be outside.

Cal opened the menu, examined it for a minute or two, then laid it down. "'The elegant rooster,'" he said. "That's what the name of the restaurant means. Although you can also translate it as 'the fighting cock.'"

"Sounds like a pretty big difference."

"Not really. It's mostly just a matter of the bird's mind-set."

A waitress appeared and placed a bowl of chips on the table, then asked if she could start them off with drinks. Cal ordered a Corona but told her not to stick a lime wedge in it. Kristin thought of another martini, then hesitated and said she'd have a glass of Cabernet. After the young woman left, Cal asked if anything interesting had happened at work, posing the question in an offhanded manner that suggested an answer in the affirmative was unlikely if not impossible.

That afternoon, following lunch at the faculty dining hall with the provost and the director of institutional advancement, she'd returned to her office and logged into her e-mail. Her inbox was full of the usual detritus: communications from the athletic department about upcoming soccer matches and volleyball games, a reminder that all full-time employees needed to attend one diversity workshop each month, messages from students complaining about professors and from professors complaining about administrators, an invitation to the library's biweekly brown-bag lecture—this week's entitled "Ruminations on the Cape Town Climate Conference." She scrolled through them quickly, deleting all but a couple, then logged out and, giving herself no chance to reconsider, typed *umich.edu* in the browser's address bar. From the University of Michigan's home page, her heart pounding, she navigated to the English Department and clicked on PEOPLE.

And there he was.

It had been years since she'd seen Philip's face. She'd gotten rid of every photograph of them together, as well as all those she'd taken of him alone. He'd aged—of course he had, since everyone does—yet the damage displayed on her LCD made her recall an article she'd seen the other day in the *Globe;* underneath a photo of a badly breached breakwater wall in Gloucester, the headline announced "The Battle Against the Sea Is No Contest." Phil's chin, once so well defined, had merged with his neck, the skin on his jaw had grown flaccid, his hair was completely gray and, though he'd once bragged it would always remain thick, had thinned considerably. You couldn't see much more than his face and the top of his torso, but the bunched fabric around his shoulders made it clear he was wearing a hoodie. One thing, at least, had not changed.

He'd been wearing one the first time she saw him, on a bench in front of the Bull's Head Bookshop at the University of North Carolina. She wouldn't have given him a second glance were it not for the book in his hands, a paperback of Alfred Döblin's *Berlin Alexanderplatz.* Seeing a guy who dressed like he did holding that, you couldn't help but stop and stare. In addition to the hoodie, which read OLE MISS across the chest, he had on threadbare jeans and a pair of cowboy boots.

He looked up before she could look away. "Have you read this?" he asked, flourishing it. "Or just seen the movie?"

"I read it in Continental Fiction. I don't think I could survive a fifteen-hour film."

"I'd go see it," he said, "if I lived anyplace where they showed it."

It had played at a Cleveland art house when she was an undergraduate, but she'd passed up the opportunity even though her favorite professor said it was one of the three or four greatest films of all time. "Do you like the book?" she asked.

He shrugged. "It's got its virtues, though you can't escape the fact that it's warmed-over Joyce."

She'd been in graduate school for all of six weeks, living by herself in a tiny studio in Carrboro, in what was shaping up as the worst period in her life. Her father had called several times, but she kept hanging up on him, so eventually he quit. Her mother checked in every few days, though her voice sounded as thick as if her mouth were full of peanut butter, and most of what she said made no sense. Sometimes Kristin didn't even bother to answer the phone.

He scooted over, so she sat down on the bench. "Döblin claimed he hadn't read *Ulysses*," she told him.

"Faulkner said the same thing from time to time, but I've seen the dog-eared copy he had in his library. While he claimed to be influenced by Döblin, there's no evidence he ever read him. Anyhow, *The Sound and the Fury* came out the same year as *Alexanderplatz,* which didn't appear in English until 1931. And Faulkner couldn't read German."

"Are you in graduate school?"

"Yeah. I've seen you sitting in the critical-theory seminar. You didn't look particularly engaged."

They'd been plowing through an anthology of works by Jameson, Derrida, Cixous and de Man, and she had yet to understand a single line of what she read. The course was required for all new comp-lit grad students. "I wouldn't say I'm exactly overjoyed. I like novels and poems, and so far we haven't read any."

Comp lit was more theoretical than English, he said, but he didn't like his classes any more than she liked hers. When she asked if he planned to become a Faulkner specialist, he laughed and said he wouldn't be caught dead doing that. He told her he didn't like bourbon, either.

What he did drink, she discovered that evening at a place called the Four Corners, was lots of beer. Specifically, Pabst Blue Ribbon, the cheapest brand on tap, a big frosty mug going for a dollar twenty-five. The pub was jammed with loud male undergraduates watching the World Series, both Philly and Oriole fans, and occasionally they jeered one another as if they were participants rather than observers. Later, she came to think it appropriate that their first evening together began in a contested environment.

When it came to books, he talked a great game. He'd grown up in a small Mississippi town, but he preferred Elizabeth Bowen to Eudora Welty and was a lot more interested in Ford Madox Ford than Robert Penn Warren. He'd read foreign authors she'd only heard of, like Ignazio Silone and Theodor Fontane, and he knew much more about poetry than she did. He was thinking of writing his dissertation, he said, on Pound or Eliot. Unfortunately, she'd always been attracted to slim guys who displayed a certain degree of taste when it came to food and clothing. Phil had the build of a linebacker, the position he said he'd played at Ole Miss, and he dressed like he was getting ready for a rodeo. He ordered a greasy hamburger for dinner along with French fries that he doused not in ketchup—that would've been bad enough—but mustard. Yet this naked disregard for social niceties might have been his most beguiling trait.

After their third or fourth beer, she asked, "Do you like the taste of this stuff?"

"PBR?"

"Yes."

"Not really."

It reminded her of castor oil, and she said so.

"Beats the hell out of the stuff I've got back at my place," he told her.

"What's that?"

At the time he was sporting a beard, so she couldn't tell if he was blushing when he dropped his gaze to his mustard-streaked plate and said, "There's only one way to find out."

He had an entire house to himself, a boxy little prefab in a cul-de-sac off East Franklin. As he unlocked the front door, he said signing the lease on the place had been a terrible mistake. The monthly rent ate up half his assistantship and didn't even include utilities.

"Why'd you do it?"

"Living in an athletic dorm for four years is like being in a zoo, except animals behave better. Guys would flip out the lights when you were in the shower and squeeze off a few rounds from a .38. Or they'd put a dead rattler in your bed. I wanted some peace and quiet."

When she stepped inside, she experienced a shock. She'd expected a mess, not a sparely furnished but spotless living room. A love seat and sofa, a teakwood table, a single standing lamp with a white bell shade, a wicker basket full of newspapers, all of them neatly stacked. No TV, no stereo. "My grandmother bought me the furniture as a graduation present," he said. "It was marked down after being damaged in the Pearl River flood."

She followed him into the kitchen, which had a small Formica-topped table and a pair of ladder-back chairs. He opened the fridge and pulled out two white cans on which the word BEER appeared in black letters. "Generic suds," he said, handing her one. "This makes PBR taste like Lafite Rothschild."

They went back into the living room and sat down on the couch. He kicked off his boots and put both feet on the coffee table. "See the water stains?" he asked, pointing.

She wouldn't have noticed otherwise, but there were a couple amoeba-like spots. "That doesn't look so bad," she said.

"It looks like hell, but I don't care. To me, this is the lap of luxury. I'll have to live someplace cheaper next year, but I'm keeping all my stuff."

On his couch, time crawled and conversation moved in a circuitous fashion, just as it used to with Patty Connulty. She learned that his mother worked for the health department, his father delivered propane for a petroleum company, and most of his clothes had been bought by his grandmother, who favored polyester and rayon over cotton because they were "man-made." He'd been a great high school football player—first team all-state, with six scholarship offers from Division I schools—though in college his interest in it declined as his passion for literature consumed him. From his sophomore year on, he just went through the motions, serving as scout-team fodder to keep his scholarship. He did most of his reading in library carrels because teammates ridiculed him when they saw him with a book of poems in his hands. An assistant coach who badly wanted to get rid of him wrote doggerel and taped it to his locker:

> *Some can block, some can pass.*
> *I can read Shakespeare super fast.*

She told him about the open-grate bridge spanning Penns Creek, how dogs couldn't cross it, and about the time the Susquehanna overflowed its banks and they had to leave their house in a rowboat. She did her best to describe her hometown, enumerating the businesses along South Market Street, telling him about Little Norway, the winter theme park where she used to go skating. When he asked about her parents, she was less forthcoming, telling him only that they were still alive and were both teachers.

They argued about T. S. Eliot, whose work she deemed cold and inaccessible. He said it was the most intellectually charged poetry he'd ever encountered, that "accessibility," in a culture guaranteed to value trash over work of substance, ought to be regarded as a dirty word by people like her and him, that if he could save only ten works from "the dustbin of history," or whatever Trotsky called it, at least three would be by Eliot, *The Waste Land,* "Ash Wednesday" and *Four Quartets.* He opened yet another beer and quoted several lines from "Burnt Norton," then paused for a moment and said, as if conducting a cross-examination, "Tell me, please, what's cold about *that*?"

Before long, his face began to fade into a bunch of pixels. Through numbness and fog she heard him say something about running out of brew. He'd taken off the hooded sweatshirt, so she knew what to expect and had decided she'd let him do whatever he wanted to tonight and worry about it tomorrow. She hadn't had sex for more than a year and never had a boyfriend who really mattered. When he finally stood up, she waited for him to offer his hand and lead her into the bedroom. Instead he said he'd take her home.

"Too drunk to drive," she heard herself protest.

"I don't intend to drive. We'll walk."

On occasion she swayed, and in each instance he kept her from falling. By the time they reached her place, he was the only thing holding her up. He must have asked for the key, because the next morning she recalled that he'd been the one who unlocked the door. Evidently, though she didn't remember this part, he'd chastely covered her with a plaid blanket. Around three, when she woke up in order to throw up, she was still fully clothed, the blanket neatly tucked under her side and feet. The next time she rose, it was eight thirty and light enough for her to see the note propped up on the kitchen counter against her teapot:

I shouldn't have let you drink as many beers as I did, because I'm twice your size. I'm sure you're going to be sick when you wake up. But if being sick doesn't make you sick of me, I would like to see you again. I'll wait outside your seminar on Thursday afternoon. If you're angry or just uninterested, it's okay. But maybe even then we could still be friends? Either way, I enjoyed our discussion, and I hope I didn't get too insistent about Eliot. His poetry means a lot to me. It's so full of risks, and it displays such disregard for convention. He was a very conflicted man and a pretty unhappy one too, but I believe that was the source of his greatness. I suspect it's probably the source of most great writing and music and painting. I say that without ever having known a novelist, poet, composer or painter, except through his or her work and what I read in biographies. It's an opinion I could possibly be talked out of. So who knows? Maybe you'll try?

Her mouth tasted like metal, and the odor of vomit hung in the air, yet a feeling of warmth settled over her. She finally had something to share with someone. And her first thought, even after everything that had gone wrong, was that she must call Patty, who during the summer had married a guy she met at William and Mary and was living in Silver Spring, Maryland. Her second thought was that of course this was impossible. There was no one she could speak to with such scarcely concealed excitement—not Patty, not her father, not even her mother.

But this sad realization was displaced within seconds by an altogether different notion, one that would account for almost everything she did or didn't do over the next eleven years: there *was* someone to share her excitement with, someone she already knew it was safe to hand a key to, and he would be waiting for her outside her seminar the following afternoon.

"No," she told Cal, "nothing really interesting happened at work. Just the usual. Five meetings. Maybe six. I've forgotten."

"Didn't have to crack the whip on anybody?"

"No."

"Anybody try to crack it on you?"

He was mounting an effort, but it made her feel like a piece of wood being probed for rot or termite damage, each thrust a reminder of all she'd lost. "No. No whips anywhere. That won't really start until spring."

"What happens then?"

"Retention, tenure and promotion. Or termination."

"Oh. Didn't that stuff happen sooner back home? Around Christmas?"

"No. It's the same time it happens everywhere, every year. Departments make their recommendations in the fall, and the administration takes over in the spring."

He lifted a chip and crunched it, swallowed, shut his eyes for a second. When he opened them again, it was as if he'd shed forty years and turned back into a boy. "That's some chip," he said, nudging the bowl toward her. "Try one."

She ate a couple, and they really were good. Then the waitress brought their drinks and asked if they were ready to order. Kristin wasn't especially hungry, but she glanced quickly at her menu and picked the chicken fajitas. Cal studied his for a moment or two, then asked the young woman about the *pescado frito*. She said it was excellent, so he ordered it, and she left them alone.

After that, they sipped their drinks, and Cal showed her that the nail on his right thumb was again torn and jagged. Having played the guitar with a flat pick for most of his life, he was now teaching himself to fingerpick, and in order to strengthen his nails, he said, he'd begun eating gelatin. "It's made out of keratin, and it turns out that's the protein in fingernails and horses' hooves. I never knew it before, but they actually used to *use* horses' hooves when making gelatin." The contrast between where she was now, and where she'd been a short time earlier, was too painful to contemplate, so she pushed it out of her mind and was relieved when the waitress brought their plates.

Her fajitas were good, if nothing special. Cal, on the other hand, said his fish was magnificent and insisted she try it, so she took a small bite and had to admit he was right. It was spicy but delicate—exactly how this kind of fish ought to taste, he said, if you fried it properly. He asked her to give his compliments to the colleague who'd suggested they come here.

As they were leaving, he stopped at the hostess's booth to tell her how great his meal had been. She was in her late fifties or early sixties, her face the color and texture of old leather, but she fluttered her eyes girlishly. "Thank you," she said. "I'm pleased that you liked it."

"Who owns this place?" he asked.

"My husband and I."

"Well, I'm from California," he said, "and I've been eating Mexican food most of my life, and this was as good as any I ever had."

"We're originally from California, too," she said.

"Whereabouts?"

"A small town near Bakersfield. Delano. Have you heard of it?"

He didn't say if he had or not. He didn't say anything at all. To Kristin's dismay, and the puzzlement of the hostess, he stood there mutely for an embarrassingly long time before mumbling good night, then he opened the door and stepped onto the sidewalk.

When he was sure she'd fallen asleep, he climbed out of bed, went downstairs in his bathrobe and, on the pad they kept by the home phone, wrote his neighbor a note. *Dear Vincenzo, I am sorry but I won't be able to make it to the dinner with your friends. I have too much to do over here. Best, Cal Stevens.* He thought for a moment, then crossed out the last name and stepped outside.

The BMW stood in the driveway. Through the front window he could see one of the big flat-screens, Bill O'Reilly running his mouth and pointing a finger at the camera. Vico was probably in another room watching the Red Sox. He climbed the steps as quietly as he could and dropped the note through the mail slot.

When he got back home, he poured a couple inches of Booker's into a glass. He was about to push the cork plug back into the bottle when he thought better of it. He filled the glass to the brim, opened the basement door, pulled it shut behind him and sat down on the stairs. In the darkness he drained about half of the glass, the whiskey searing his throat and making him gasp. At 127 proof, it would soon do what he needed it to. Until that happened, he'd have to sit here recalling how hot the southern San Joaquin got in summertime, heat rising from the pavement and the packed hardpan. The creek beds would have been bone-dry for months, and if you stepped down into one you'd need to be careful where you walked because it would be full of trash—aluminum cans, scrap metal, needles, broken glass. Anything you did required great care. You could lose your wits when it got so dry and hot. In weather like that you couldn't even sweat.

in the fall of that year, leading up to the midterm elections, the country seemed gripped by malaise, with unemployment hovering close to 10 percent. In Massachusetts it had fallen to 8.4 percent, but improvements were hard to detect on a day-to-day basis. Downtown Montvale saw three Main Street businesses close: a liquor store, an Indian restaurant, a laundry. Even Frankie's business had dropped off. He was still selling plenty of sandwiches, though he'd noticed lifelong customers buying their cold-cuts for less at Stop & Shop.

Everyone agreed the electorate was in a volatile mood, and not just in the red states. The Republican candidate for governor, a former insurance executive, was running a dead heat against the Democratic incumbent, and the local seventeen-term congressman faced serious opposition for the first time in years. The Republican victory in the January special election for Ted Kennedy's old senate seat had weakened the knees of Massachusetts Democrats.

Matt Drinnan hadn't voted since 2004, when he and Carla were still living in Cambridge. It wasn't that he didn't care about politics. He prided himself on being a man of the left and, back when he could afford it, had subscribed to both the *New York Review of Books* and the *Nation,* eschewing the *New Republic* because Marty Peretz kept making intemperate remarks about the Palestinians. In effect, Matt had quit voting because for a long time he hadn't felt like he had a stake in anything.

So it was a sign of more than civic duty when he entered the Montvale Town Hall on a weekday morning in mid-October, barely beating the registration deadline. The clerk who handled his request, Sara McDonough, was someone he'd known all his

life. At one time she'd been slim and pretty in the hippie manner, with straight red hair that fell almost to her waist. But in
recent years she'd put on a lot of weight; and her hair, though
still long, was streaked with gray. She and her husband lived
directly behind Cal and Kristin.

While he filled out the form, she asked if he'd met the new
neighbors.

"Yeah," he said, hoping his cheeks weren't as red as they
suddenly felt. "I had dinner with them over there one evening."

"I haven't met either of them yet," she said. "But every day,
right around the time I get home, the guy's up there on the top
floor playing the guitar. First time I heard it I thought it was a
record. He's really good."

He pushed the form back under the glass. "Maybe it is a
record."

"No, I've seen him through the window. The whole time
he's playing he keeps his eyes shut."

She wore some of the thickest lenses he'd ever seen, even
when she was a kid, and he remembered hearing she'd had
trouble getting her driver's license because she couldn't read
the wall chart. "I'm surprised you can tell his eyes are closed,"
he said.

She checked his form, then rubber-stamped it, tore off the
bottom portion and pushed it toward him. Grinning, she said,
"I've got a pretty good pair of binoculars."

Until lately, the urge to escape scrutiny was one he'd seldom
felt. His efforts to mask his drug use had been cursory at best,
and while he'd convinced himself he was taking all possible pre-
cautions to conceal his embezzlement, the truth was that he'd
been far too cavalier in his choice of targets. He'd often asked
himself how and why things had gone as wrong as they had,
and the only answer he'd ever arrived at didn't reflect well on
him: having always succeeded, he'd assumed he always would.

If you considered yourself a success, shame staked no claim on you. Any failure, of whatever nature, could easily be explained. If you quit on yet another book project, the time just wasn't right. After *The Corrections,* hadn't Franzen stopped writing fiction for several years? If you woke in the middle of the night to find your wife tossing from side to side, grinding her teeth and groaning in her sleep, you could always tell yourself that a couple of days ago the two of you had gone sailing around Boston Harbor on a PEN New England cruise with Chris Cooper, whose films she loved. Being with you had its rewards. So what if you were snorting her life up your nose?

Then all the evidence got collected, and multiple failures were confirmed, and for a while he did want to hide his face in shame. But now even the shame didn't matter any longer. The only thing that did was making sure nothing denied him a few more martinis with Kristin Stevens in North Reading.

The night the hurricane blew by offshore, when he mounted the stairs in her basement and she looked down at him and asked him to hold her, he'd wrapped his arms around her and let his head come to rest on her breast. Her heart was pounding wildly, the beats disturbingly irregular. "You're out of rhythm," he said.

"It only happens when I'm upset."

"Don't worry. Your basement will empty out."

"I'm not just worried about my basement."

As he stood there holding her, he believed he understood what had happened to her. Moving across town is traumatic enough. Moving across the continent, leaving all her friends behind after losing her job, probably called everything into question. She must have lost interest in her husband. The guy seemed nice enough, if a little dry, but he was large and ungainly and had a ghoulish quality—as if, though obviously still alive, he really ought to be dead. Matt wondered if maybe he'd fought in the First Gulf War. He looked like a man who might have taken a life or two and in the process surrendered a chunk of his own.

As for himself, Matt Drinnan was undergoing the acute physiological distress that results from touching a grown woman. Two minutes earlier, he'd found her annoying. Now he was clinging to her like Gorilla Glue.

"That book," she said. "Why did you give it to me?"

His right hand began to caress her spine. "Because it's a good book."

Over the droning sound of the sump pump and the chugging noise of water rushing through a hose, she said, "Remember that passage about what happens when we quit longing for joy, how our lives are almost over? 'One day we wake up and rub our eyes and do not know why we have woken. We know all too well what the day offers: spring or winter, the surface of life, the weather, the daily routine. Nothing surprising can ever happen again.'"

He broke the embrace and stepped back as far as he could without falling into the water. The opening at the top of the stairwell framed her perfectly.

"I've probably made you think I'm crazy," she said, gazing down at him. "We don't even know each other."

"We know each other better than we did a few minutes ago."

She wiped the smudged mascara off her face, then turned and led him up the stairs. He stepped into the harsh light of the former dining room, where there were two leather-covered armchairs with bentwood frames. When she lowered herself into the closest, the black Lab lumbered out of the kitchen and collapsed near her, taking no note of his presence.

"You gave me a novel," she said, "in which the long-dead lover who's the source of all the trouble and discord is named Krisztina."

Half the novels ever written in Central Europe probably had

a character named Krisztina, or even Kristin, but he sensed that pointing this out might interfere with whatever she planned to say next. He stepped past the dog and dropped into the chair beside hers.

"I've never caused trouble or discord," she said. "But I do feel like nothing surprising can ever happen again."

"Something just did. It surprised the living hell out of me, anyway."

She bent over and removed one shoe, then the other, finally leaning back and closing her eyes. "I'm tired," she said. "I feel put out and petulant. And I hate petulance more than just about anything."

From where he sat he could see into the kitchen. On one of the counters was a bottle of red wine, about three-quarters full. A single empty glass stood beside it. "I don't suppose you're going to offer me a drink, by any chance?"

"No, Matt, I'm not. I hope you'll forgive me. I appreciate the help. And I appreciate the hug."

If she'd said "your help" or "your hug," he might've reacted differently. But he felt as if his face had just been slapped. Even the fucking dog had dismissed him. He sprang out of the chair and said, "I'll send you an invoice."

"I didn't mean—"

He didn't wait to find out what she didn't mean, knowing that much already. Instead he stormed away without his umbrella.

He thought maybe she'd drop by to apologize the next day or the one after that, and if she had he might have apologized himself, perhaps even told her he'd just experienced a humiliating nosebleed in front of his ex-wife, her new husband, his best friend and what seemed like half of Montvale, that he felt completely lost, at a dead end, and was thinking maybe he ought to buy himself a cockatiel and teach it to perch on his shoulder.

But she didn't come by. He didn't even see her or her husband walking the dog, though he peeked out the window numerous times over the weekend.

When Monday rolled around, he was seething. He snapped at Dushay and behaved abruptly toward several customers. Frankie kept watching out of the corner of his eye and might have offered some sage advice, or at least asked him what the fuck was the matter, if Matt hadn't doffed his apron at the end of the day and left without helping him clean up.

He drove to the gym and sat in his car for a few minutes, trying to decide whether or not to go in, then turned back to Main Street and headed up Route 28 toward Andover. When he reached the train station, he didn't even bother to park in the commuter lot and pay the fee, just stopped at the curb, cut his engine and jumped out.

She was standing alone on the platform, waiting for the next train with her back to him. Her shoulders were slumped, and her briefcase rested on the concrete near her right leg. There were two benches a few feet away, both unoccupied. If you were so tired, he wondered, why wouldn't you sit down?

As if she'd detected his presence, she turned toward him. Her face gave away nothing. She looked neither surprised nor disturbed nor pleased. She didn't ask what he was doing there, and he didn't tell her. She just leaned down and lifted her briefcase and walked past him, and he followed her to his car.

They surveyed each other across the roof. "The drink I didn't offer you on Friday night," she said, "I'd like to make up for today. If you know someplace, we could have one en route."

"What are you in the mood for?"

"Alcohol."

The place they stopped at used to be a popular hangout among kids up and down the North Shore when Matt was in high school. Back then it was named Mister Mike's after the guy it belonged to, and as long as you looked like you were out of junior high you never got carded. These days it was called the Electric John, since both the men's and women's bathrooms boasted Incinolet toilets capable of reducing human waste to germ-free ash. The current owner was a committed environmentalist.

Inside, they took seats at a corner table underneath a banner promoting Mayflower golden ale. Only four or five others were at the bar. "The martinis are pretty good here," he said. "At least they used to be. I haven't been in since my divorce."

She pulled the plastic drink card from the salt-and-pepper rack. "You used to come here with your wife?"

"Sometimes. We never lived around here—we had a place in Cambridge—but once or twice a month we drove out to see our folks, and occasionally we'd stop in for a drink. It already had a new name and owner. But it's the space itself that used to matter."

She looked up from the plastic card. "It still matters to you. We wouldn't be here otherwise, would we?"

As he tried to decide how to respond, a waitress strolled over and asked what they'd like. Kristin placed the card back in the rack and ordered a martini, so he did too. After she left, neither of them was in a rush to speak again. On the TV above the bar somebody was interviewing the quarterback Brett Favre, who'd gotten in trouble for sending a woman lewd texts and videos. He kept trying to change the subject, wanting to discuss the Bears' secondary.

"Do you ever watch football?" Matt asked, since somebody needed to say something.

"Hardly ever."

"I don't watch it much myself. The guy I work for stays glued to the tube every Sunday. He's a big Pats fan, but he's got a soft spot for Favre."

"Who's Favre?"

He motioned at the TV. "He plays for the Vikings now.

Used to play for the Packers. He's never lost a game when the temperature's below freezing. You wouldn't expect a guy from Mississippi could adapt to cold weather."

"My first husband was from Mississippi," she said, "and he could adapt to anything. Or anybody."

Once she started talking she didn't stop, except briefly when the waitress brought the first round of drinks and then again when she brought the second. For many years now, she confessed, she'd mostly read junk. "Dan Brown or even worse." Yet books had been her first love. They had led her to her second love, a childhood friend named Patty, and then to her next love too. She lost both of those for reasons she didn't care to delve into. And then the books, as a matter of course, seemed to follow.

She said she initially found the novel he pressed on her boring. Beyond the conventional suspense of the unexpected guest, soon to arrive, there was nothing compelling. Then something eerie happened once she started to feel as if *Embers* had been written with her in mind. Two boys become inseparable in the waning days of the Austro-Hungarian Empire. They love each other, each in his own manner. They grow up, a woman comes between them, and then she, too, is lost. Portraits figure prominently in the text—those that grace the wall in the old general's castle as well as the one that has been removed from where it hung beside all the others. "When the general's still a boy," she said, "and the nurse is talking with his mother, worrying what might happen if he and Konrad become estranged . . . well, do you remember what she says?"

He took another sip of his second martini, then shook his head. When he read a novel, he might admire it for its language, for the vividness of the characters or the setting, the urgency of its ideas, the pithiness of its dialogue. But novels no longer made him cry or lie awake at night like they used to. He hadn't been aware of the change until now, and it made him feel deficient. "No," he said, "I'm afraid I don't. It's been a couple of years since I read it."

"'That is our human fate,'" Kristin said, in the same deliberate voice she'd used on the basement stairs. "'One day we lose the person we love. Anyone who is unable to sustain that loss fails as a human being and does not deserve our sympathy.'" That very afternoon, she told Matt, she'd gone online and looked at a picture of her ex-husband. She hadn't seen his face for sixteen years.

"You didn't keep any photos of him?"

"No. I destroyed every one of them. And you know what's most amazing? I chased the images out of my own mind. There were no photos of him there, either."

"I don't believe you," he said. Images of Carla flooded his mind. He thought of her all day long and dreamed of her at night.

"I'm just like the old general in the novel," Kristin said. "There's a blank space on his wall where Krisztina's portrait once hung. And there's a blank space in my mind where Philip's image used to be."

The conversation had taken an unexpected and unwelcome turn. He assumed when she climbed into his car that having a drink was the prelude to an affair, and while he'd never conducted one himself he'd read about them and believed he understood the dynamic. Each of them would use the other for a while to satisfy some unmet need. Her husband, it went without saying, would pose a big problem, as would the proximity of their houses and the neighborhood itself. You couldn't do anything on Essex Street without everyone else knowing about it. He foresaw a series of Updikean trysts up and down Route 28. Things would end as they always do: one day they'd just stop. There would be a few bittersweet encounters in the aisles at Shaw's or Stop & Shop, an embarrassing moment when he had to shoot the breeze with Cal in line at Dunkin'

Donuts. That's all these things were and all they were meant to be.

Now here was something else, an unburdening he hadn't reckoned on, and he had no idea how to respond. It was as if he were back in the basement of the bookstore and surrounded by millions of words, all of them useless. "I thought we were going to have an affair," he said.

The tension ever present on her face ebbed away. As the lines disappeared, they ceded space to her eyes, which seemed to grow larger as he sat there. He'd never seen her smile before, and that was all it took to make her beautiful.

"I wondered if you might not be thinking that," she said. "But I told myself it was silly. I must be at least ten years older."

Nabokov once noted that an optimum number of words exists for every simile, and once that number is passed the simile begins to lose its power. Discussion of a potential affair, Matt intuited, couldn't last too long without making the affair impossible. So he reached across the table.

She didn't jerk her hand away to avoid contact with his, just let it lie there with his on top of it. She studied them as if they were forensic evidence.

To her mind, this represented indisputable proof that if conversation, even of the most intimate nature, was all she could offer, he wouldn't be sitting there across the table. He'd made a mess of his life, and even though he hadn't gone to jail he acted like a newly released inmate. On the basement stairs, when she'd asked him to hold her and he put his arms around her, she knew immediately she'd made a mistake. But she couldn't bring herself to break the embrace. Right then, she needed it that much.

Because she continued to look at his hand atop hers, she was spared having to witness the moment when the willingness to take a big risk and make a fool of himself deserted him. As far as he was concerned, his foolishness belonged in the electric toilet where it could be disinfected and turned into ash. He removed his hand and placed it beside his empty glass. "I'm sorry, Kristin," he said. "I used to be better than this, though I don't expect you to believe it."

"I used to be better than this too," she said, then did something that she could neither explain nor justify, reaching across the table, lifting his hand and bringing it to rest once more on hers. They sat like that for a moment or two longer, then she caught the eye of the waitress and asked for the check.

In the car, as if it were a normal request, she asked him to drop her close to the train station rather than driving to her house. Before climbing out, she said, "That was the nicest hour I've spent in a long time, Matt."

He said he felt the same way, but the question of whether it would happen again was never posed, much less answered.

The next day he didn't drive to Andover. The day after that he did.

Following the town hall conversation with Sara McDonough, he walked into the deli to find Frankie and Dushay engaged in heated debate. Their dispute concerned the Supreme Court's refusal to hear the case of Massachusetts inmates who'd challenged the law prohibiting incarcerated felons from voting in state elections. Unlike Frankie and the Supreme Court, Dushay was persuaded by the inmates' argument that the law had a disproportionate impact on minority voters because more of them were in jail.

Frankie shoved a porcelain tray of roast beef into the deli case. "Be that as it may," he said, "we adopt a color-blind policy when it comes to alcohol. If somebody's in the slammer, he can't get drunk on Saturday night, even if that has a disproportionate impact on liquor stores owned by Hispanics. You're not making shit for sense, Douche, though there's nothing new about that."

"I believe in everybody's right to rehabilitate himself, and taking part in the political process is a good start."

"You wouldn't be standing here if I didn't believe in rehabilitation. That's what you're doing every time you ogle some high school girl and slice your finger instead of a bulkie roll. Your rehab's costing me eight bucks an hour, my friend, and that's leaving aside the possibility that the girl's mom might see you leering at her daughter, which could also cost me a customer. So don't tell me, Douche, that I'm hard-hearted when it comes to our caged brethren. I'm softhearted to the point of insanity. And like it or not, I'm the main thing between you and a ticket back to Shirley."

"The judge released me on my own reconnaissance."

"Recognizance—that's what he released you on. But he also said you had to remain gainfully employed. And that's what you're doing, Douche. You're gaining. I'm losing."

Matt pulled his apron off the peg and strapped it on. The morning passed slowly, the mood of most of the customers relentlessly downbeat. Ryan Kelly looked bleary-eyed. His wife, a medical technician, had gotten laid off by Hallmark Health, and word around Montvale was that his heating and plumbing business was in trouble too. He was working evenings now at the Cedar Park Walgreens, prowling the aisles in one of those little blue vests. "I spend my days," he told Matt, "clearing plugged toilets. Now I spend my nights stocking Preparation H and Anusol. Looks like I was created to deal with shit in some form or fashion."

Matt Drinnan was out of step with the times. Having lost everything before everybody else did, he was now on the road to recovery and had come up with his own stimulus plan. And while it required bipartisan support, it wasn't subject to the vicissitudes of public opinion since it took place entirely in secret. His weekday afternoons all ended at a bar in North Reading with a woman who wasn't his wife. Since that first day when she'd laid his hand back on top of hers, they hadn't touched even once. They made ample eye contact, but otherwise all they did was drink and talk. And if the talk ran out, though that seldom happened, silence sufficed.

Much of the conversation was trivial. One day she told him that she'd looked his last name up. "It originally meant 'blackthorn,'" she informed him, "and it's often changed to 'Thornton.' One of your ancestors was the poet who first referred to Ireland as the 'Emerald Isle.' So you see? You've got poetry in your blood. No wonder you wanted to be a writer."

He voiced curiosity about her life in academia. When he was a student at Tufts, he told her, the English professors always seemed to be at war with one another. An Americanist he became friendly with said it was "because never before was so little at stake."

She laughed, then remarked that there sometimes was quite a bit at stake. After the O. J. Simpson trial, she said, the chair of the philosophy department at her former university went to a conference in Los Angeles. In the cab back to the airport, the driver asked if he'd like to detour through Brentwood and see O.J.'s house. "So he says why not. An amateur photographer, he takes his Nikon everywhere and figures he'll get a nice picture of a place in the news. The taxi pulls up front, and while our philosopher's got his camera aimed at the house, out comes guess who?"

"O.J.?"

She nodded. "He ambles over and starts chatting them up and eventually asks, 'Want a picture with *me*?' So the department chair has the taxi driver snap his photo with the most reviled man in America, both of them with huge grins on their faces, and when he gets back home he has a nice glossy eight-by-ten printed up that happens to be framed and sitting on his desk the day he calls a lecturer in to tell her that her contract isn't being renewed. She sued him for creating a threatening environment in the workplace."

"Did she win?"

"We never let it go to court and settled for around four hundred thousand."

"You thought she had a valid case?"

"I wasn't willing to bet she didn't. Sometimes you have to cut your losses."

As the afternoons and the martinis multiplied, the talk took a serious turn. He once asked her if she'd ever missed having children, and she said, "I don't know that I could answer that question honestly."

"Why not?"

"Because I might well have lied to myself about it for such a long time that I don't even know the truth anymore. Maybe we should leave it for later. Why don't you tell me about your girls?"

"They couldn't be more different from each other," he said. "Angie's got Carla's complexion and hair color, and she also runs her mouth a mile a minute. And you know what else? She's the world's worst arachnophobe. I'd hear a shriek, and by the time I got to their bedroom she'd be up on the windowsill, pointing at some little bug you couldn't spot with a microscope. Lexa, on the other hand, is blond and fair-skinned, the kind of girl who'll sit for two or three hours with a book and never make a sound. Her favorite writer's Larry McMurtry. How she got hooked on him, I don't know. She's never set foot in the state of Texas, but she's nuts about those *Lonesome Dove* novels. Before the divorce, I promised to take her to Archer City one day and see if he might be hanging around his bookstore so she could ask for his autograph. That'll never happen now."

"Why not?"

He sipped his martini. "I get them twice a month and only on weekends."

"Wouldn't your wife let you take them on a trip?"

"I don't know. I feel like I'm kind of fading away as their father, given Nowicki and all. It's a little scary."

"Isn't that a good reason for you to work up the courage to ask about having more time with them?"

"Maybe I should," he said. "After all, I worked up enough to track you down in Andover."

"Did it really take that much, Matt?" she asked.

"Yeah, it really did."

"Well, that makes me feel important." She brushed a loose strand off her forehead, and he saw that she'd just had a manicure. "It also calls to mind June Lockhart."

"Who?"

"She played Timmy's mom on the *Lassie* series. Later on she hosted the Miss USA pageant—until they fired her for taking up with a younger man."

"But you haven't taken up with me. We're just having a few drinks."

"No, but people notice our age difference."

"What people?"

She motioned toward the bar. "Our waitress. And anybody else who comes in here."

"Does it bother you?"

A little extra color appeared in her cheeks. "I can't actually say that it does."

Clearly she'd cut her own losses, settling for less than she'd sought in every respect, becoming an administrator rather than the professor and literary critic she'd set out to be and leaving a top-tier university for a third-rate state college because she had no other choices. She'd lost the man she loved and married another one for something less than love. Matt knew as much even though she never said so.

What he didn't yet know, and wondered if he'd ever find out, was whether what was happening to him was also happening to her.

one morning in mid-october Cal woke late. He'd again spent the night on the third floor after drinking too much whiskey, falling asleep around three on the daybed in his music room. The bed wasn't quite long enough for him, so he'd slept on his side with his legs drawn up, and when he swung them off the mattress he felt a twinge in his lower back. Because of that, he sat there a little longer than he otherwise might have and absorbed details he would've missed if he'd bounced right up.

The air in the room, he noticed, felt bracingly crisp like it never had in California, where autumn brought tule fog that seeped inside your house and into your bones. And then there was the tree in the neighbors' backyard. It was a maple, but not a silver maple like he was used to. The leaves on this one had turned a rich, winey red and were toothy around the edges. He tried to remember if it had looked like that yesterday, and he was certain it hadn't.

He finally stood and moved toward the window. As the boundaries of his vision expanded, so did the range of colors. Red, orange, yellow, gold, pumpkin spice, tobacco sunburst. He'd never seen so many different hues outside a Renoir. Yet his neighbors were all climbing into their cars and trucks and heading off to work as if nothing miraculous had happened and this were just another ordinary day. He laid his hands against the chilly pane, then let his forehead rest there, too, until his breath began to cloud the glass and fade the impression that while he slept the world had caught fire.

Of the many different tasks involved in constructing or maintaining a home, the ones he liked least all involved electricity.

He'd witnessed a horrible accident as a young man when he was working for a company in Modesto.

They were building a new house for one of the bigwigs at Gallo. Though he was trying to steer clear of personal entanglements, spending most of his free time alone in a rented room where he taught himself to play guitar and mandolin, he'd recently become friends with a guy named Ernesto, who'd moved to the valley from Salinas. Somehow, maybe because he found his own jokes funny and always broke up when delivering a punch line, Ernesto had managed to make Cal laugh a few times, which lifted him out of the dark hole he'd fallen into. On Friday nights they began going out for a few beers and chile rellenos, and Cal was beginning to think of unburdening himself. "I made a real bad mistake a couple years ago," he imagined saying, at which time—he was sure—Ernesto would lean closer and say, "Tell me about it, amigo."

That never happened because one day at the construction site his friend told a joke that amused him so much he slapped the side of a crane just as the beam swung around and made contact with a pole where several power lines converged, each conducting twenty thousand volts. Ernesto's mouth opened wide like he intended to laugh once more, but nothing came out and nothing ever would. When he dropped to the hardpan, everyone thought he was playing a trick. And then they smelled his scorched flesh.

After that, Cal tried to avoid messing with wiring. The old knob-and-tube stuff in the house on Essex had long since been replaced, but he'd already found several problems. Instead of connecting the case grounds to water pipes in the basement, somebody had left several of them dangling in the air, and in the breaker box neutral wires and ground wires had been paired together under the same screws. Just the other day, the kitchen's recessed lights began to flicker. It didn't matter how low or high you set the dimmer switches, the result was the same. Somebody had fucked something up somewhere, and it was becoming harder to ignore, so after he ate his bowl of oatmeal and drank enough coffee to clear his head he set out to identify what and where it was.

He went down into the basement, grabbed an aluminum stepladder and the sack of 120-volt floodlights he'd bought yesterday at the hardware store and went back to the kitchen. If the lights were wired in series across the load, something as simple as a loose filament in one bulb could account for the annoying fluttering. He mounted the ladder, removed each of the old bulbs, replaced it with a new one, then climbed back down and walked over to the wall switch. He flipped it on, and the lights shined perfectly. He looked at his watch, waited two full minutes and was reaching for the switch when the lights flickered again. He stood there timing them. The fluttering came at odd intervals: thirty-five seconds, three and a half minutes, twenty seconds. "Shit," he said.

He returned to the basement and grabbed a screwdriver. Some fool had probably interrupted a neutral wire and put the switch in neutral; that could cause the ground-fault interrupter to cycle on and off, depending on how much voltage was hitting the bulbs.

In the kitchen, he turned the lights off and removed the wall plate. The switch was wired normally, so he flipped the lights on, laid the metal plate on the windowsill and went downstairs again. The breaker box was in the corner, but he forgot to duck and smashed his head into the aluminum ductwork. It was quite a lick, and after he put a hand to his forehead it came away bloody.

He pulled the box open and turned off every breaker on the main panel except the one feeding the kitchen lights. Then he took the stairs two at a time and stood in the kitchen staring at the ceiling for ten minutes. The lights failed to flicker. So he went back down and turned on all the breakers again, but by the time he got back to the kitchen they were flickering once more.

He spent the next few hours running up and down the basement stairs, turning off one breaker at a time before standing in the kitchen and gazing at the ceiling, trying to identify which one might have a pulsating load that drew peak current at the same rate as the blinking lights. After the final breaker failed to yield an answer, he slammed the box shut.

When he got upstairs again, he was shaking. Lunchtime had come and gone, and he knew he ought to eat something, maybe drink a beer to settle down, and then start looking for other solutions. The source of the problem might not even be inside the house. If he was dealing with the power in general, he'd have to call NSTAR.

Rather than making himself a sandwich, he decided to go out and buy one, just to get a change of scenery. There was a convenience store about half a mile away, on East Border Road, so he put Suzy on her leash, threw on his fleece jacket and went outside.

A breeze off the ocean was sweeping up the hill through Cedar Park, and as he walked along with Suzy they were showered by falling leaves. The day was bright, with a little bite in the air. Until now he'd never really known what autumn meant. One year when he was growing up it hit ninety-four degrees in Bakersfield on Thanksgiving Day. The leaves there went from green to brown overnight. Something about that had never seemed quite right. It was like you were being cheated of two seasons, since it started getting hot again in March.

The convenience store's parking lot was empty except for a white SUV. When they got to the door, he told Suzy to sit, then pushed it open and stepped inside.

If he'd been the kind of guy who paid a lot of attention to cars, he might have noticed that the SUV was identical to the BMW owned by his neighbor, whom he'd waved at once or twice but avoided conversation with since he'd bailed out on his dinner invitation. If he'd noticed that, he probably wouldn't have gone inside. He had plenty of stuff at home to make a sandwich with, and just getting out of the house had been the point. He would've walked back up the hill and fixed himself something to eat. And then what was about to happen wouldn't have, though he later guessed that maybe something worse could have.

Vico was standing with his back against a floor-to-ceiling refrigeration case filled with soft drinks, Gatorade and bottled water. Hugging a big sack of Cape Cod potato chips, he was sweating badly. That didn't make much sense because the day was cool and he was wearing only a light sweater. His eyes looked abnormally large, and the left one was twitching.

To Cal's right, behind the counter, were two other men. One was about twenty-five, with light brown skin that made Cal think he might be Pakistani. He was wearing wire-rimmed glasses and had his hand in the cash drawer.

At first Cal didn't see the third guy, who was crouching behind the display case containing the sandwiches and pre-packaged cartons of potato salad, coleslaw and marinated peppers. Now he stood up, waved either a .38 or a 9 millimeter at Cal and said, "Move your ass over there beside Robert De Niro." He was in his midfifties, short and gray-haired, and had on a long-sleeved gray work shirt. Even his face looked gray, covered as it was in stubble.

Cal had never been threatened before by a weapon more lethal than a stone or a crowbar. Both could kill you if the person wielding them knew what he was doing, but the odds were much lower. This was something different, in a year filled with new experiences, and he felt himself coalescing around a center whose existence he'd begun to question. "Where?" he said.

"Whatta ya mean 'where'?"

"I don't see Robert De Niro."

"I'm speaking about the wop of the day," the gunman said, nodding at Vico. Three weeks earlier, he'd been released from the New Hampshire State Prison in Concord after serving five and a half years for armed robbery. He'd done time in Massachusetts and New York State, too. "Get over there next to the guy looks like he aims to fuck that bag of chips."

"All right," Cal said. He had fifteen dollars, an ATM card and a Visa in his wallet. There was nothing on his person he couldn't afford to part with, which was kind of a shame. He'd left home without his cell phone. He didn't even have on his watch, a stainless-steel Rolex Explorer that Kristin had bought him for his forty-fifth birthday. It cost close to four thousand dollars, and had it been on his wrist the burglar might've noticed it and come close enough to take it off him. If he'd just had something a thief badly wanted, he would've been in a much better position. It went without saying that if you set off to rob a convenience store, you couldn't expect to come away with a Rolex. It also went without saying that the guy with the gun would probably rather get the money and run without pulling the trigger, though it was by no means certain he wouldn't kill somebody if he needed to.

The man stepped out from behind the case, his eyes scanning the parking lot, the gun in his right hand acting as a director's baton as he waved Cal along toward his neighbor. Suddenly there was a loud crash, followed by thunderous barking. Cal turned to see Suzy hurling herself at the glass door, slobber flying from her tongue.

"Make that fucking dog shut up."

Cal, Vico would later tell reporters from the *Boston Globe* and the *Cedar Park Independent,* seemed strangely calm when he addressed the burglar, whose name was Andrew Saucer. "He looks at the guy and says, 'I'm not sure I *can* make her shut up. She didn't do real well at obedience training.' And that's when the fellow goes apeshit."

Neither paper printed the expression "apeshit" in its account. From Cal's perspective, it wasn't accurate anyhow. "Apeshit" meant you completely lost your wits, forgot about consequences and acted without reason, whereas Saucer was behaving pretty rationally, despite holding a gun in his hand and trying to rob a convenience store in the middle of the day while an eighty-pound black Lab flung herself at the door and barked so loudly people could hear her several blocks away. If he'd truly gone apeshit, things might have worked out better for him, or maybe not, you could never really predict. You did what you did, and things happened as they happened.

"You son of a bitch," Andrew Saucer said. "If you don't stop her from barking, I'm gonna shoot you *and* your fucking dog."

"The only way I might be able to stop her," Cal said, "is if you let me go out and take her home. I think she's formed a low opinion of you."

"You arrogant fuck," Saucer said, his gun hand starting to tremble. "You think I'm playing around?"

On the far side of the parking lot, next to East Border Road, a couple of schoolkids were walking by. Both of them stopped to look at Suzy, who continued to bark and throw herself against the door.

"This is all kind of new to me," Cal replied. "I really haven't had time to find out what I think."

Big drops of spittle had formed in both corners of Saucer's mouth. The first couple of weeks after his release, he'd stayed in Montvale with his brother and his sister-in-law. Then he'd lifted a pair of twenties from her purse, and even though she didn't see him do it and couldn't be sure he had, they told him to clear out. Last night, he'd ridden the Orange Line from Oak Grove to Forest Hills and back three times, and when the trains finally quit running he'd shivered for a few hours on a bench near Pleasant Pond. This morning, after his brother and sister-in-law left for work, he'd gone back and forced a window, eaten a sandwich and swiped his brother's gun. They'd hidden it in a tool chest, but he knew how that asshole's mind worked.

Cal decided later that if he'd been in Saucer's position, he would've shot the dog first. That would've made the most sense for at least two reasons. To begin with, Suzy was raising holy hell, already attracting attention, and because of her size it wasn't inconceivable that she might jar the door open and lunge into the store. She'd never bitten anybody, but Andrew Saucer didn't know that. Second, Cal was on the far side of the counter and deli case from Saucer, a good seven or eight feet away. If he was a decent shot, Saucer could have killed the dog and then turned to fire at Cal before he was able to take more than one stride.

But for whatever reason, Saucer, who'd aimed plenty of weapons at people but never shot anybody, made the opposite choice. He stepped back behind the deli case and braced the butt of the pistol on top of it, between two big jars of Lakeside Red Hots.

According to the article in the *Globe,* the deli case weighed 543 pounds when it was empty, and all the stuff inside and on top of it probably added another 40 or 50 pounds. Yet when Cal lowered his head and threw himself against it, the case moved enough to disrupt Saucer's aim, so he fired a round into the ceiling before losing his grip on the gun, and the glass in the case shattered, several shards ending up in Cal's left arm and shoulder.

What occurred next was never clear to Cal. Unlike Andrew Saucer, he'd gone apeshit.

"My neighbor's on the floor with blood streaming down his arm," Vico told two of his friends that night, sitting in over-stuffed chairs in his "man cave" in the basement. There was yet another wide-screen TV down there, and the Yankees were playing the Rangers in the American League championship series, New York up two games to one, but he didn't feel like watching, and his friends understood. It was the drunkest he'd been in years, which wasn't saying much, since normally he never got drunk. The ex-cop from Everett kept drawing him glasses of wine from a big box of Franzia Cabernet that stood on the wet bar. Vico hadn't drunk such bad wine since college. "I mean, for all I know it's his jugular."

"If it'd been his jugular," the ex-cop said, "he never would've made it to his feet. See, body posture's got a lot to do with how fast you lose blood. If you're in a prone position, your ticket's punched. I saw a guy bleed to death like that down in the Dirty E."

"He didn't stay down long," Vico said. "It was like he shot off the floor. He just kind of high-jumps the counter—that's the only way I can put it. Like he's doing the fucking Fosbury Flop."

"He went over *backward*?" the ex-coach asked.

"What do you mean?"

"Fosbury jumped backward—that's why they called it the flop."

"I don't know if he went over backward, forward, sideways or upside down. That's what I'm trying to get across. It all happened so fast it's like one constant blur. He's over that counter in a flash, so fast the poor Pakistani can't move aside in time and gets knocked like a bowling pin. And when he throws the first punch at the skid, the bastard just disintegrates. I mean he crumbles before my very eyes."

"And the whole time this is happening," the ex-cop said, "you're doing what?"

At some point during the ordeal he'd wet himself. He was on prostate meds, and most of the time he did well to squeeze out a couple ounces, but he hadn't needed Flomax today. "What do you mean, what am I doing?" he asked, downing the last of his wine.

The ex-cop got up again to refill his glass, and this time he had to tilt the box. "Like maybe you grabbed the gun?"

"I didn't have to. When the clerk got to his feet, he darted around the counter and picked it up and ran out the back. Then he called your former colleagues."

"That still doesn't tell us what you were doing," the retired coach said. "And that's what we're interested in, my friend, because tonight you're not yourself. You look like Vico Cignetti, but right now you're acting like somebody else."

"I was *watching*," Vico said. And then he told them what he couldn't get out of his head. "He pulls the poor limp fuck off the floor, props him against the wall and hits him so many times, so freakin' fast, the guy can't even fall back down. It's like the force of the blows is what's holding him up.

"Then my neighbor grabs him with both hands and begins ramming his head into the wall, throwing him into it again and again like he's on some kind of assembly line, picking up metal parts and jamming them into a punch press. He's still doing it when the cops pull up."

"And then what happens?"

This was the part Vico found most troubling. He'd think about it later that night and off and on again for many weeks afterward. It would repeatedly disrupt his sleep, leaving him wondering if he was safer, or more at risk, than he'd been before Cal Stevens and his wife moved in. He'd never even considered safety before. Around here, stealing a hubcap made news, and slashing a tire could land you on the front page of the *Montvale Sun*. "What happens then is, my neighbor"—he gestured in the direction of the house next door—"my *neighbor* who damn near just killed a man turns to me and asks if I'm all right. His face is a little red, and he's got blood all over one arm, and his knuckles are bleeding too, and there's a gash in his forehead and a Band-Aid dangling down over one eye. But just like that, he's as placid as if he's eaten a bottle of Valium. So I nod at him, though I'm anything but all right because I've pissed my own pants, and he says, 'I'm sorry I didn't make it over to watch the game that night with you and your friends. That was rude of me. Maybe you could ask me again?'"

The ex-coach was chewing tobacco. He looked at the ex-cop, then spit a long brown stream into his Styrofoam cup. "Sounds like my kind of guy," he said. "But he might be more fun to watch boxing with than baseball."

that night, when she returned from the shower, she found him in their bed. For the last few weeks he'd been sleeping on the third floor, which he explained by saying that he knew she had to rise early and was worried about waking her if he came to bed late. Around two or three, when he climbed the final flight, she always woke anyway and lay there thinking just how easy he was making it for her to disengage. She'd come here hoping that starting over in a new place would bring back whatever it was she'd felt in the crossroads grocery the first time she heard him play. But it was as if he intended to convince her that what she'd felt was nothing at all and that marrying him was simple expediency, like changing a guitar string after you broke one.

He lay on his back in a pair of black jogging shorts, his right knee raised, his left arm bandaged and folded over his chest, his right arm hanging down off the bed so far his fingertips grazed the floor. The only light came from the Himalayan salt lamp she kept on the dresser, and for a moment she thought he was asleep, but as her eyes adjusted she saw that his were wide open and staring at the ceiling. "I almost killed that guy," he said.

She pulled her bathrobe off, opened the closet door and hung it on the hook. When she received the call from the hospital, she assumed he'd injured himself with a power tool. No one told her until she walked into the emergency room and found him sitting on a gurney that he'd broken up an armed robbery. And it wasn't until they were riding home in the taxi that she learned someone had tried to shoot him. "Well," she said, "he almost killed you before that."

"On the news, they said he's spent eighteen of the last

twenty-one years in prison. He's fifty-two. Just a couple years older than me. That'd be like me being in jail all but three years since I was twenty-nine."

He was lying on her side of the bed, or the side she'd come to think of as hers since he began sleeping upstairs. As she walked around the foot of the bed, she noticed what the raised knee was apparently intended to conceal: a huge bulge in his shorts, where she hadn't seen one in ages.

The sight caused her to pause, and her reaction didn't go unnoticed. "We don't have to make anything of it," he said, "if you don't want to."

"I don't know if I do or not," she said. "I mean, it's the juxtaposition I find troubling. You go out and almost get killed and then proceed to beat somebody senseless, and then you get an erection for the first time in . . ." She couldn't finish the sentence.

"Ten months," he said helpfully. "If you could call what I got that night an erection. I'm not sure it qualified."

She wasn't sure it did either, but agreeing would have been unkind. She went around to the other side of the bed and sat down with her back to him. The clock was over there on the bedside table, and she set the alarm. She had a meeting at eight thirty the next morning with the chair of the history department on a matter he'd termed extremely urgent, and what she really wanted more than anything was to go to sleep.

Sleep wasn't the only thing she wanted, though, or the only thing she needed, a truth she found disquieting. She sat there for a moment longer, her bare feet on the cold floor. Then she pulled her nightgown up over her thighs, raised her arms and lifted it off.

"I probably better stay on my back," he said. "My left arm and hand aren't too useful right now."

"That's all right. You're not going to chord me."

When she turned toward him, he said, "Jesus. I forgot how beautiful you are. I feel like I did when I saw you the first time."

"You've seen me every day for fifteen years."

"Some days I see better than others."

"Almost dying's sharpened your vision?"

"I imagine that's what it does to most folks." He raised his head long enough to stare down the length of his torso. "Kristin," he said, "I'm scared I'll lose it."

"Well, we can't let that happen, can we?" She reached under his waistband. "You're fine." She knelt and pulled his shorts down over his legs and feet and dropped them off the side of the bed. Then she straddled him.

It hurt when he went inside her, and also that he failed to acknowledge her discomfort, pushing hard rather than allowing her a moment to recover. She bit her lip and closed her eyes, but it only got worse. When she opened them again and looked down at him, she saw that his jaw was clenched, that he was hurting too, though where his pain came from she couldn't imagine.

His hand closed on her left breast, kneading, squeezing. She leaned over him, flattening her palms against the mattress, struggling to find her own rhythm. No one was in control. They were equally helpless, two lost bodies.

From his vantage point all Matt could see was her shadow, but that was more than enough. She bent forward, then seconds later rocked backward. He stood beneath the maple at the corner for another moment, then turned up the collar of his windbreaker and walked down the hill into Cedar Park.

He'd waited at the station in Andover for close to an hour. Waiting was all he could do, because he had no way of reaching her. When he'd suggested they swap cell numbers, she said it was a bad idea, and her home phone was unlisted. His wasn't, but when he got back she hadn't left him a message. Just to hear a voice, he turned on the TV and, while eating leftovers, saw the report about the attempted robbery. They said her husband was treated for minor injuries and released.

He sat on a bench next to Pleasant Pond, where he'd learned to ice-skate. He couldn't have been more than three or four when his mother brought him here to teach him. He'd wanted to zip across the glistening surface like the bigger kids, because it looked like so much fun. But when the day finally arrived he woke up crying, claiming he had a sore throat, that it was too cold out and his ear hurt. She paid his protests no mind, just bundled him up, took him by the hand and led him firmly down the street. While he sat on this same bench, she squatted before him and strapped on his skates, then sat down beside him and strapped hers on too. After that she again clasped his hand, and together they stepped onto the ice.

"When you start skating," she told him as he clung to her, "don't look at your feet. Hold your arms out straight, like you're about to lay them on the dining room table. If you feel a fall coming on, bend over and grab your knees. That will lower your center of gravity. And most importantly? If you *do* go down, get right back up." She towed him around in front of herself and gave him a gentle shove.

though no one ever came right out and said it, Kristin gradually understood that Sarah Connulty's religion was of another order than that practiced by her parents and Mr. Connulty and Patty and everyone else she knew growing up. The only prayers Kristin heard at home were the perfunctory graces her father used to say over dinner at Thanksgiving, Christmas and Easter. Eventually, by the time she entered high school, he'd even quit saying those, and neither she nor her mother ever missed them. The Connultys themselves never prayed over their meals, so it was a while before Kristin noticed that once she sat down to eat Mrs. Connulty would quickly shut her eyes, her lips moving wordlessly.

When the two families gathered, there was always a predinner drink, and a couple bottles of wine would be consumed during the meal. Afterward, the adults decamped to the living room, where they had yet another drink—brandy or cognac—and while Mrs. Connulty always joined in these activities, she never appeared to do more than wet her lips. When the girls cleared the table, an inch or two of wine usually remained in her glass.

If Kristin's mother noticed these tendencies, she never remarked on them. Her father made at least one reference, asking his wife, after the two of them went to New York to see *Jesus Christ Superstar,* if they'd run up much of a bar bill at their Midtown hotel and if Mrs. Connulty agreed with those born-again Christians who considered the Broadway musical blasphemous. Her mother ignored the first question but responded sharply to the second: "If she did, do you think she would've gone to see it?"

"Maybe she didn't know what she was letting herself in for."

"She was the one who suggested it. Did you forget?"

"I guess I did." He was dressing up as Santa for the school Christmas party when this conversation took place. Their bedroom door was ajar, and as Kristin walked past she could see him pulling on his red velour pants. His beard and stocking cap lay on the bedside table.

"Yes, I guess you did," her mother replied. "For someone who teaches literature, you're far too quick to stereotype."

That response pleased Kristin. She felt oddly protective of Mrs. Connulty. The source of this impulse was hard to identify, but it had at least something to do with the fact that Patty's mother differed from the other women in the town in a number of respects and that she never could've concealed these differences, no matter how she tried. And try to conceal them she did.

One February morning when Kristin was in junior high, she woke up with an earache. Her mother insisted on taking her temperature and discovered it was already 101. She offered to stay home with her, but Kristin assured her she'd be fine until the school day ended. They made a doctor's appointment for four fifteen. She went back to sleep but woke up again around eleven with her face on fire and her ear feeling as if someone had stuck a power drill into the canal and was doing his best to drill right into her brain.

When she got out of bed, she felt dizzy and had to steady herself against the bedpost. As soon as the world quit spinning, she looked out the window and saw that Mrs. Connulty's car was in the driveway. She stepped into her shoes and wrapped herself in her warm bathrobe, then went downstairs and outside. Later, she wondered why she didn't just pick the phone up and call her.

She knocked on the door, but nothing happened. People didn't lock their houses when they were home during the day, and some probably didn't even lock them at night, so she opened the door and stepped inside. "Mrs. Connulty?" she called.

Sarah would claim afterward that she hadn't heard her, but she said this with no small amount of embarrassment, her face the color of an August sunset as she stuck a thermometer into Kristin's mouth. She hadn't heard anything because she herself had been speaking so earnestly.

The voice came from the pantry, where Kristin had first tasted those homemade wafers. Initially she assumed Mrs. Connulty must be in there talking on the phone, which hung on the wall near the electric range but had an extra-long cord. When she entered the kitchen, however, the receiver was in its cradle. If she hadn't been in so much pain, she probably would have turned around and gone home to call her mom, but she needed to be comforted and knew that Sarah Connulty wouldn't disappoint her.

When she parted the curtain, she saw her friend's mother on her knees, her back to the entrance and her forehead resting on her hands, which were squeezed together atop a twenty-five-pound sack of Martha White flour. "Please, Jesus, please," she was saying in that thick mountain accent, "don't let folks find out I'm such a awful fraud. Help me keep it hid. Forgive me, Jesus, please, my God in heaven."

She didn't say what she needed to be forgiven for, presumably because God and Jesus already knew. Kristin let the curtain fall and turned to run from the house, but then stumbled into the electric range, at which time Sarah realized she had uninvited company and called for her to stop.

After she'd taken her temperature, she made her lie down on the couch under a blanket while she phoned the school and asked for her mother. With her good ear, Kristin heard her speaking calmly. "Yes, it's awful high, and her ear's red and hot to the touch. . . . No, I don't think you need to do that. I'll just call them myself and take her right in. . . . Yes, of course, I'll let you know the minute we get back. . . . It's no bother, I love her too."

It turned out she had a bacterial infection. They told her to lie on her side while they put some drops in her ear. Then they prescribed an oral antibiotic, gave her an extra-strength pain reliever and let her go.

It was snowing hard when they left the doctor's office. She sat in the car with the heater on while Mrs. Connulty used an ice scraper to clear the windshield, and looking through it Kristin could see the tears in her eyes. She didn't think they were caused by the cold. She believed they'd been brought on by her fear of exposure.

That episode was on her mind the morning after the foiled robbery, as she waited for Donna to show the chair of the history department into her office. She had a public e-mail address, and lacking any other means of contacting her than walking up and knocking on her front door, Matt Drinnan had chosen to use it. Around three a.m. he'd written to say he was in love with her—*It seems impossible, but it's happened*—and her inclination, after reading the lengthy message, was to delete it immediately, because messages sent to a university address were never private, especially if you were a personnel officer. In California, hers had been subpoenaed so often it seemed like the techies were rummaging through her inbox at least once a week. On the other hand, deleting it wouldn't accomplish anything. It was still on the server. And it was still in Matt's heart.

Donna ushered the chair in, then stepped out and closed the door. Kristin rose and offered him her hand. They'd met at a couple monthly sessions held by Academic Affairs, but had never really talked. Around forty, trim and fit, with a receding hairline, John Bell had earned his Ph.D. at the University of Delaware. Like a number of other chairs around the university, he was a tenured associate professor. This was by design, since an associate was more likely than a full professor to do whatever the administration asked, even at the risk of annoying senior colleagues. If the department denied him promotion, the administration would overturn it—assuming he'd done its bidding. That's how things worked both here and at any number of other schools.

"I saw the *Globe* article this morning about the attempted robbery in Cedar Park," Bell said. "That was your husband who broke it up, wasn't it?"

"I'm afraid so."

"He must have real cojones."

The academic cop in her noted his willingness to use that particular word in the presence of a female administrator. "That's one way of putting it," she said. "The other is to say it was foolish as hell. The guy pointed a gun at him and was obviously prepared to use it."

"Is he all right?"

Wanting to get the meeting over with so she could decide what to do about Matt, she gestured at the seat opposite her desk. "He's got bandages all over his arm. He won't play the guitar for a while, which is a problem for him."

Bell sat down. "He's a musician?"

"Among other things."

"I play a little guitar, though I'm not very good."

She made a point of glancing at the wall clock. He hadn't come to discuss musicology, and she had more momentous things on her mind.

Bell finally cleared his throat. "I don't know you well," he said, "but I've got a problem on my hands and don't know where else to turn."

"What kind of problem?"

"It concerns a couple of my faculty members, and it's related to academic integrity."

"Well, normally that would come under the purview of the dean and the provost. And if Joanne thought I needed to become involved, she'd tell me."

"Yes, I know that," he said, and even though the morning was cool and the heat in the office had yet to trip on, his cheeks were beginning to glisten. "The thing is . . . Well, Dr. Stevens . . ."

"Kristin."

"Kristin," he said, "the thing is, Joanne Bedard is a good friend of one of these people. He's spent six years cultivating her, and she's susceptible to flattery. If I went to her with this problem, I'm afraid she'd take a chunk out of my rear the size of a Big Mac."

Kristin didn't want to have this conversation any more than Bell did, but they clearly were going to, so she might as well try to ease his discomfort. She stood, walked over to the window and cracked it open. When she sat down again, she said, "Whatever you're about to say to me is confidential. I won't discuss it with anyone else without first asking your permission. Does that help?"

"Yes," he said, "it does. My wife just lost her job, we've got two kids, and I was hoping to go up for promotion next year. I'd rather not be here this morning. But if I didn't address this situation, that would be negligence. There's only so far you can go in protecting your self-interest. That's what I said to my wife, anyway, and she agrees."

Last week, Bell told her, the department had met to vote on tenure and promotion for Robert Dilson-Alvarez and Gwen Conley. They'd satisfied all the requirements, and though neither was particularly well liked they'd gotten positive recommendations, in both cases on a seven-to-two vote. Then, a couple days ago, he'd found a large manila envelope in his departmental mailbox, with his name typed on a label. It had neither stamps nor a postmark. Inside were two photocopied articles, each of which had several additional pages paper-clipped to it. The first article was a piece by Dilson-Alvarez titled "Neocolonialism and the Media in the West Indies Federation: 1958–1962." It had appeared three years ago in a Canadian journal. Someone had used a yellow marker to highlight various passages—some as short as two or three sentences, others as long as a few paragraphs. The attached pages were taken from three other articles, each by a different author, all published prior to Dilson-Alvarez's piece, and each attached page had highlighted passages identical to those in his article.

"Identical?" she asked.

"Word for word."

"And he didn't identify the passages as direct quotations?"

"No."

"What was the second article?"

"One of Gwen Conley's. Same thing. A number of passages highlighted in yellow—some short, some long—and each of them appeared verbatim in the attached pages from previously published work by other authors."

"Did either Dilson-Alvarez or Conley cite the other works in their bibliographies?"

"I'm afraid not."

"So we're not dealing with simple sloppiness."

"No."

"You didn't bring the pages with you?" Bell hadn't been carrying a briefcase when he entered her office.

"No." He looked sick, his face taking on a hue that wasn't green, exactly, though it was pretty close. "I actually thought . . . No, that's the wrong word. I'm afraid I *hoped* you'd tell me to forget it."

"What in the world made you think I might do that?"

Bell laid both hands on his knees and leaned forward. "Kristin," he said, "do you fully understand where we are? The provost at this university was twice turned down for tenure before she came here and worked her way into the administration. She has no standards whatsoever but can run rings around the president, and she's surrounded herself with sycophants."

"So you assumed I was one too?"

"Well, let's just say many of us were stunned when you got hired. People don't come here from the UC—Bedard doesn't want them. She wants people from places like Black Hills State."

"Is there really such a school?"

"That's where our dean worked previously. Bedard and Norm Vance have been friends for about forty years. She's the one who hired him."

She picked up her pen and started making notes on a legal pad. "Do you know who voted against Dilson-Alvarez and Conley?"

"Yes."

"How?"

"Because we have signed ballots, and I'm the one who counts them and records the results."

"Was it the same two people both times?"

Bell nodded.

"Where are the ballots now?"

"The provost has them."

"*What?*"

"We're required to turn them in to her office immediately following the vote."

"According to the faculty handbook, Joanne's not supposed to have anything to do with the tenure and promotion process until she receives the recommendations of Dean Vance and the school committee in January."

"That's what I've been telling you. We're supposed to follow the handbook, but we don't. The provost already knows who voted against her pet."

"Is the faculty aware that the ballots have gone to her?"

"I doubt it. They probably think I have them."

"As department chair, you don't vote, right?"

"No. But I have to submit an independent recommendation next week. And that's why I've swallowed about half a bottle of Xanax since I got that envelope. Somebody on my faculty knows I have this information. If I give Robert and Gwen positive recommendations after seeing evidence of academic misconduct, I'm open to serious charges myself. But if I give them a negative, Bedard's going to—"

She laid her pen down and held up her hand. "Let's back up," she said. The handbook, she reminded him, stated that evaluations could be based only on the materials in the file submitted by the candidate. Since the pages in that manila envelope weren't part of anyone's file, he couldn't consider them even if he wanted to. There was a mechanism for adding material after the departmental vote, but it involved notifying the candidate of what you planned to do, and whoever delivered this information certainly hadn't.

"In other words," he said, "you *are* telling me to ignore it?"

"Absolutely not. In fact, I'm instructing you to bring me the contents of that envelope."

"So you can do what with them?"

"So I can begin an investigation into possible academic misconduct."

"And in the meantime?"

"In the meantime," she said, rising, "it's strictly my problem."

He stood up too. "Well, given the size of it, I hope it's the only one you've got."

"It's not," she said.

Something in her voice must have revealed more than she intended. Instead of leaving, he continued to stand there. Then he stepped around the desk and hugged her. "I'm glad you're here," Bell said.

Once he left she opened a Word file and wrote a one-page account of their meeting, leaving out the hug. Then she popped in her USB stick and saved the file there. As soon as she received the material Bell had been given, she'd start investigating every aspect of Conley's and Dilson-Alvarez's careers. She felt certain that nothing she discovered could possibly faze her.

Her more immediate concern was Matt's message, which she went to her inbox and reread. In it, he absolved her of all responsibility for his feelings, asserting that he knew she never intended to lead him on, that she hadn't been sending false signals, that from the moment he reached out and touched her hand at the ridiculously named bar in North Reading he'd understood she wanted only to be his friend. The blame, if it had to be assigned, should all accrue to him. He was in love with her, but that was his problem, not hers.

He said it had come to him lately that he must once have taken joy in something as simple as the sight of a familiar face hovering over his crib when he opened his eyes in the morning, the creaking of a particular floorboard as he stepped through the front door after a long, boring day in first grade, his friend Frankie's voice on the phone when they were eight or nine or ten: "Hey, Drinnan, you wanna go see the Sox on Sunday with me and Pop?" The process by which small pleasures had lost their power to deliver happiness was as mysterious to him as ever—maybe even more mysterious, since their value now seemed so essential that only a fool could fail to grasp it.

He'd seen the news report about her husband last night, and he knew they'd been together a long time, and he was not out to disrupt their marriage. But couldn't they keep meeting for drinks? he asked. If not every day, then whenever she had time? She'd helped him become engaged in life again, he said. He'd recently given his car a good cleaning. The house too.

He was going to repair everything that had fallen apart there, and he was beginning to think about the future and had even registered to vote. He didn't have any money, but if he ever got his hands on some he'd do something smart with it. Around the corner, for all he knew, lay stocks and bonds, mutual funds.

She read the message four or five times. At some point, she propped her elbows on the desk and put her head in her hands. When she shut her eyes, she could see him sitting there in the house down the street from hers, alone in the middle of the night, telling a woman he'd only known for a couple months that all his thoughts now revolved around her. Even if he was asking for more than he acknowledged, he was offering more than he asked and at no small risk to himself. He couldn't know that last night, when she'd made love to her husband, it was his hand rather than Cal's that she'd felt on her breast, or that afterward she'd lain on her side with her back to the man she'd lived with all this time so she could imagine what it might feel like if it were Matt she was in bed with.

For fifteen years, up until she lost her job, her life had been without significant complication. She'd risen each morning, made herself breakfast, glanced at the local paper, then showered and dressed. She'd walked into the garage, pressed the door opener, climbed into her car and driven to work. At the university, she'd attended innumerable meetings, mostly with people like her, who'd started out as biologists, literary critics, painters or chemical engineers and ended up in administration. They talked now about budget shortfalls, mission statements, outcome assessments, five-year plans. All of them earned corporate salaries. For the most part, they were bright people, and generally speaking they liked one another.

Cal didn't say much about music, but when he did it was usually because he'd heard another musician whose playing excited him. "That guy's really tasteful," he might remark. "He never plays too many notes, and his improvisations are fresh and unpredictable. He delivers lots of color." Every now and then, usually when she was driving home in the evening, often after going to dinner with a couple other administrators, a job candidate or some wealthy alumnus being courted by the development office, she would think about Cal's comments and assess things accordingly: she was living her life tastefully—she never played too many notes—but it lacked color. And she never departed from the melody. Improvisation was for others.

She had no idea how much time had passed before she reached for her mouse and clicked Reply. She wrote only a few lines.

Forgive me, Matt, for not contacting you yesterday. As I'm sure you understand, what happened to my husband was disturbing, and I rushed to the hospital once I found out. I could have left a message on your home phone to explain, and I should have.

And forgive me for what I am about to say now, because we will surely both come to regret it, probably quite soon: I'm afraid I might be in love with you too.

when matt was seventeen, he read a short novel by Richard Yates called *A Good School* and was so moved by the struggles of the book's adolescent characters that he'd scoured the Montvale and Cedar Park libraries for all the author's work, blazing through one title after another. Shortly afterward, an article in the *Globe* reported that the semifamous writer lived in Boston and often ate dinner at the Newbury Steakhouse, which Matt recalled having seen on his numerous trips to Fenway with Frankie. So one late-summer evening he rode the Orange Line into the city and hung around the corner of Mass Ave and Newbury, where the restaurant was located, hoping the novelist might happen along. He'd justified the endeavor by telling himself he simply wanted the author to know how much he loved his work.

He was about to give up when a man resembling Yates walked around the corner. Matt wasn't sure it was him: he looked both older and taller than expected. But he had the right face—gray beard, sad lines—so before he could enter the restaurant, Matt stepped up and said, "Mr. Yates?"

The man paused, glanced at him, then dropped his gaze as if he needed to consider the question. In the ensuing silence, Matt noted that his slumped shoulders made him look like a hunchback. Finally, he said, "Yeah?"

Matt's heart began to race. He felt as if he were offering testimony and that if he hit on the right words he'd walk away with tangible gain. He didn't know why he thought so, just as he wouldn't know fifteen years later, when he sat down to dinner with Jonathan Franzen or Ian McEwan or any of the other writers with whom his job allowed him to rub shoulders. "Mr.

Yates," he stammered, "I just wanted to tell you how much I love your books. I've read them all. *Revolutionary Road, Eleven Kinds of Loneliness, The Easter Parade, Cold Spring Harbor, Disturbing the Peace . . .* every single one of them. My favorite's probably *A Good School.*"

Again the author dropped his gaze. Later, whenever Matt related the story of the encounter to other novelists, they invariably asked if Yates had been drunk. He didn't know for sure, but he didn't think so, and that was what he told them.

"*A Good School*'s an étude," Yates finally said. "*Revolutionary Road*'s a symphony. The closest I ever came to writing one, anyway."

Matt just stood there awkwardly after hearing that, and once the novelist realized his young fan had run out of words, he stuck his hand out. Matt shook it—it felt dry and chilly—and then Yates disappeared into the steak house.

Lately, he'd been thinking a lot about that experience. He'd heard a man with five or six more years to live speaking of himself and all his efforts almost in the past tense. It was like he already knew he'd never produce another book. And unlike many of the writers Matt had met at the Emporium, he didn't insist that his most recent novel was his masterpiece. Instead, he thought his first one was, or that it had at least come close, and Matt believed this was something Yates had known for a long time, that even when writing it he might've suspected it represented the best he had in him. Though he used to think his hero was disparaging *A Good School* by calling it an étude, he now saw things differently. No one could write a symphony every day, and no one could live one either.

The first time he spoke to Kristin after she returned his declaration of love with a halfhearted one of her own, she informed him she was worried about her husband's reaction to the robbery he'd broken up the previous day and that Matt would either have to be patient with her preoccupations or write her off before things went any further. She made those remarks over the phone, having divulged her cell number in exchange for his. Her tone suggested that if he chose the latter course she'd be relieved, if not pleased.

He felt as if he'd stepped into the realm of last chances, where the ice is thin and apt to break and caution is no currency. "I saw you last night," he said.

"Where was this?"

"I saw you making love. Your shadow, anyway. Those blinds of yours must be thin as paper."

"Is that why you wrote to me?"

"It's one reason."

"If that's the only reason, why don't we hang up?"

"It's not."

"What's the other reason?"

"I need you."

"That's not enough."

"I want you."

"That's better. Because while you might've seen what I was doing, you couldn't see what I was feeling. There's a lot you don't know about me, Matt. I'm afraid there's plenty I don't know about myself."

"When can I start learning?"

"Maybe we could meet for a drink on Friday."

"Why not today?"

"Like I said, I'm concerned about Cal. His arm's in bad shape, and his mind's even worse."

Having no choice, he agreed, and the delay left him time to think. Among other things, he thought about routine. For him, it had always resulted in ruin. He'd lulled himself into assuming that because he'd ripped the store off ninety-nine times, he'd sail on into the hundreds. Because Carla hadn't left him each time he slipped into the bathroom and snorted a line, he thought she'd stay forever. The best thing that could've happened to him, he thought now, was if somebody had walked into the bookstore and pointed a gun at him. Maybe, if he'd survived, he would have made more of his life.

She waited on the platform, intending for him to climb out of his car and come find her. If it cost five dollars and fifty cents to park in the lot across the street, so be it. If the lot was full, he could park illegally and risk a ticket as he had the first time. She wanted to be sought, and for the seeking to be a constant activity, taking place every hour of the day and also the night.

Each time she thought of him standing on Essex Street in the dark, watching her rocking shadow and wishing he were the one who lay beneath her, her throat constricted and her face flushed. It had occurred this afternoon during a meeting with the academic deans and Joanne Bedard, that tiresome woman droning like a window unit and disgorging one acronym after another—AO, RTP, DPTC—until she noticed the redness spreading over Kristin's neck and cheeks. "Are you feeling all right?" she asked. "You're looking a little . . . overheated. Want me to call one of my assistants to bring you a bottle of water?"

"No," Kristin said, "I'll be fine."

Everyone in the room probably assumed she was caught in the throes of menopausal malfunction, but she could care less. Nor did the provost's smirk trouble her.

Matt walked around the corner and onto the platform at four thirty. He was wearing a heavy black fleece jacket she'd never seen before, and instead of his usual jeans or khakis, he had on a pair of black sweatpants. She was still dressed for work: tweed skirt with matching jacket, white blouse, brown leather riding boots. Nobody who saw them together this evening would ever forget it. She was about to express her dismay when he threw his arms around her and kissed her on the mouth.

Seven or eight people were waiting on the platform, and

while she didn't recognize any of them, she couldn't swear that
none of them worked at the university. She placed her palm
against his chest in an effort to back him off. "What are you
doing?" she whispered. "Have you lost your mind?"

"Absolutely. Haven't you?"

"I guess so. But does everyone else need to know it?"

He let go of her, and she followed him to the car. When
she opened the passenger-side door, she saw another sweat suit
lying on the backseat, new, along with a jacket just like his and
a box with the Nike symbol on it.

"I bought you size eights," he said. "I was just guessing."

"So our first official date, after we've both gone insane, is a
trip to the gym?"

He laughed and told her to get in, so she did. He started
the car. "Not the gym," he said. He gestured over his shoulder.
"Back there on the floor there's a portable cooler with a jug
of premixed martinis. We'll have to drink from plastic cups,
though. I have something special in mind."

"And it requires me to wear jogging clothes?"

"Afraid so."

"And where am I supposed to change into them?"

"At a gas station."

The one he chose was grungy enough to make her feel like
she was back in high school, except she'd never done anything
like this then. It was unheated, with a concrete floor and a bare
lightbulb dangling from the ceiling. The toilet bowl abounded
in botanical activity, so she lowered the seat cover. She pulled
her blouse off and folded it, then laid it on the lid, reminding
herself it would need to be washed. Slowly, she removed the
rest of her clothes, then took a moment to look at herself in
the mirror.

In her hips and thighs she saw the first hint of heaviness she
had long associated with Sarah Connulty. She'd once assumed it
came from a preference for sweets, but when she thought back

on it she hadn't really seen Mrs. Connulty eat that many sweets. In pictures around the house of her and her husband when they were younger, she was tall and slim. The weight crept in over time, and the day she died she weighed close to two hundred pounds. Kristin's mother was the one who found her half buried in the snow at the foot of the back steps. According to the coroner, she'd slipped, and the cause of death was blunt trauma. Why she'd fallen forward, he said, was anybody's guess. When your feet slid out from under you, you usually landed on your back.

She shrugged into the sweat suit, then laid her clothes on the edge of the sink, sat down on the toilet and began to lace up the new Nikes. He rapped at the door. "What's taking so long?"

"I'm almost finished. This is crazy, you know? I can't believe I'm doing this."

"Me neither. Are you sure it's happening?"

"I guess so. The odor in here's definitely real."

They drove back toward Montvale, the traffic moving slowly as it always does on Friday afternoon in autumn, when people pour out of Boston toward New Hampshire and Vermont. A major jam had formed near the I-95 interchange. While they sat there, she couldn't stop herself from glancing at the cars on either side, to see if anyone from work was nearby. Cal had reluctantly attended a couple of functions at the school, so at least a few people knew what he looked like.

Her anxiety didn't escape Matt. He was feeling plenty of it himself, though his was of a different nature. She'd never done anything like this—he knew that without being told—and he hadn't either, and it was likely, if not certain, that they'd fuck it up through sheer ineptitude. He began to question his plan, wondering if they shouldn't turn around and head back to their usual spot. Maybe that was their romance setting, the only place where anything that mattered could happen between them. Maybe two martinis at an environmentally conscious roadhouse was all the future they could hope for.

"Would you mind telling me where we're going?"

"Ever heard of Penny Hill Park?"

"No."

"Technically, it's part of Montvale, though it's right at the edge of the Fells Reservation. There's something there I want you to see."

He was trying to sound confident, but his voice faltered, and she knew he was afraid she'd ask him to let her change back into her work clothes and drive her to the train station so she could walk home. Strangely, she gained courage from his fear. If she chose to, she could seize control of the situation, though for now she would cede it.

Their destination proved close to Essex Street, no more than four or five blocks from her house. He turned onto a narrow lane that she and Cal had noticed while walking Suzy. The road wound steeply upward for a couple hundred yards. Then they came to a heavy chain with a sign suspended from it banning automobiles beyond that point. Off to the right lay a gravel lot big enough to accommodate three or four cars. A marker said PENNY HILL PARK. DOGS MUST REMAIN ON LEASH. He pulled in and stopped near the lone garbage barrel.

Darkness was falling, so he reached under the seat and grabbed a large flashlight. "Hop out," he said. "I'll snag the cooler."

When she got out, she discovered that the temperature had dropped ten or twelve degrees. A plume of smoke escaped her mouth. She'd initially thought the sweats and jacket silly, even childish, but now she realized she would have frozen in her work outfit, and his concern for her comfort was touching. "I don't know if a cooler's what's called for on a night like this," she said. "Maybe you should've brought a thermos."

"We don't have to drink martinis. There's a bottle of brandy, too, if you'd prefer it."

Philip had drunk a lot of brandy during their last couple of years together. By then he'd achieved tenure and was no longer called Phil. He still walked around campus in jeans and a hoodie, but he'd developed a preference for expensive wines and small-batch bourbons, and on their sideboard there was always a decanter of Germain-Robin XO. "What kind of brandy did you get?"

He shrugged. "I don't know." He opened the rear door and looked inside, then lifted out the bottle and examined it. "Christian Brothers."

"Let's take that instead."

"Want me to bring the cups?"

"No. If you've got germs, you infected me in Andover."

They stepped over the chain and walked uphill into the gathering darkness, Matt holding on to her arm. Her natural tendency to resist seemed to have been left in the parking lot. After the first few yards, she leaned in against him.

"Are you really in love with me?" he asked.

"I've decided," she said, "to behave as if I am. We'll see where it takes us."

"You realize that's not the most romantic answer."

"I'm not the most romantic person."

"Did you used to be?"

Looking back, it seemed that maybe she had been at certain points in her life. But since being a romantic was a character trait that presumably you couldn't switch off, she supposed the answer was no and was about to say so when he said, "Forget I asked."

"There's nothing wrong with asking. It's just that I'm not sure."

"You've never quite gotten over the end of your first marriage. Isn't it as simple as that?"

"Not exactly." Up ahead on the left she spotted a pitched roof. Through the shadows a mansion emerged, and she recognized the Tudor Revival elements: half-timbers and herringbone brickwork, dormer windows and wall plates. There was a high, patterned chimney on the side nearest the path. "This is what you wanted me to see?"

"Yes, because it means something special to me."

"Another place you came with your ex-wife?"

"No. It's one of the few places in Montvale that I didn't come to with her."

The place looked fairly well maintained except for some missing roof tiles, but there were no lights on anywhere, and it seemed deserted. A second-story hallway with a single dormer window connected the main house to a two-car garage, and beneath it was a wrought-iron gate. He pushed it open—"Follow me"—and they stepped through it into a garden. A few pieces of heavy patio furniture stood there—a table, three or four chairs. The lawn and sparse landscaping were surrounded by a brick wall seven or eight feet high.

He placed the brandy on the table, pulled a chair out and told her to make herself at home.

"We're going to play house," she said, "but we can't get inside?"

"We could if we ever wanted to."

"How? By breaking a window?"

"No. By unlocking the back door. I've got a key. I've had it for almost twenty years."

He screwed the cap off the bottle and handed it to her. She took a swig that burned her throat, making her cough. She wiped her mouth and handed the brandy back. "Let me get this straight," she said. "About twenty years ago, somebody gave you a key to this place? Or was that the first thing you ever stole?"

He took a swallow from the bottle and set it on the table. He told her he'd found the black cast-iron key while going through the file cabinet at his father's office after he died. It was in a folder labeled PENNY HILL HOUSE. "The woman who used to live here was named Penelope Hill," he said. "She died back in 1983. I was thirteen, and I still remember her funeral. I think it was the first time I cried over somebody's death."

His father had carried the insurance on the house, Matt said, and he'd come over here with him once when he was ten or eleven years old, on a day when his mother was down on the Cape visiting an old college friend. He and his father and Mrs. Hill sat in the library, and while the two adults drank something that might have been brandy or whiskey but was definitely brown and contained alcohol, he had a glass of milk and ate a few cookies and then perused the books, many of which were big leather-bound editions of classics. She had all of Dickens up there, as well as Thackeray and Hardy and de Maupassant and Chekhov.

He'd noticed her downtown a few times before. She was a striking woman, tall with frizzy hair that he suspected had once either been red or blond but had long since turned gray. He didn't know precisely how old she was that afternoon, but if he'd had to guess he might have said fifty. As it turned out, she was in her midsixties, though he wouldn't learn that until she died, and he saw what was engraved on her headstone. That was also when he learned her husband had been a lot older, and that he'd been dead for close to thirty years by then.

"His family owned one of the shoe factories. Both Montvale and Cedar Park used to be mill towns. By the time I was a kid, the mills had either been razed or, in a few cases, converted. That long building near the train station that now has all those luxury condos? They used to make rubber boots there. Anyhow, shoes are where her husband's money had come from. And then when the mills shut down, he sold the land to developers."

At some point during that first visit, Penelope Hill noticed how interested he was in her books. Not that there weren't plenty at his own house; both of his parents read, his mother more than his father. But Mrs. Hill's books had a heft and elegance the ones at home lacked. She asked if he'd like to borrow some of them, and his father said that wouldn't be necessary, but she waved the objection aside, and he left with *A Christmas Carol* and one or two others.

His father never mentioned her to him again, but Matt said he took to dropping by her place every few weeks. She gave him milk and cookies and let him leave with as many books as he could tote in his backpack, and he always returned them in perfect condition. Somehow, he understood that the books she loaned him should never be shown to anyone.

"She drank a lot during the day," he said. "I think probably she was an alcoholic, though I didn't know it at the time. She always had a glass in her hand, and it was always something brown, with no ice. She didn't talk to me much. I didn't think she knew how to talk to a child because she'd never had one of her own.

"She got scared a lot at night. If you start asking people my age or older what they recall about Penny Hill, that's all most of them can tell you. About once a week, for God knows how many years, she'd call the Montvale Police Department at two or three in the morning, claiming she heard somebody in the woods outside and they were trying to break in. She was always horribly apologetic with the dispatcher, and when the cops showed up and assured her the property was empty, she invited them inside and offered them a drink.

"When she died, she left her house and the surrounding land to the city of Montvale and even bequeathed some money for upkeep. She wanted it turned into a conservation center. There used to be bird feeders all over the place, and the grounds were lush for a while, but the endowment couldn't keep pace with inflation and now the city's letting it go. There's a guy who mows the yard and picks up the litter, and I guess somebody must do some basic maintenance from time to time. Otherwise it just sits here. Most people don't even know it exists."

It was dark now. Through the mostly bare tree limbs, she saw a plane beginning its descent into Logan. A few seconds later, they heard the sound of the engines. When that died away, the evening again became still. You couldn't even hear traffic on 93, though the freeway couldn't possibly be more than a mile away. "Why's it so quiet?" she asked.

"I don't know," he said. "It just always has been. There're a lot of trees and bushes in the Fells. I guess they soak the sound up."

He passed her the brandy, and she took another swallow. "What did you think when you found the key in your father's desk?"

"Well, I didn't know what to make of it," he said, "so for a while I chose not to think anything. Then one night when I'd been to Montvale to visit my mom, I drove over to the place we just parked and walked up here. The key didn't work in the front door, so I walked around back, figuring surely the city'd changed the locks when they assumed title. But when I stuck it in the lock on the back door, it fit. Next thing I knew, I was inside."

He said when he switched on the lights, he found things more or less as he remembered them, but the bookshelves were empty. "Apparently, they'd sold her collection off in an estate sale or something. All the furniture, though, was still right there."

He'd gone upstairs, he admitted, just to see what it looked like—having seen only the entryway, the living room and the library when Mrs. Hill was alive. There were four bedrooms on the second floor. The three smaller ones had identical full-sized beds, but there was an enormous canopied four-poster in the master bedroom. He didn't know why he did it, he said, but he flipped off the light and sat down on it, then kicked off his shoes, drew up his feet and rolled onto his back.

Lying there, he'd experienced the oddest sensation: his father's presence. It was all the more unsettling because they'd never been particularly close. When he was growing up, he said, his dad worked a lot and was gone a lot, and rarely did with him the things that Frankie and his father did together. They'd never gone to Fenway, or the Garden, though he'd been to both venues with the Zizzas. He realized that night that his most vivid memories of his dad almost all centered on holidays—Christmas or the Fourth, Thanksgiving or Easter. Those were the only occasions you could expect him to remain home all day. He even went to work sometimes on Sundays, though he always waited until the family had returned from Mass and eaten lunch.

Kristin expected him to continue the narrative, but it broke off there. For several moments he sat beside her with his arms crossed. Then he reached out and grasped the bottle and took another hit.

He was only inches away from her, but in the dark she couldn't make out his features. She laid her hand on his forearm. "Why are you telling me this?" she asked.

"Because I want you to know that I don't take tonight lightly."

"You mean you're not just out to get laid?"

"That's a rather reductive assessment."

She let go of his forearm. For a moment she was back in the boxy little prefab in the Chapel Hill cul-de-sac, offering herself to a man who'd decided to walk her home. She shook her head. She wasn't aware of having made a sound, but she must have.

"What's funny?" he asked.

"Twice in my life," she said, "I thought a man was about to treat me like a piece of meat. And both times they turned into vegans. If that's not funny, what is?"

Viewed in a certain light, the following information would be: in his pocket lay the key to the house that formerly belonged to Penelope Hill. In reality, the old woman had indeed been a drunk, and he had come to this house with his father, though she hadn't offered him milk and cookies and he hadn't left with a book after that first visit or any other visits, either, because there had been no subsequent visits. He'd wandered over and laid his hand on a leather-bound book on a side table, but she'd snapped, "Don't touch that!" His dad, who hadn't been offered a drink that day, had gone there to inform her that he no longer could insure her home. She'd filed three claims for water damage in the last two years alone, having left her bathwater running until the tub on the second floor overflowed, ruining the walls and ceiling in two ground-floor rooms—probably befuddled by drink or even passed out in the tub. After she'd rudely commanded him to keep his hands to himself, Matt noticed the black key next to the book and, when she turned her anger back on his father, stuck it in his pocket.

When she died and the town took over the property, which she really had left to Montvale in perhaps the only generous act of her life, he and Frankie tried the key, and to their surprise it unlocked the back door. Periodically, as teenagers, they'd come to sprawl on the furniture and drink beer or smoke weed. They never worried too much about getting caught, because everybody knew the caretaker left around four. Matt had once suggested to Carla that they come inside on Friday night and avail themselves of the big four-poster, but she said he was out of his mind.

He was out of it now too. He hadn't intended to tell the lies he'd just told. About ten or fifteen minutes ago, gravitas seemed called for, so he'd summoned it from the thin, cold air, and his skill at doing this forced him to draw a pair of conclusions. First, maybe he did possess enough imagination to write a novel one day. Second, though no longer a thief, he was still an asshole.

The only decent thing to do, he knew, was tell her right now that he'd invented a sentimental crock of shit to lure her upstairs. He was always stumbling into stupidity, he would say. His personality obviously wouldn't stabilize. Sometimes he thought he lacked a core, that he was all flank and edge. "Listen," he began, "that stuff about my dad and Mrs. Hill? It just came to me a few minutes ago, when you suggested maybe I'd brought you here because I'd done the same thing with Carla. It felt like I needed to say something to convince you otherwise. So I made all that stuff up. Well, not all of it . . . but most of it. I did actually come here with my dad. Only that one time, though. He drove over to cancel her insurance, and she wasn't nice to him or me either, and in a fit of mischief I stole her key. If you want to slap my face, or pick up that brandy bottle and bash me over the head with it, or just walk off and leave me here by myself, it's all right. I'm deserving of whatever. But the bottom line is, my dad never had an affair with Penelope Hill or anyone else. He didn't do things like that. With him, what you saw was what you got."

Since he couldn't bear to watch her process this information, he kept his gaze aimed straight ahead at the brick wall on the far side of the garden. Unable to look at him either, she did too, thinking that what you saw was never what you got, and that it was sad he'd reached forty without attaining this basic insight. Then she corrected herself. It wasn't sad at all; it was simply outrageous, especially after he'd read so many goddamn novels. "Let me ask you something," she said.

His Adam's apple made a clicking sound. "Sure."

"When your dad died, did you really find a file labeled PENNY HILL HOUSE?"

"Yes, I did. That's the truth."

"By then, how long had it been since he canceled her homeowner's insurance?"

"I don't know. Maybe twelve, thirteen years."

"Did you find any other files on people whose coverage he'd dropped that long ago?"

"No. I mean, I don't think so."

"So why do you think he kept a file on *her*?"

"I don't know."

"What was in it?"

"Some papers. A few pictures."

"What kind of pictures?"

"The ones he always took when he insured a property. Photos of the house and grounds, interior, exterior, nothing special."

"Did Penny Hill appear in any of them?"

His dad had been the best man he ever knew. He was the kind of man who won the respect of everyone he encountered and gave you something to live up to. Hundreds attended his funeral. "I have no idea," he said. "I can't remember. Maybe she did. But so what, what's your point? What is it you're trying to prove?"

Since she understood she was discomforting him by casting dark doubts on a truth he held dear, she declared a unilateral truce. They could argue tomorrow or the next day or even later on tonight. Or else they could both decide to go home at the end of the evening and ignore each other for the rest of their natural lives. The possibilities were various, the consequences undefined.

Rather than answer his question, she rose, her chair legs grating on the patio stones. In a practiced manner at odds with everything he thought he knew about her, she slowly began hugging herself, each hand caressing the opposite elbow and working up to her shoulder, then inching down over her breasts to her stomach, where it lingered for a moment with the other before moving again toward her breasts.

in the days following the failed robbery, Cal stayed home. His photo had appeared in the Cedar Park and Montvale papers, though thankfully not in the *Globe*, and he'd had to provide personal information to the Cedar Park police. They took his driver's license number, then asked how long he'd been on Essex Street, where he'd lived before that, his birthplace and so on. One of the cops told him he had an uncle in Bakersfield—"Service supervisor at the Mercedes dealership"— and when Cal failed to respond, the guy looked miffed. But Cal's dad used to buy a new Mercedes every year and at one time or another had probably abused the cop's uncle, since that's how he always treated those he considered beneath him, which included almost everyone alive.

Cal's reluctance to leave the house was due in part to his fear of being recognized by people who might want to praise his bravery, which he obviously wasn't worthy of. He'd just reacted like a pissed-off redneck. If he hadn't, Andrew Saucer might have made off with a couple hundred bucks, but in all likelihood nobody would've gotten hurt.

He'd been wondering what sort of suffering Saucer had experienced that made him willing to kill for petty cash. A certain amount of background was available online: six-year-old articles from the New Hampshire *Union Leader* and the *Keene Sentinel* and even older pieces from papers in upstate New York and the *Worcester Telegram & Gazette*. Mostly, they detailed his criminal actions and reported his sentencing. Cal was able to glean a bit more than that, though, from the earliest articles.

Unlike a lot of career criminals, Saucer had lived what appeared to be a normal life, up until a certain point. According to the Worcester paper, he'd served two years in the army after graduating from Montvale High, then worked for almost a decade as a maintenance man at Assumption College. Due to cutbacks, he'd lost that job in 1989, about six months before sticking up the country's oldest hardware store, Angus James, on Main Street in Worcester. The piece said he wasn't armed when he entered, though he'd fortified himself with enough alcohol to be legally drunk. He grabbed a spade with a diamond-point blade and held it over the cashier until he emptied the register of $344.17. About an hour later, he was arrested. There were two customers in the store when Saucer robbed it, and unfortunately for him one worked in the dining hall at Assumption.

After he went to jail that first time, it was as if he'd ceased to exist until he committed another felony. Except, of course, that he hadn't. Just as he'd had a life prior to burglarizing that hardware shop, he had clearly remained alive between his crimes, and it was those stretches of undocumented existence that interested Cal.

Saucer was a small man, and based on his inability to defend himself the other day, it was unlikely he'd ever learned to fight. So what happened to him in jail? Had he been regularly preyed upon by bigger and stronger inmates? That he hadn't seemed unlikely, if not impossible. And what about those brief periods when he wasn't incarcerated or making yet another bad choice? Was he watching sports on television, cooking or drawing, tinkering with engines? Preferring Pepsi to Coke, Budweiser to Coors? None of these questions could be answered without sitting down and talking to the man, and while he knew this would be both illegal and insane, he couldn't quite rid himself of the urge to do so.

If they'd been able to converse, he might've asked Saucer whether there was a single moment he could identify when things began to go wrong. If he hadn't lost his job back in '89, would he still be repairing broken toilets and replacing damaged screens at the college? Or did he think that sooner or later he would've started using master keys to enter the rooms of rich kids, stealing their laptops and making off with their credit cards? Was he who he was because bad things happened to him, or did those things happen because he was bad? These were the interesting questions, at least to Cal, and he suspected they might well be to Saucer himself. If he had to put money on it, he would've bet the guy woke up every morning asking many of them and fell asleep each night doing the same thing.

He decided to quit drinking anything stronger than beer, and while not going to bed in a stupor had its virtues, he again was having terrible dreams in which he was descending a steep slope into a gully, his skin as dry as paper, the manzanita scratching his shins and flaying him alive with each halting step.

Fearing the nightmares, he fought off sleep as much as he could, though since he was trying to behave like a normal husband in an average marriage, he stayed in bed beside Kristin rather than prowling the house and attempting to wear himself out. Due to his size, he couldn't shift position very often without waking her up, so he lay on his back, still and stiff, his right hand gripping the railing.

During the day he often felt disoriented and lethargic, and he'd stopped working on the house. When he wasn't parked on the couch thinking about Saucer, he spent time with his friends on the third floor. At the hospital they'd told him not to play for several days, since that might cause his stitches to work loose, but he'd never been able to keep his hands off a stringed instrument if one was nearby. Figuring he was most likely to hurt himself on the guitars, he generally played one of his mandolins for a little bit, mostly open chords that didn't require any big stretches. Even if you weren't trying to improve your technique or learn something new, you could simply appreciate tone. He had a vintage Gibson F-5 that cost him a staggering eleven grand and a four-year-old Bitterroot, made in Montana, that he'd bought new for twenty-nine hundred. The F-5 sounded pretty good, but the Bitterroot sounded great, delivering such a piercing treble that you didn't have to attack it hard on single-note leads. He sat with it on the daybed for an hour or two at a time, strumming D's and A's and listening to the strings sing.

The Bitterroot was very basic, something very few professional musicians would ever play. Most, if they saw one hanging on the wall of some high-end shop, would walk right on by and reach for the oldest F-5 in sight or, if they couldn't swing that, would settle for a Gilchrist or a Monteleone. Andrew Saucer was the kind of man you walked right on by, unless he was waving a gun in your face. Practically a definition of basicness. But the Bitterroot had a great tone, whereas Saucer's was off. He didn't sound good, didn't look good, couldn't think well, and as soon as Mass General released him from intensive care he'd be right back in jail.

When Cal finally laid the Bitterroot in its case, he was drawn to the window, where he stood looking at the neighbors' maple. After searching online, he'd decided the tree was of the Autumn Blaze variety, and even though he could see others in the distance that looked almost identical, this one fascinated him. He wished there were some means of determining how long it had stood there, how many times it had burst into color or its leaves had turned brown and fallen off and whether it had suffered any significant storm damage. Surely, the snow must weigh it down. Even on a tree this big and sturdy, a branch would have to break eventually.

Over the next couple of weeks, Kristin began to return late—sometimes after nine—but he'd grown used to that in California. The further she got into her school year, the more meetings she'd have to attend. And those meetings meant it was more likely that things would go wrong. Though he lacked evidence, he suspected the main activity university administrators engaged in was coming up with stuff to administer. Like contractors, they got paid twice: first for building something, then for repairing it after it began to fall apart.

Each day, when she left, she'd tell him if she'd be coming home late. If so, around six thirty or seven that evening he'd put on a warm jacket, then go out and light a fire in the Smokey Joe. While waiting for the coals, he sat by the grill and enjoyed the crisp air. There were leaves everywhere now, brittle and crunchy, and each evening he promised himself that the next day he'd drive down to the hardware and buy some of the tall brown lawn bags he'd seen standing on the sidewalk throughout the neighborhood, awaiting curbside pickup. But when the next day came, he again stayed home.

One night toward the end of the month he was out there with Suzy, sipping Sam Adams and debating whether he wanted to throw a steak or a couple of chicken breasts on the grate. He'd just about decided on red meat when he heard someone call his name, and stood up.

In the light from the kitchen window he could see his neighbor standing at the fence, holding a comically large wineglass. You could have poured half a bottle into that thing, and it looked like the older man had.

"How you doing?" Vico asked.

"So-so," Cal said. "Just trying to figure out what to eat."

"Haven't had a chance to talk to you lately."

"I've kind of been keeping a low profile."

"That business at the store shake you up?"

"I guess maybe it did. A little bit."

"Scared the living shit out of me." With his free hand, Vico gestured at his own house. "I mean, I've always assumed I'd die right there, in some mundane way. Know what I'm saying? Have a heart attack and fall down the stairs. There's a rug right at the bottom that's about six inches thick, so I'm hoping that'll minimize disfiguration. I got some relatives that went into their boxes in poor condition—bullet wounds, water damage, you name it—and since it's my buddies who'll most likely find me, I don't want to cause them any loss of appetite."

"That's considerate of you."

"Well, these guys appreciate a good meal."

The level of disengagement Cal felt began to frighten him. For an instant, he forgot almost everything he knew about this guy—his former profession, what kind of car he drove, who the hell he was. He remembered only that the man had watched him beat another person half to death. His neighbor would never forget it, and in his eyes that was who Cal would always be, just as Cal would always see him as someone who'd witnessed it.

The fence between them suddenly seemed to say it all. He himself had ended up on the far side of the continent from everything and everybody he could plausibly call familiar. The individual he knew best wasn't even a person—she was only a dog, and she was old. She couldn't be expected to stick around much longer.

All over the country people were being dislocated, heading off to places they didn't belong, hoping to somehow find themselves another home. Some of them, like Andrew Saucer, probably couldn't fit in anywhere. Cal was beginning to suspect he was yet another, that there was nothing left for him, that one wrong turn he'd taken a long time ago had landed him right here, trying to remember the stranger next door.

"Speaking of a good meal," Vico was saying, "I believe you could use one. You've ingested a lot of lighter fluid over the last couple of weeks. My pals and I lost interest in the Series when the Yankees dropped the pennant and denied us the chance to root against 'em, but the Pats play the Vikings on Sunday, which means Randy Moss is back and we've got him to hate.

How about it? Want to come over? Game starts around four. We'll drink all the way through it and chow down when it ends."

Over many years of playing fiddle tunes on guitar and mandolin, Cal had learned to prize those fleeting instants when his wrists loosened up and his hands were moving at just the right speed: not picking so hard that he had to smear notes, instead allowing each one to exist as its own separate creation, according it the dignity it deserved. When this happened, the most wonderful sensation came over him, as if at least for a while everything was as it should be, the tune he was playing and the instrument he was playing it on both belonging to him and, even more important, he to them. It couldn't last forever, but that's exactly how he felt now.

"Sure, Vico," he said, "I'd like that."

donna taff would've preferred to go through life thinking others wished her well, but she'd noticed that this notion often led people to become prey, losing their savings to Bernie Madoff or their cell phones to some young hoodlum because they'd stupidly pulled them out on the subway as the train neared their stop. Whereas if you were like her and regarded those around you with keen-eyed suspicion, you wouldn't easily get fooled.

So she was suspicious of her husband, Charlie, who kept hatching schemes to improve their financial situation. A few years ago, after his best friend drowned in the *Starbound* disaster, he'd sold his trawler, taken out a second mortgage on their Gloucester home and opened a bar called the Screeching Gull. His reasoning went something like this: new groundfishing regulations, combined with reduced limits on a number of species, made it unlikely he'd see any growth in catch levels over the next decade or so, too many of his friends had died at sea anyway and he didn't want to leave her a widow. Furthermore, the film version of *The Perfect Storm* had just been released about eighteen months earlier, and people were flocking to town wanting to see where the crew of the *Andrea Gail* had lived, worked and hung out. Since a great many of the scenes in the movie were set in a Gloucester bar called the Crow's Nest, he was convinced that simply opening a pub named after a bird would draw tourists by the score.

The tourists never came. The pub was only a block off Main, but it was a block that few outsiders ever ventured into. While over time it developed its own clientele, primarily old friends from the fishing industry who'd tired of all the thrill seekers continually crowding the Crow's Nest, business had been slack now for at least a couple of years and even showed signs of getting worse. If she hadn't been one of only three administrative assistants at North Shore State to receive a raise last year, she and Charlie might have shown up in the foreclosure stats.

She was suspicious of Finn and Cara Martone, who worked at the Screeching Gull and told too many stories that didn't add up. They'd met in Kansas, Finn said when the two couples were sitting at a table after the bar closed, finishing off a keg. Yet another time, Donna overheard Cara tell a customer that she'd first laid eyes on her husband on a beach in Orange County, California. Surrounded by all that tan SoCal perfection, she proudly remarked, he'd still stood out. How could he not? Even in dank and foggy Gloucester his skin remained as bronze as a penny, his stomach was flat, and his biceps rippled when he reached for the tap to draw a pint. He'd earned a degree in PE, he said, and coached football for a couple of years at a Michigan high school. But Charlie, who seemed enamored with both of them, once noted that when he and Finn watched a Pats game together, his younger friend seemed stumped by pretty basic terminology like "cover two" and "skinny post."

Her suspicion also extended to her boss. At first, it was rooted in her fear that a woman as well educated as Kristin Stevens, with her background at a top research university, would look down her nose at her from the moment she walked in. Happily, that hadn't been the case. Grudgingly—because it was not Donna's habit to give things away—Kristin earned her trust. She was kind. And you could sense she'd known her share of hardship.

As the semester moved into the middle of November and a number of nettlesome issues loomed, her boss looked far less stressed out than she had when she began work back in August. Rather than appearing each morning with her hair askew and bags under her eyes, she now came in with every strand in place, her makeup carefully applied, her face relaxed. Some mornings she brought Donna delicacies she'd picked up at the bakery across the street from the Bradbury bus station: vanilla-custard babas, lemon *anginetti*. One day she even invited her to lunch at a small place called Café Polonia, which served three different kinds of pierogi and a tangy hunter's stew.

Her current suspicion of Kristin was rooted in the belief that when a fifty-year-old woman stops looking miserable and harried and seems relaxed and happy, it's usually for one reason only. If they'd ever had occasion to go out after work for a few drinks, she eventually might've looked her boss in the eye and said, "Whatever it is you've found for yourself, you better not let it come to light."

What comes to light when you launch an investigation of academic misconduct is seldom surprising. People pad their CVs, listing as "publications" articles that are simply under review. They reward themselves with consultantships at companies in foreign countries. They claim membership in Phi Beta Kappa. They name themselves to leadership positions in professional organizations that, at best, they're only members of. They list "presentations" at conferences they didn't attend. Back when student evaluations were turned in on paper, they delivered forgeries; now that the process has gone online, those with the technical know-how hack into the system and replace poor evaluations with good ones, taking care to make at least a few of their students sound representatively inarticulate.

When Kristin was a professor, she hadn't expected to qualify for tenure. Her teaching evaluations were spotty, and the book based on her dissertation had been turned down by several presses. Shortly before she would've had to stand for tenure, she'd been asked to join the administration on an interim basis. She accepted, since that would stop her tenure clock. If she'd gone through the process, though, she wouldn't have lied about her lack of accomplishment, so she'd never felt any sympathy for those who did. If they lied and she discovered it, they'd get what they deserved.

After John Bell delivered evidence damning Robert Dilson-Alvarez and Gwendolyn Conley, she went over it carefully, then pulled the professors' personnel files and reviewed their CVs.

Dilson-Alvarez listed an undergraduate degree from Heidelberg, and a master's and doctorate from McGill. Prior to his arrival at North Shore State, he'd held visiting professorships at SUNY Binghamton and Colgate, followed by a lectureship at Appalachian State. One could argue that his career had spiraled steadily downward. But so had Kristin's.

According to Gwendolyn Conley's vitae, she'd taken her B.A. at Cal State, Fullerton, then earned an M.A. at Northern Arizona University in Flagstaff. There was a gap of six years before she'd enrolled in the Ph.D. program at the University of Nevada, Reno. During this period she'd taught for three years at a community college in Porterville, California.

Conley had the kind of background you expected to encounter at North Shore State: degrees from second- or even third-tier public schools, a spotty teaching résumé, minimal publications. Dilson-Alvarez didn't. He'd started off hot, attending prestigious universities and publishing a book a decade ago with a press in Great Britain. She flipped back to his résumé and saw that *"To Shoot Down a European": Frantz Fanon's Theory of Therapeutic Violence* had been issued in the fall of 2000 by Caylor and Hill, International Academic Publishers. She hadn't heard of the press, so she opened her browser and typed the name in on Google.

The company had gone out of business in 2003. She found a couple of articles in British trade journals detailing its various financial problems, and one of them reported that the press had specialized in titles that dealt with liberation movements. A couple had been fairly successful, with a paperback edition of one having been brought out in the United States by Picador.

Oddly, the only mention she could find of Dilson-Alvarez's book was on the North Shore State website. It wasn't listed on Amazon UK, and no reviews came up anywhere, even in JSTOR. The only pertinent reference was a quote from the preface Jean-Paul Sartre had written for Fanon's *The Wretched of the Earth:* "The rebel's weapon is the proof of his humanity. . . . For in the first days of the revolt you must kill; to shoot down a European is to kill two birds with one stone, to destroy an oppressor and the man he oppresses at the same time."

Dilson-Alvarez's tenure documents would have reached the dean's office by now, and the file should have included all relevant publications. But given what Bell had told her of Provost Bedard's coziness with this professor, she decided not to call her just yet.

Instead, she phoned the chair. "Listen," she said, "I've got a question for you."

"Okay. Can you hold on for a moment? My office door's open."

While waiting, she saw the red light blink on her Black-Berry. A new text message from Matt: *Making a foot-long tuna melt and thinking of you.* He sent them to her off and on all day, and she frequently reread them. In each instance she felt augmented, as if digesting the words for the tenth or twelfth time added yet another layer to the entity the rest of the world knew as Kristin Stevens. The messages might not keep coming forever. She was fifty years old, her hair beginning to turn gray, her body losing its tone. But something surprising had happened just when she thought nothing ever could.

"All right," Bell said, "I'm back."

"When Dilson-Alvarez submitted his tenure documents," she asked, "did he include his book?"

"No. He wasn't required to. He published it before we hired

him. All he had to submit in the tenure file was the work that's been accepted or come out since he got here."

"Have you actually seen the book?"

"Yes."

"When?"

"When we interviewed him. I was on the hiring committee. He submitted it as his writing sample."

"Did you read it?"

"Some of it."

"What did you think?"

He sighed. "I was an assistant professor at the time—actually up for tenure myself. Some people on the committee were very taken by it. I mean, it was a *book*. Nobody else in the department had ever published one."

"In other words, you weren't impressed?"

"Since you're asking me questions," he said, "might I risk one myself?"

"I suppose the least I can do is say yes, right?"

"You could say no, but I suspect you're too nice a person."

"Okay. Fire away."

"What made you quit being a literary critic?"

Still holding the phone, she pushed her chair back from her desk and looked through the window at the quad. The morning couldn't have been more beautiful. The sun was out, and a brisk breeze sent leaves swirling through the air as students strolled between classes. It was the kind of day that made you happy to be here, even if it wasn't where you thought you belonged. "I despised all the jargon," she said. "I blamed it for destroying my love of literature. In retrospect, this was unfair. That didn't have to happen."

"Granted," he said. "Better things can always happen. But academic discourse, especially in fields like yours and mine, has become a long, tiresome exercise in obfuscation. That's what's in. What I love is decidedly out."

"What do you love?"

"I'm an old-fashioned proponent of event-based history who clings to the simple-minded notion that what's most interesting is a well-told story. The writers I go back to again and again are people like Shelby Foote, Bruce Catton, David McCullough, Doris Kearns Goodwin. And they're anathema to academic historians. Robert's book's okay for what it is, I guess. But I only made it through about five or ten pages. Why do you ask?"

She told him she couldn't find any mention of the title online. The publisher was defunct, and the book had apparently never been reviewed anywhere, which she found unusual.

"So given the plagiarized passages in his article," Bell said, "you're wondering whether or not the book exists. I can relieve your mind on that score. Seven years ago, I held it in my hands."

"For all of ten or twelve minutes."

Bell burst out laughing, and it sounded as if this was the first release of tension he'd experienced in days, if not weeks. "Kristin," he said, "the most amazing thing has occurred."

"What's that?"

"I've become fond of an administrator."

That night, as she lay on her back in Penelope Hill's bed, staring at a ceiling she couldn't see, in a house she had no right to be in, she told Matt about her two plagiarists and said she was in a quandary about what to do next.

"Just get rid of them," he said.

"It's not quite that simple."

"It was pretty simple when my boss caught me."

Both of them smelled of sex, brandy and Szechuan beef. After making love, they'd eaten Chinese takeout in the glow of a lithium flashlight he'd bought at Paul Nowicki's hardware. He no longer felt any inclination to avoid the place, he'd told her. The other day his ex waited on him, and they'd chatted like old friends.

"You worked at a bookstore," she said. "My plagiarists are employed by a university. A shitty one, but still a sort of institution with all the usual rules."

"Breaking the law's generally accepted as wrong. I fail to see the difference."

On this sagging mattress that hadn't been slept on in decades, she'd done and said things that she could neither condone nor disown. Soon she'd go home and face her husband, and when he asked how she'd spent her day and evening she would look him in the eye and lie, and his willingness to believe her would diminish him a bit further. He was six foot four but shrinking daily, a decent man with huge hands that became delicate only when he laid them on a mandolin.

"We're breaking the law by being here," she said.

"Well, that *is* different. In our case, hearts are involved."

He rolled toward her and rested his head on her breast. She loved it when he did that. Though it shamed her to acknowledge this even to herself, it made her wish, as she used to, that she could have a child. Phil always maintained they should wait until they both got tenure, but once he did he left. She was in her midthirties when she met Cal. When he broached the subject she told him it was too late, that her job wouldn't allow for child rearing. The truth was she didn't want to have a baby with him, though she knew that unlike Phil he would've made a good father. How irrational her choices had been, none more so than being where she was right now. "I actually have a feeling hearts may be involved in my plagiarism case, too," she said. "Gwendolyn Conley's heart, anyway."

She told him that the first time she'd seen the two of them together, she suspected they were lovers. From John Bell she'd learned that Conley was divorced, with two young children, and that Dilson-Alvarez was married, though no one in the department, as far as the chair knew, had ever met his wife. It was said she came from someplace in Eastern Europe. Slovenia, he thought, or maybe Slovakia.

"So what does being lovers," Matt asked, "have to do with being plagiarists?" It accrued to his credit that he took her concerns seriously. Try though Cal might—and he sometimes did—he'd never been able to conceal his belief that about 90 percent of what transpired at universities was bogus. He once remarked that the only people he respected at her previous school were those in the Department of Viticulture and Enology. When she wondered why, he said, "At least they admit they're producing an intoxicant."

"I don't know," she told Matt. "But I have a feeling that somehow Dilson-Alvarez has entrapped her."

"Well, if she let him talk her into plagiarizing, she'll pay with her job."

"I'm not so sure."

"Are you serious? Your provost might be an idiot, but I doubt she's suicidal. Once you've shown her the evidence you just described to me, she can't afford to ignore it. That'd make her guilty of misconduct herself. I read a book about plagiarism—*Stolen Words*, I believe it was called. It's pretty cut and dried in academia. You should know that."

"You've read a book about everything," she said, then told him she still needed to confer with the editors of the journals in which the disputed articles had appeared, to alert them of her discovery and take their statements. She also hoped to contact the editor in chief of the British house that published Dilson-Alvarez's book; she'd seen his name in one of the online articles, so unless he'd died in the meantime, she ought to be able to track him down. She couldn't help but wonder why the book had never been reviewed anywhere.

"Under ordinary circumstances," she said, "I'd also call the

National Student Clearinghouse and ask them to check their degrees, since official transcripts can be faked. But that's tricky, because the clearinghouse requires written permission from the individuals whose records you've requested. Normally, you get that before hiring anybody, but North Shore didn't have the foresight and asking for it now would tip my hand. This is just a horrible mess, and I can't tell you how badly I wish it hadn't come up. If I could ignore it, I would."

He lifted his head, then sat up in bed. She'd been surprised when she first saw him with his shirt off. His torso looked frail, the bones of his ribs visible through his skin. He didn't have much chest hair either, just a faint downy fuzz. There was something so boyish about him, a vulnerability that made her feel many things, one of which was a desire to protect him, even from herself.

Though no musician, he wasn't tone-deaf. "You're not thinking of letting it go, are you?"

She'd once overheard a friend of her mother's pose the same question, with exactly the same inflection. As if an affirmative answer would cast doubt on her mother's sanity.

The occasion was a visit home from Chapel Hill, on the Thanksgiving of her first fall in grad school. She'd gone because her mother practically begged her to come. By then she and Phil were spending all their nights together, drinking his generic beer and talking books, making love and talking books some more. He wanted to accompany her to Pennsylvania but couldn't; his grandmother was seriously ill in Mississippi, and he hoped to see her once more before she died. "Just keep your chin up," he advised. "Your mom needs you. Otherwise she wouldn't ask."

The friend who'd asked her mother the question wasn't aware that Kristin was within earshot. The house she'd grown up in had become a place in which one lurked, stopping and listening before moving from one room to the next. Her mother often sat alone in dark corners, talking on the phone with the lights turned off and the drapes drawn tightly so she couldn't accidentally catch a glimpse of the property next door. Her father was renting a room in one of the row houses at the end of South Market. She'd never known anybody who lived there, but evidently he did. Who could say who he did or didn't know or how long he might've known them?

"You're not thinking of letting it go, are you?" her mother's friend said. "You'd let him move back *in*?"

"I didn't say that," her mother said. Her voice no longer sounded as if her mouth were full of peanut butter. She'd quit taking whatever the doctor had been giving her but was on the mend, though no one understood that then, least of all Kristin. "I said I'm considering picking up the pieces and moving on."

"With him?"

"Possibly. Next semester, when I go back to work, I'll see him at school every day. If I see him there, I might as well see him here."

"But what about her? She's right next door."

Her mother sighed. "She won't be a problem."

"She sure was before."

"She won't be anymore."

"How can you be certain?"

"Because she told me she wouldn't."

"And you trust her?"

"I always have."

"And look where that led."

Where it had led was to the bedroom or, more precisely, as Kristin's friend said the day she called her in Cleveland, to Patty's own bed. That was where Patty's father had found them. He'd entered the house around four in the afternoon and slipped upstairs, knowing what he would discover before he ever saw the proof. He'd spared Patty most of the details, she said, but implication is the most potent of all poisons: when she began to cry at the notion that they'd made love in her bed, her dad said, *No, honey, it wasn't like that, they weren't in the bed, exactly.* So Patty then imagined her mother bent over, clutching the foot rail while Kristin's father slammed into her. She wouldn't have been on her knees, since the room had no carpet. *You know what she said to my dad?* Patty sobbed. *When he asked her if she loved your father? She said not only didn't she love him, she didn't even like him very much.*

"Sooner or later," her mother told her friend, "trust always leads to disappointment. You think you'll wake up tomorrow, because you always have. But one day you won't. Sarah's already disappointed me, but she hasn't got it in her to do it again. She didn't really have it in her the first time. She just ended up living on the wrong man's street."

Her mother's assessment seemed so cynical that for a while Kristin couldn't forgive her. Strangely, it was easier to forgive Mrs. Connulty. The last time she ever saw her, in the checkout line at Food Giant the year before her mother found her in the snow, they spoke as if none of this had ever happened. Kristin's father had died several years before, and Tom Connulty had long since returned to PP&L's home office in Allentown. Sarah Connulty's grocery cart held only a small sack of red potatoes, a head of lettuce, a package of spaghetti noodles, some ground beef, several cans of cat food.

"How are you, honey?" she'd asked.

"I'm fine," Kristin said, because at the moment it was true. She and Phil had just bought a nice house in California, he'd gotten early tenure, and she'd become an associate vice president. They were happy. She enjoyed each new day. "And you?"

"I'm all right," Mrs. Connulty said. She'd lost her figure, but the flowing skirt she wore hid her vast bulk from view, and her hair was still dark and thick and beautiful. "I think of you all the time," she said. "Your mom keeps me up-to-date."

She held her gaze and might have said more had Kristin not

reached out and wrapped her arms around her. "I love you, Mrs. Connulty," she said, her own means of finally, irrevocably, letting it go.

Now she was lying in bed, in a musty room where the accumulated dust on the coverlet made her sneeze each time she crawled under it, and a man who could have gone to jail for embezzlement was asking her if she could possibly overlook academic mischief. This time last year, if someone had dared to ask a similar question, she wouldn't have dignified it with an answer. Misconduct was misconduct, and it came with a price tag. "I didn't say that," she responded.

"You said she might not pay with her job."

Using her elbows, she leveraged herself into a sitting position, the headboard against her back. She watched him admiring her breasts. To her great bafflement, guilt was not an altogether unpleasant sensation; it brought with it a sense of expansion, as if you were still who you thought yourself to be as well as someone else you never knew existed. "If we're to keep coming here," she said, "we'll need to wash these bedclothes."

"I'll take them home this evening and clean them and bring them straight back. I should've done it before now. You deserve a clean bed."

"Eventually we'll be discovered. You know that, right?"

"I prefer to look on the bright side. Tonight I'm here with you."

"I prefer to do the same thing. But remember the bright side's got a flip side."

"I know that all too well," he said.

An octagonal clock hung on the wall closest to the four-poster. She always looked at it when they entered the room, and she turned to it again now. But the absence of light left the black hands indistinct. She saw only the face, which the night rendered gray.

the kristin stevens file

"see what i was saying?" Dave, the ex-cop Cal had met at his neighbor Vico's house, was sitting in his living room and displaying the third finger of his left hand.

Cal leaned over to get a closer look. The last joint was bent, and it hooked toward his pinky. "How'd it happen?" he asked.

"One night, my first or second year on the force, me and my partner get called to this domestic disturbance. Somebody's neighbor's heard a hell of a racket, some guy's screaming his wife's a cunt. Next thing the neighbor knows, glass is shattering and furniture's going over, and it sounds like somebody's getting the shit beat out of 'em. Now, in that kind of situation, which is still very much in progress when Esposito and yours truly show up, we don't knock but once. And in this case knocking wouldn't do any good anyway. Somebody in there's getting a royal ass kicking, so I say one, two, three, and each of us puts a shoulder to the door.

"In the hallway, this guy's going at his wife with all he's got, and she's got a busted lip, but her fingernails must be at least three inches long, and she's giving as good as she's taking. Her old man's bleeding from his cheeks, neck and forearm where she's sunk those claws into him. But they've got a kid that plays football, and his dad's put his helmet on for protection so he can keep at it.

"Since Esposito's smaller than me, he goes after Catwoman, and before he pins her arms she does some interesting etchings on his jaw. This leaves the helmeted fuck for me. When I reach out to grab him, my finger gets caught in his face mask and bent sideways. Next morning the damn thing's purple and I can't straighten it out."

"You didn't have it looked at?"

Dave shrugged. "What kind of cop goes to the doctor for a broke finger? Besides, how was I to know someday I'd have a chance to play the mandolin?"

And how could Cal have known that when he agreed to go over to Vico's for a few drinks and a bowl of pasta, he'd run into Dave? If someone had told him what was going to happen afterward, he would've begged off.

There had been four of them: him and Vico and Dave and a guy named Jimmy who used to coach football. He'd had a lot to drink—only beer, it was true, but after a while even beer adds up—and by the time they were through with dinner, he had a nice buzz and was virtually defenseless when Vico turned to him and said, "By the way, what kind of music did I hear you playing in the backyard? Country? Celtic? Blues?"

He hadn't imagined he could produce enough volume for a neighbor with a hearing aid to tune in. Otherwise, he wouldn't have risked playing on the patio once or twice back before it got too cold. "I guess it's a little bit of all three," he said. "Which I suppose means it's bluegrass, but I'm not real big on labels."

That was when Dave rapped the table with a meaty palm and said, "You like bluegrass?"

Cal knew immediately that he was in trouble. He'd stepped around the fence into his neighbor's yard, and now a wall was truly being breached. He took another swig of beer, then held the bottle up to examine it while trying to figure out how to suggest he didn't know shit about bluegrass, that he was just a bum with a guitar who couldn't tell Bill Monroe from Bill Clinton. "Harpoon," he said, studying the brightly decorated label. "This is local, right?"

"My neighbor's a modest guy," Vico said. "You should hear him play. Hey, maybe we could have a little music. How about it?"

Cal drained the rest of the bottle. As the beer went down,

something equally bitter was coming up, and to call it anger would hardly do it justice. He was about to stand up and excuse himself, to say he'd had too much to drink and needed to go home and lie down before he got sick and puked all over Vico and his excellent intentions.

But before he could, Dave said, "For maybe thirty seconds, back in 1985, I was no more than this far"—he held his chunky hands about eighteen inches apart—"from Tony Rice and that D-28 that once belonged to Clarence White." He shook his head. "I knew right then I'd never forget it." The ex-cop turned to Cal. "You know what I mean?"

This could have gone differently, but instead of leaving, Cal stayed seated. "Yes," he said, "I do."

It turned out that Dave had first heard live bluegrass in Everett in his midtwenties. He said Cal probably wouldn't know about the fellow who'd brought him to the bar, but he was a local guy who repaired typewriters for a living and played bluegrass on the side.

"Joe Val," Cal said.

Dave grinned and shook his head. "Vico, this dude's fucking hard core."

When their host beamed, Cal suspected he was the sort of person who'd always mystified him and made him feel mistrustful. On the surface, it looked like he enjoyed bringing folks together for the simple pleasure of seeing them talk and drink and have a good time. Cal's father had brought people together too, and they probably thought he enjoyed their company, but he issued invitations only because he wanted something from them. The house had teemed with those he hoped to buy, bamboozle or otherwise fuck over, and he was seldom disappointed. Cal knew that seeing this day after day, year after year, had damaged him. What he didn't know was how to overcome it. Changing his name hadn't changed who he was.

He and Dave talked about Joe Val. Cal said he'd never heard

him play live, but he owned a couple of his CDs and admired his work on the mandolin. Dave said he'd met Val the way he had met almost everybody else he knew down in Everett. "He used to drive around in this old beat-up van, and one day he leaves it parked on the street and forgets to lock the door while he goes in to pick up somebody's Smith and Corona. You don't leave a vehicle unlocked down in the Dirty E. He comes out of the building, and every fucking typewriter in the van's been snatched. Me and Esposito knew right where to look, and within the hour we'd recovered all but two of 'em. Joe was so grateful he invited us to hear him play—this is after he'd formed the New England Bluegrass Boys—and he made the house waive the cover. I didn't even know what bluegrass was, just didn't have anything better to do that night, but man, it really grabbed me. I went nuts and started buying so many records my wife put me on an allowance. Got to be good friends with Joe, too, and all the guys in his band. That's how I saw Rice. When Joe was dying, the Boston Bluegrass Union organized a benefit concert, and Tony played with Jimmy Gaudreau."

He said that some years ago he'd taught himself to play the guitar and had become competent enough to strum chords and pick a decent G run. He'd tried the mandolin as well and still owned a cheap one, but he'd finally concluded he just wasn't a musician. "Loving it's not enough, you know what I mean? Sad, but that's how things go."

"Did you ever take any lessons?"

"Nah. My work schedule didn't allow it. And after a while, I lost heart anyway. I know what good sounds like, and it don't sound like me."

Cal was still drunk, but he knew what he was doing when he said, "Want to see my instruments? I've got quite a few."

Kristin had gone shopping for winter clothes at the Burlington Mall, so when they stepped into the house, after assuring Vico and the ex-coach they'd return before long, no one greeted them except Suzy. Dave knelt in front of her, letting her sniff while he scratched behind her ears.

"You got a dog?" Cal asked.

Dave laughed. "Don't own one. But when I was on the force, every pooch I met was mine. You want 'em on your side." He stood and looked around. "Nice house. Vico says you're remodeling?"

"Was," Cal said, and flipped on the staircase light. "I kind of got off track after the thing at the convenience store."

"Shit like that takes awhile to get over. Someday, maybe I'll tell you some stuff I saw being a cop. Some of it's funny. But most of it ain't."

Cal led him upstairs. A few minutes later, they were down on their knees in the room on the third floor, surrounded by instruments. Dave was particularly drawn to the F-5. He ran his hand over the fretboard, letting his fingers linger on the abalone position markers. "This looks just like the mandolin Joe used to play," he said.

"Wouldn't surprise me. That's what everybody wanted back then."

Dave handed it to him. "Would you mind?" he asked.

Cal had recently begun to suspect he'd never again play for anyone else. Back in California, the audience, such as it was, consisted mostly of people just like him—fairly skilled amateurs who considered Friday nights an opportunity to stretch out with kindred spirits—but around here, the Berklee College of Music disgorged scores of real musicians who could play rings around him in their sleep, and while most of them had to give lessons or sell guitar strings and mandolin straps to earn a living, he'd felt so daunted when he stepped into Elderly Acoustics in Lexington and heard a few of them play that he was reluctant even to pick up a mandocello he wanted to try.

Had Dave phrased his question differently, he would have

demurred. But the request was expressed with such humility that it was impossible to say no. He only wanted to hear something that might remind him of his dead friend Joe Val.

"Okay," Cal said. He sat on the edge of the daybed, checked the tuning, then closed his eyes and began playing tremolo on the A and E strings, waltzing into "Blue Moon of Kentucky." He played the A part once and decided to do it a second time, because he'd muffled a note or two and he hated to move on until it sounded just right. What he hadn't counted on was the aid of a vocalist.

> *Blue moon of Kentucky keep on shining*
> *Shine on the one that's gone and proved untrue*
> *Blue moon of Kentucky just keep on shining*
> *Shine on the one that's gone and left me blue*

Dave's voice was a tenor, clear and unaffected. He rolled "moon" and "of" together in the manner of Monroe, and his voice rose a full octave before he let the note go. Like Val, he didn't bother to pretend he was anything other than a North Shore townie, so "shining" came out "shine-un." To someone else it might have sounded funny, but just as Cal had always thought a house should belong to the person who built it, he believed music should belong to those who could make it. And in some elemental sense, the retired cop knew how to.

When they finished the chorus, he quit playing. "I like your voice," he said. Then he offered Dave the mandolin.

The other man had fat lips, tiny eyes and a bulbous nose with huge pores, yet for a moment, as he basked in the compliment, his face was beautiful. "I can't play it," he said. "Those chop chords that stretch out over four or five frets—they whipped my ass years ago. It's a shame, because I'd give almost anything to be able to do what you just did. I swear to God, you sound like a pro. You're just as good as Joe was."

Cal laid the Gibson back in its case. "If you'd like to learn," he said, "I could try to teach you."

When Dave came for his first lesson, Cal discovered that he actually knew the shapes of the major and minor chords. He just had trouble playing them cleanly, due to that mangled ring finger. "For bluegrass rhythm playing," Cal told him, "that's not such a problem. Mostly what you're doing is damping the strings anyway, to get the barking effect. The mandolin takes the place of a snare drum." He explained that eventually he'd start teaching him simple fiddle tunes. "Playing those forces you to learn scales. Once you've done that, you can improvise over almost any melody. It's kind of like building a house. First you lay the foundation. Then the walls go up. It's a good while before you're installing light fixtures and slapping on paint."

He was perched on the coffee table with his mandolin on his knee, and Dave was sitting on the couch. The instrument he owned—a fifty-year-old Harmony Monterey—wasn't worth much, but Cal said it had a nice sound.

"You really think so?" Dave asked. "Me, I can't tell."

"A lot of them actually improve when they get older. Once the lacquer develops a few hairline cracks, it frees the wood. Every year or two, I'll make a tape using each of my instruments, and it's amazing how the sound changes from one time to the next. And they all sound better here," he said, "than they did in California. It's bone-dry out there in the valley, and they need moisture."

"That won't be a problem around here," Dave assured him. "Man, wait till you experience a New England winter. I just hope you won't split."

Cal had been wondering if he'd leave or not, swinging back and forth on a daily if not hourly basis. Sometimes, sitting on the daybed up on the third floor and looking out at the neighbors' tree, now a leafless, twisted gray skeleton, he felt he could never belong here, not least because the distance between Kristin and him had been easier to ignore when his days were busy and his surroundings familiar, back before the economic contraction sent them packing.

At other times, when he leashed Suzy and took her out for a stroll in the rolling hills of Cedar Park, he could almost imagine making a go of it here. The notion that every house had a history, that people had been living in most of them for well over a hundred years and in some instances double that, made the place seem permanent like California never had. You'd see peeling paint and rickety steps on a big Queen Anne with a Lexus or Mercedes in the driveway; the folks who lived there could obviously afford to repaint it, and probably every few years they would, but in the meantime they just let it stand, secure in the belief that it would weather whatever nature threw at it. And everybody seemed to know everybody else. He'd see neighbors talking to one another as they bent over in their yards bagging leaves, and while this didn't include him he began to envision a gray-haired version of himself bending over in his own yard five or ten years down the road, gathering leaves and swapping pleasantries with Vico. He hadn't had a real friend since Ernesto got electrocuted when they were building that mansion in Modesto.

"I doubt I'll be leaving," he told Dave. "For one thing, I don't have anywhere to go. But you're retired now. Ever think of taking off for a warmer climate?"

Dave opened his case and laid the mandolin back inside it. "Nah, not really. I mean, I've been to Florida a few times, and it's a nice place to vacation. I even went to California several years ago, visited a guy I knew in the marines who lives in San Diego. But my brother's up in Billerica, my sister's down in Bridgewater, and I got grandkids scattered from here to the Berkshires. This is where I belong. What about you? Got any family besides your wife?"

"No," Cal said, pulling the strap off his mandolin. "I was an only child. My mom's been dead for years." He bent over to place the instrument back in its case. "My father died in 1999." While his head was down, he added, "Actually, he got killed."

"In an accident?"

"No. In federal prison." He sat up and laid his hands on his knees. "He'd been involved in a bunch of crooked land deals, and he built a lot of shitty houses that started causing health problems and falling apart, so plenty of people had reasons to hate him. The guy that did it wasn't one of 'em, though. He was just somebody my dad shot his mouth off to. He had a little trouble adjusting to jail."

"Most people do. I've known a few that breathed their last breath in Walpole." Dave thought about his wording for a moment, then said, "Not that your old man was a perp, in the conventional sense."

"But he was in the grand sense," Cal said.

That made the ex-cop chuckle, so Cal did too. He tried to remember the last time he'd laughed, but couldn't. It might have been a year. Probably more.

"Well," Dave said, standing up, "at least you can say your pop didn't lack ambition."

"Nope. He wanted to own as much land and as many people as money could buy."

Dave thanked him, and they agreed they'd have another lesson the day after tomorrow. Earlier, when his new student insisted on paying him, Cal said absolutely not, that he was doing it for fun and wouldn't mind having someone to play with.

They were moving into the hallway when hinges creaked, the door swung open and Kristin stepped inside. He'd reminded her about the session this evening but assumed she'd forgotten, because she looked surprised: face flushed, even damp, though the temperature had dropped into the low thirties. She must've speed walked all the way from the station.

"Oh," she said, "hello."

Cal introduced them.

"Pleased to meet you," Dave said. He stuck out his hand, and Kristin gave him hers. "Your husband's a saint," he said, "for putting up with the noise he heard tonight."

"I'm sure you're better than you admit."

"No, I'm even worse."

"Oh, I doubt that," she said, stepping over to the closet and pulling off her coat.

Cal noticed a purple bruise on her neck, between her hairline and blouse, and intended to ask about it, but by bedtime he'd forgotten, and the next day it was gone.

north shore state closed on the Wednesday before Thanksgiving. She'd hoped to sleep in but woke around eight when
Cal headed downstairs. She lay there alone for a few moments,
waiting for the heat to come on. A rime of frost coated the
windows, and the wind rattled them.

During the night she'd had a strange dream. She was back
in the grocery store in her hometown, and Christmas music
was playing over the sound system, though it seemed to be
either Halloween or Thanksgiving. Pumpkins were piled up
in the display window and were floor-stacked at the end of the
aisle into which she'd pushed her cart. Just ahead of her was a
blond woman with two small children. She could only see the
mother's back, but she wore professional attire: wool skirt and
jacket, sensible shoes. The boy had on blue knee shorts, and the
blue-and-gold scarf knotted at his neck identified him as a
Cub Scout. The girl, however, looked like a character from the
Walker Evans album of Depression-era photos that Philip used
to haul out when he got to his second or third brandy.

The woman reached out to lift a can or jar off the grocery
shelf, and drawing closer Kristin recognized she was Gwendolyn
Conley. Her face was pale, as though she hadn't slept for days,
and her eyes were red. When she saw Kristin, her face turned
red too. Kristin expected her to apologize, to explain or to beg
for mercy, but all she did was look away. That is exactly what
she herself had done when her provost in California, her boss
and friend for ten years, had called her into his office and said,
"Kristin, I'm afraid I have some bad news for you."

The journal that had published Conley's disputed article
was based at a large midwestern state university. The other

day she'd contacted the editor, and in a matter of minutes he'd progressed from skepticism to bafflement and then terror. His voice broke when he observed, "This could cost me my job."

"*Your* job? You didn't plagiarize the article."

"No, but I published the goddamn thing. Listen," he said, sounding as if he were about to choke, "could I call you back from my cell?"

"Sure."

He didn't phone for at least fifteen minutes. When he finally did, she heard traffic in the background, a barking dog. He explained that the state legislature had proposed a 12 percent cut that might well eliminate his journal. "This kind of mistake," he said, "could be a strike against us. And so could the fact that it took this long for anyone to discover it. They'll just say it's proof almost nobody reads us anyway."

She did her best to soothe him, promising to let him know before she took any further steps. In the meantime, she said, she'd send him all the information she'd collected, including JSTOR citations for the pilfered articles. He requested she use his Hotmail address.

When she reached the editor of the Canadian journal that had published Dilson-Alvarez's piece, he sighed and said, "I was expecting your call."

"You were?"

"From you or someone else. Where'd you say you worked—Shoreline State?"

She corrected him, then asked why he'd anticipated a call.

"Because," he said, "just yesterday I received a little present from someone down there." It had arrived in a regular manila envelope, he said, postmarked Bradbury, Massachusetts, and probably wouldn't have been opened for several months, the editorial staff assuming it contained a submission. "Those lie around forever awaiting screening," he told her. "But this was addressed to me, and since it looked like real correspondence, the interns laid it on my desk." Inside was a typed note inform-ing him that the article he'd published by Robert Dilson-Alvarez had several plagiarized passages. "Whoever sent it to me," he said, "was kind enough to list the articles he'd lifted stuff from, as well as the relevant page numbers."

"Have you already compared them to the article you published?"

"Yes, I did that last night."

"And?"

"And?" he said.

"I'm just wondering what your reaction was."

"Doctor . . . I'm sorry, what did you say your last name is?"

"Stevens."

"Dr. Stevens, my reaction was extreme weariness. I'm seventy-one years old. I should've retired at least ten years ago—although even that would've been too late for me to avoid becoming disgusted by the whole enterprise. I'm sick and tired of it. I even hate the word 'profession' because whatever it is we're doing now, it is not *professing*. We may be provoking, we're definitely proliferating, but mostly we're prevaricating. We lie to the young, and we lie to ourselves. We've ceased to disseminate wisdom. So the discovery that your faculty mem-ber stole someone else's words neither angers nor surprises me. He has simply recycled garbage. Would you be upset if you saw somebody raiding a stranger's trash bin?"

Two or three years ago, she might've said that if he felt like that he should've quit right then. But she seemed incapable, lately, of even feigned outrage. People had flaws. They ignored the law, broke hearts and violated all norms of decency and ethics, engaging in academic misconduct, financial malfea-sance, political chicanery, sexual transgression. Spending a good part of your life trying to stamp that out would exhaust any-body, especially if you were guilty yourself, and in some form or fashion who wasn't?

Her conversation with the elderly editor had taken place on Monday. Then, just when she walked into the office yesterday morning, Donna told her that somebody named Julian Blatchford had called her half an hour earlier. "I asked if he wanted your voice mail, but he said no. He left you a number in London and said he'd be home until six his time."

She took the slip of paper from her assistant, stepped into her private office and closed the door. Blatchford had been the editor in chief of the house that published Dilson-Alvarez's book. Tracking him down had taken some doing. He apparently hadn't landed another job and had an unlisted phone, but a former graduate-school classmate who worked for Oxford University Press in New York had helped Kristin locate him.

When she dialed the London number, a woman answered. Kristin asked to speak to Julian Blatchford, and a moment later he said hello. "You'll be expecting a British accent," he said, "but I'm actually a Yank. Born and raised in Brattleboro, Vermont."

He sounded British to her. She thanked him for getting in touch, then asked if her friend at OUP had explained why she wanted to speak to him.

"Well," he said, "she told me it concerned a highly confidential matter of academic integrity. Which made me suspect it involved Robert Dilson-Alvarez. So I poked around online and discovered he's washed ashore there. That's entirely too bad. For you and your school, I mean."

During the few months she'd occupied her new office, she'd discovered that rotating her swivel chair so she could gaze out the window always produced a pleasant effect. The quad was a contained space, redbrick buildings visible on three sides, the green strewn with brittle leaves. Everything was where it should be, and the students strolling in twos or threes looked happy. Twenty percent of them might be clinically depressed, 15 percent probably had serious drug issues and a handful were most likely suicidal, but you couldn't know this from looking out the window. It was a great view, since you could see what you wanted to and miss what you didn't.

Blatchford said Dilson-Alvarez's book on Frantz Fanon and therapeutic violence was primarily the work of a Finnish academic. "I can't recall the name of the press that originally published it because, as you might imagine, I've repressed a good bit of this. But I believe it was located in Tampere. Robert simply translated the text into English, inserted a few passages by other writers here and there, tweaked the title and submitted it under his own name. It would've been a fine book. We had great hopes for it and ordered a first printing of six thousand copies, which was a lot for us. There'd been a surge of interest in Fanon around that time, and we'd already secured distribution in the U.S. through Yale. It was actually someone there who alerted us it was stolen. It turns out a woman in their marketing department could read Finnish, and in researching the subject she came across some references to the original text that made her suspicious. So she tracked it down, and we managed to halt the release. Robert evidently did a magnificent job translating it. He's married to a Hungarian woman and speaks that language, which is of course related to Finnish."

"So you mean you didn't actually publish it? One of my faculty members swears he's seen a copy."

"Oh, I don't doubt that. We'd sent Robert a carton of author's copies, and he never responded to our request that he return them. I might've predicted what he'd do with them. We could've gone after him, but our solicitor said that would be costly. I just decided to let the whole thing go. And hoped I'd never hear his name again."

She asked if he could send her a brief account of what had happened. "An e-mail," she said, "would be fine."

"Gladly," he replied. "He'll be getting the sack, I take it?"

"I don't have the final decision, but I can't foresee any other outcome."

"Well, that's quite wonderful."

"Mr. Blatchford—"

"Julian."

"Julian. Do you have any idea what prompted him to do something so stupid? He seems like an intelligent man. He has a fine education and speaks a number of different languages. He decided to become an academic, but he could just as easily have pursued a career as a translator, a diplomat, I don't know what else. There had to have been all kinds of options, at least in the beginning."

He laughed. "Do you ever listen to the country singer Hank Williams?"

"Not really. My husband plays his music sometimes, though."

"Well, ask him to play 'Your Cheatin' Heart.' Therein lies the answer. Robert simply has the heart of a cheater. Doing things normally would most likely bore him to death, so he becomes a midnight man. But you know Williams's final word on such behavior, don't you?"

"I'm afraid not."

"Sooner or later," Blatchford said, " 'your cheatin' heart will tell on you.' "

She climbed out of bed, stepped into her slippers and shrugged on her robe. She might as well get going. That guy Dave was coming over this morning for another mandolin lesson. Cal had actually begun calling him "my friend," and while Kristin was happy he'd found one, the phrase sounded so strange on his lips that it made her feel unsettled.

In the kitchen, he was sitting at the table with the *Globe* spread out before him, next to his coffee mug. "Hey," she said. "Good morning."

"Good morning to you," he said, "dear."

He'd begun using the term lately, and it troubled her. Whatever else Cal might be, he wasn't expressive unless he had an instrument in hand. She walked over to the counter, poured herself a cup of coffee, then split an English muffin and popped it in the toaster. "What's the news?" she asked.

"The worst thing so far is that somebody in Lawrence murdered his pregnant girlfriend because they disagreed about the baby's name." He read her part of the account, in which the Essex County district attorney concluded, "She insisted the name be hyphenated, and he was opposed."

She lifted the top off the butter dish. "That's horrific."

"Well, folks can go crazy over a lot of things. Names being one." Laying the paper aside, he asked if she had any special plans for the day.

She carried her coffee and her muffin to the table and sat down. They were supposed to have Thanksgiving next door at Vico's, along with Dave and his wife and another guy, and since she'd agreed to bring dessert she told Cal she thought she'd drive up to the Whole Foods in Andover and do some grocery shopping.

"You'd better get going," he said. "It'll be a madhouse later." She agreed and, once she finished her breakfast, went back upstairs, took a shower and got dressed.

She hadn't driven much since they moved here. The unmarked streets and aggressive drivers made her reluctant to, but she knew she'd have to adjust to both if they stayed. The Volvo sounded sluggish when she started it, so she sat in the driveway awhile, letting it rev up a little, then finally backed out.

The deli stood at the intersection of East Border Road and Main Street. Waiting at the traffic light, she glanced through the plate glass, hoping to spot Matt, but too many customers were in line. He said you'd be surprised how many people opted for sliced turkey to avoid the trouble of roasting a whole bird.

When she asked if he had plans for Thanksgiving, he told her he'd be spending it at his boss's home. They invited him every year, he said, but until now he'd turned them down. When she wondered why, he said, "Because I had nothing to be thankful for. Just a lot to regret."

Both of them had begun talking about the future as if it didn't preclude their present behavior. In her rational moments, she knew the affair couldn't continue. Sooner or later, Vico or Dave would see her climbing out of Matt's car and tell Cal. Or someone else—a caretaker, a policeman—would discover their sanctuary and, in the best scenario, change the locks on Penelope Hill's house. In the worst case, they might find themselves in jail.

Once Cal learned her secret, what he would do was anybody's guess. She could imagine him leaving in the middle of the night, disappearing from her life forever, but she could also see him walking down the street, kicking in Matt's door and beating him to a pulp. Even before he prevented the robbery at the convenience store, she'd known he was capable of violence if pushed far enough. You could just tell he had it in him, and over the years this had given her a sense of security that now seemed perverse.

The traffic on Route 28 wasn't bad yet, and she reached Andover in just under thirty minutes. The parking lot at Whole Foods was already crowded, but she found a spot near the rear of the store and went inside.

She'd decided to bake a simple apple cake. She could still see the recipe, in Sarah Connulty's surprisingly elegant script, on an index card; her mother's best friend had collected these in a three-ring binder and presented them to her before she left for Case Western. What had happened to that little book Kristin no longer knew, but she'd cooked out of it for years, and no one loved the results more than Philip Harrington.

Unlike the Whole Foods she'd shopped at in California, the Andover store was strangely configured. Upon entry, you stepped straight into the produce department, where tables set against one another at odd angles were bracketed by vegetable coolers. If the goal was to create a massive traffic jam, it was a great success, and it took her several minutes to get close enough to the apples to select four nice-sized organic Granny Smiths. After that she picked up a carton of eggs and, just to be on the safe side, five-pound bags of sugar and flour. Then she bagged eight ounces of chopped walnuts and an equal amount of raisins. Finally, she went to the butcher's counter and ordered a duck and some grass-fed beef chuck, thinking that on Saturday she might make a pot roast.

All six checkout stands were staffed today, but the line at each was eight or nine customers deep. The store had a café, so even though she didn't really need another cup of coffee, she decided to have one. If the situation didn't improve in a few minutes, she'd line up like everyone else. She ordered a latte, then pulled her cart over to the only unoccupied table, sat down and began to sip her drink.

Cal once told her she was unobservant. He didn't mean it as a criticism, though it sounded like one. He said it when they were driving by a neighbor's house in California and she noted that the shake roofing had been replaced by tiles. "They did that about five years ago," he said, then remarked that she often saw things without actually *seeing* them.

The washed-out blonde had been standing in front of the espresso machine for some time, part of the background detail. But to toss her empty paper cup into the trash, Kristin had to walk past her, and that was when she realized it was Gwendolyn Conley.

She paused at the exact instant the barista placed a drink on the counter in front of Conley, who wrapped her hand around the insulating sleeve and turned around, now facing her directly, giving Kristin no chance to get rid of her cup and walk away as fast as she could.

After a few awkward seconds, Kristin asked, "Are your kids here with you?"

Conley's face was naturally pale. If she'd ever had a California tan, no trace remained. "My kids?" she said. "No. They're with their father for the holiday. Why do you ask?"

When Kristin dropped her cup into the bin, her hand was shaking. She realized she couldn't conceal it, so she didn't bother trying.

erlend withdrew his arm. *He said nothing, and so Kristin walked quietly away and climbed into bed. Her heart thudded hollowly and hard against her ribs. Now and then she cast a glance at her husband. He had turned his back to her, slowly taking off one garment after the other. Then he came over and lay down.*

Kristin waited for him to speak. She waited so long that her heart seemed to stop beating and just stood still, quivering in her breast.

But Erlend didn't say a word. And he didn't take her into his arms.

At last he hesitantly placed his hand on her breast and pressed his chin against her shoulder so that the stubble of his beard prickled her skin. When he still said nothing, Kristin turned over to face the wall.

Matt laid the book on the floor next to his recliner. He'd just begun the second volume of *Kristin Lavransdatter*, which from the very start had made him edgy, possibly because of the character's first name or maybe due to its problematic title, *The Wife*.

He lifted his empty coffee cup and walked into the kitchen. Ten thirty on Thanksgiving morning, and he hadn't seen her since Tuesday. Usually, all he had to do was get through a weekend, but now he'd embarked on a stretch of six days in which he couldn't hope for anything more than a random sighting. If he'd gone to work, it might have been easier to pass the time, but Frankie always closed the deli on Thanksgiving and didn't reopen until the following Monday. He needed those days off, he said, to lie on the couch and watch football.

Matt stood the cup in the sink alongside dirty dishes from last night's dinner. The deli had stayed open until eight to fill special orders, so it was almost ten when he finally got home and made *pasta alla puttanesca,* using a recipe Carla had taught him. Though it was something he loved having at least a couple times a month, by then his appetite had deserted him.

He'd tried to read after giving up on dinner, but every few minutes he kept walking over to the window, pulling the curtain aside and peeking out. The lights in Kristin's bedroom were still on at eleven thirty, but a little before midnight the room went dark. When that happened, he turned his own light off and pressed his face against the cold pane. Then he turned the light back on, whipped out his cell and wrote text messages to both of his daughters, wishing them a happy Thanksgiving and saying he looked forward to seeing them on Saturday. In reality, he all but wished they weren't coming. After their previous visit they'd told their mom that he seemed a lot happier than he'd been in ages, that the house was clean and he'd fixed the shower faucet, and this prompted her to stun him with the first e-mail she'd sent him since marrying Nowicki. *Sounds like your life has taken a turn for the better. I can only guess what that might mean. But I'm happy for you, Matt. Clue me in when the time comes?* This weekend, he'd probably act so gloomy that Angie and Lexa would go home and tell Carla he was as miserable as ever.

He had a hard time understanding what had happened to him. During those afternoons at the bar in North Reading, when he and Kristin drank their martinis and talked, he'd sometimes felt a tightness in his chest. It wasn't pleasant, nor was it exactly unpleasant. He knew perfectly well what it meant: a new feeling existed where none had for a long time, and it needed a little space. When that opened up, and then got filled up, his chest could go back to feeling normal. If he'd been forced to bestow a name on this new sensation, it would not have been "love," though that's what he called it when he wrote Kristin that long e-mail.

The first time they went to bed together at Penny Hill's, he'd expected reticence from her, even embarrassment. Yet after drawing the curtains shut, she felt for the light switch and flipped it on. While he stood there shivering in his underwear, the sweats in a ball at his feet, she pulled her top off, reached around behind herself and unhooked her bra. It fell to the floor and then she stepped out of the pants, and to his amazement she wore nothing underneath. The whole time she held his gaze. "Well," she said, her arms at her sides, her long, slim fingers grazing her thighs, "what do you think?"

His voice failed. He knew he ought to say something, but he couldn't find any words. She turned sideways, letting him study her profile. Her breasts were still firm and full, and she had only the trace of a belly. "I'm asking," she said, "because I would guess this is the first time you've ever seen a fifty-year-old woman naked."

He stepped out of his underwear, then moved toward her and wrapped his arms around her from behind, his fingers locking just above her navel. He smelled a hint of fragrance. "I haven't made love in a long time," he said.

"I haven't either," she told him. "All I've done is have sex. But very little of it."

He'd thought that was what they were going to do that night, that two people who liked each other would share pleasure in a bed belonging to the city of Montvale. Maybe it would happen once, even twice, maybe ten times or more. As long as it was nice and they didn't get caught, what was the harm?

He flicked off the light and held her hand as they stepped toward the canopied four-poster. The coverlet was dusty—when he pulled it back, she sneezed. She crawled in first, then he lay down beside her and tugged the sheet over their shoulders. "You might think I've done this before," he said, "but I haven't."

"It's patently clear that you haven't."

She said nothing else, leaving room for the obvious question, so even though he already knew the answer, he asked it. "What about you?"

"This is the one thing I always promised myself I would never do."

"So we're both rookies. We'll probably botch it."

"I don't think so," she said, then reached between his legs and began to stroke him.

That this had happened only six weeks ago now seemed impossible. Or that he'd make it through Thanksgiving at Frankie's, then somehow survive tomorrow when almost everyone else would either be watching college football or using pepper spray on one another in the crush at Best Buy. And that on Saturday and Sunday he'd be playing father to his daughters, looking for a movie to take them to before ushering them into LA Fitness on guest passes, followed by dinner at Montvale Pizza—trying the whole time to convince them of his newfound contentment, so they wouldn't have to worry about their dad. It felt like Monday was years away, not just four days.

He washed his coffee cup and last night's dishes and read for another couple hours before going upstairs to take a shower. When he got out and dried off, wrapping the towel around his waist, he stood beside the bedroom window, pulled the curtain back a few inches and peered out.

She and her husband were on the sidewalk in front of Vico Cignetti's. Cal had a grocery sack in one hand, a guitar case in the other. She held a domed cake plate. Just as they stepped into the driveway, she looked over her shoulder toward his bedroom window, as if she knew he'd be standing there, and for an instant they gazed at each other. Then Kristin bowed her head and followed her husband inside.

VICO WAS THAT RARE MAN who looked at home in the kitchen. He wore his checkered apron with aplomb, and when she remarked on its unusual pattern—rectangles overlapping squares, eight or ten different colors bleeding into one another—he told her he owned an entire collection. "Wanna see?" he asked, then threw open a floor-to-ceiling cabinet stocked with mops and brooms, dustpans and brushes and an impressive array of cleaning solutions. Mounted at the back was an apron rack, displaying a colorful assortment: black and white, green-and-gold checks, even a frilly little thing with a blue heart sewn onto a pink-and-white-checked background. "My daughter made that one for me on my sixtieth birthday."

"Very nice," she said, though the thought of him actually wearing it was incongruous at best. It belonged on a ten-year-old girl.

She deposited her cake plate on the counter and asked if she could help.

"Sure you can," he said. "Pour yourself a glass of wine and provide scintillating company while the goons watch the Pats."

"All right, I'll be happy to."

"Try that Barbera." He gestured at an open bottle. "In the world at large, it's got a less-than-stellar rep. In my house, it's king. I started drinking it on my tenth birthday. I got up that morning, and my dad sat me down and handed me a glass. 'Vico,' he said, 'you're a man now.' I've loved it ever since."

She poured herself a glassful and took a sip. It tasted awful. "This is wonderful," she told him.

He was busy trimming Brussels sprouts. "I'm going to roast these," he told her. "See, most people don't know it, but when you boil or steam them, you lose almost all their cancer-retarding properties."

"I didn't know they had any."

"Well, most people don't. At my age, though, you learn to pay attention to anything that might prolong your time here. I don't know what comes next, but I've got a feeling finding good Barbera there might be tough."

While she sat at the kitchen table, watching him make deft slicing motions, he gave her the story of his life, all of which, he said, had been spent in Massachusetts. A graduate of North Shore State, he'd taken his first job in Gloucester, handling accounting for the Community Pier Association. "Did that till 1980 when my marriage broke up, at which point I decided I needed a change of scenery. So I moved down here and opened my own accounting firm, and it was still going strong when I retired. I sold it for a nice sum of money."

To keep up her end of the conversation, she remarked that her assistant lived in Gloucester.

"Yeah? What's her name?"

"Donna Taff."

He laid his knife down, turned around and crossed his arms. "Jesus Christ. Hard Taffy works for you?"

"Hard Taffy?"

"That's what . . . look, you probably don't want to hear this. And I probably shouldn't tell you."

"Of course you should." She figured a story was forthcoming about Donna's stern, take-charge manner.

"Well, if you insist." He refilled his wineglass and plopped down at the table, propping his chin in his hands and leaning forward conspiratorially. She saw the hearing aid stuck in his ear. "She and her husband, Charlie, used to be the biggest swingers in Gloucester."

"*My* Donna?"

He winked. "She might be yours now, but she was a community asset back then. I bet she still is."

She'd heard quite a bit of strange news over the last few days, but this was the only piece that made her need a drink. She took a big swallow of the ghastly wine, then another. And then she took another. "Donna must be sixty now," she protested, the Barbera burning her nostrils.

"I'm sixty-five. And I imagine if I saw her this minute, a couple decades would melt right away."

"So you had . . . encounters with her?"

"It was the seventies, and Gloucester's a fishing town, and in that business it's always boom or bust. You get busted, you want a little boom. Yeah, we all messed around."

"Is that why your marriage broke up?"

"You can't say why any marriage breaks up. It's a bunch of things, and then one day they all turn into one thing and you're at the end of your run. Kind of like a Broadway play."

This wasn't an easy notion for her to buy into. In her first marriage, she'd seen no evidence that anything was wrong until Philip came home and told her he was leaving. They'd had a wonderful breakfast that very morning at the local farmers' market, croissants with strawberry preserves, and her Southern gentleman stood behind her while she finished her coffee, resting his hands on her shoulders and kissing the top of her head. "You're a great lady," he'd said.

She pretended to examine the label on Vico's wine bottle. "So what did you do," she asked, "to reach the end of yours?"

"I forgot to put the seat down on the toilet."

"You can't be serious."

"It's hard for me to be serious, but it's not impossible. What happened was, it's the middle of the night, I'd had a few beers, so I go to the bathroom and do my business, then stagger back to bed. About an hour later I hear a shriek. She fell into the toilet and couldn't get out, and that was the end of that. We're still friends, though, and talk every few days."

He lifted the bottle and topped off her glass, and she took another swallow. She'd heard enough about the end of his marriage. She was afraid he'd ask if she'd been married before, and she didn't want to lie and wasn't about to tell the truth. "Why did you call Donna Hard Taffy if she was so . . ."

"Hot?"

She nodded.

Vico laughed. He had sparkling white teeth, large and well formed. "'Hot,'" he said, "doesn't mean soft. She could be pretty insistent."

"About what?"

"Everything. She had no trouble telling you what she did or didn't like. She wasn't above critiquing your performance, either." He drained his own glass, reached for the Barbera and poured himself another. "Isn't this great?" he asked.

"It is. I'm not sure I've ever had this variety before, but I like it."

"I'm not talking about the Barbera. I'm talking about talking. You and me sitting here gossiping about a woman who made guys do crazy things thirty years ago. Dave and Jimmy and Cal in there blissed out before the TV. Friends gathering to celebrate the holiday. That's what I mean. This is great. It's life. What else is there?"

She took another sip. Objectively the wine was dreadful, but right now it suited her just fine. The right wine for the moment—sharply acidic, no lulling velvet aftertaste. "You don't regret what you did with Donna?" she asked.

"Why would I?"

"You don't think maybe it helped wreck your marriage?"

"My marriage wasn't a wreck," he said quietly. "It was great till it wasn't. As for all that stuff with Donna and assorted others . . . well, I'd do it all again. Except for one thing."

"What's that?"

He spread his arms wide in what she would've taken as a gesture of defeat except that he burst out laughing. "I can't. I would if I could. But there's no way I can."

A great many facets of American life dismayed Cal Stevens. Among them, in no particular order: the willingness to accept shoddy goods and poor workmanship when better products and services were available; a preference for the most vapid pop music, played so loudly over someone else's iPod that you couldn't help but hear it, even if you hated it; the easy platitudes spewed from pulpits and swallowed whole by millions; the scarcely veiled licentiousness promoted by commercials, stupid movies and reality TV; the assumption that ours was the most dynamic country the world had ever known, that it would always be so, though at present one out of every ten people was unable to land a job flipping patties at McDonald's. Nothing, however, was as repulsive to him as football.

This, in fact, encapsulated many of the American traits he hated most. It was about getting and taking, about breaking the will of an opponent, who by virtue of wearing the wrong-color jersey could only be regarded as the enemy. Many of the players seemed to operate under the assumption that the Lord was on their side, kneeling after touchdowns to thank Him for leading them through the wilderness into the Promised Land. The game was preceded and often interrupted by crashing cymbals and blaring trumpets. On the sidelines, busty young women paraded their half-naked bodies before scores of thousands in the stadium and many millions on the couch. It was the kind of spectacle especially beloved by military leaders and corrupt businessmen like his father.

Sitting there with Dave and Jimmy, who frequently hopped up to high-five each other after yet another New England score, he kept his revulsion private, even forcing himself to grunt with feigned pleasure once or twice, though he virulently disliked Tom Brady, who reminded him of too many burnished beach boys he'd known in California. He downed a couple of beers fast, and while this produced the desired effect he couldn't help wondering if he was really glad to be where he was or if he was the sucker who'd accepted the low bid.

Around two thirty Dave's wife showed up. Her name was Gloria, and even if Dave hadn't already told him a bit about her background, Cal would've known the moment he laid eyes on her that she was Hispanic. Her short, frosty hair looked striking against her copper-colored skin.

When she said hello, he heard the Caribbean accent. "Dave tells me you're from California," she said. "Do you speak Spanish?"

"A little bit," he answered, hoping to Christ she wouldn't switch.

"My sister lives out there."

"Where?"

"Crescent City."

"Up on the north coast."

"You've been there?"

"Once or twice."

"I go out there every other year," Gloria said. "The off years, she comes here."

Dave rolled his eyes. "Seems like it's more like a couple times a month."

This didn't sound bitter, just like banter. Confirming Cal's impression, Gloria reached over and swiped playfully at her husband's head.

She hugged Jimmy and said she was glad to see him, then Dave led her into the kitchen and introduced her to Kristin. She dawdled there before returning with a glass of red wine. She and Cal discussed California for a few moments, and she asked if he thought he'd ever get used to cold weather and snow.

"Oh, I imagine I can handle it."

"My parents and I came here from Cuba when I was a teenager," she told him, "and they never did learn to cope with it. Some people are just made for sultry climates."

"What about you?"

She laughed. "I was probably made for that too."

"Have you ever gone back to Cuba?"

"No. It's not that easy. And I'm not sure I want to."

"I know what you mean."

"How could you? You live in the country you were born in."

"This country's not one country," he said. "It's several. And this certainly isn't the one I was born in."

"Okay, I understand your point. But you have the same language and, overall, the same customs. I mean, it's not like you grew up burning dolls on New Year's Eve, right?" She laughed and laid her hand on his arm. "In Cuba, we did it as a symbolic gesture to rid ourselves of everything bad that happened over the preceding year."

"I kind of like that," Cal said. "Maybe I'll buy a Barbie this year and light her up."

Vico soon announced it was time for dinner and herded them into the dining room, where Kristin was placing an oval platter of stuffing on the table. "Sit wherever you choose," he said, "but leave the seat at the far end for me. I'll be running back and forth between here and Armageddon."

"That's not why you want to sit there," Gloria told him. "You want to sit there because you're the *caudillo*."

Cal waited to see where she sat, then took the chair beside hers. He was on either his fifth or sixth beer, and his head was cloudy, but he retained the presence of mind to know what was going on, which was why he sat beside her rather than across the table, where he could see her face. She was in her midsixties and until an hour or so ago had been nothing more than a name—*my wife, Gloria*—but she reminded him intensely of someone he used to know.

Vico brought the turkey out to cheers and set it in the middle of the table—the largest bird Cal had ever seen, a twenty-one pounder, according to his neighbor, who promptly informed them that since each person was responsible for consuming precisely three and a half pounds, they'd better dig in.

"What about the bones?" Jimmy asked.

"What about 'em?"

"Don't you got to subtract the bones from the overall weight?"

Cal ate far too much. He didn't really like turkey, just as he didn't really like Thanksgiving, but he wanted to keep something in his mouth. Out of the corner of his eye, he could see Gloria employing a fair number of hand gestures when she spoke, often laying down her knife and fork. A couple times she appealed to him for confirmation—as, for instance, when she observed that Proposition 13, along with the prison guards' lobby, was destroying the state of California, forcing people like her sister, a public-school teacher, to retire early or be laid off. Each time she turned to him, he nodded and kept chewing.

Once, when he got up to get another beer, his thigh brushed hers and he mumbled, "Sorry."

"That's all right," she said. "I liked it."

He pulled a beer out of the fridge, stood it on the counter, then locked himself in the downstairs bathroom. After emptying his aching bladder, he flushed and put the top down and sat on the toilet for a few moments. He wanted to keep teaching Dave—easily the best thing, he'd decided, about this new life—but he'd have to limit his time around Gloria. If he wasn't careful, the next thing he knew he'd be suffering full-fledged flashbacks, like the ravaged men you used to see wandering the outskirts of Bakersfield in the early seventies, the ones who'd stayed too long in the Mekong Delta.

When he got back to the table, she was telling Jimmy he needed to remarry, that his clothes were always wrinkled and he was starting to lose weight. As Cal took his seat, she again touched his arm. "Don't you agree?"

"Absolutely," he said. "I think everybody needs to get married." He should've stopped there but didn't. "It's the only thing," he added, "that could've saved a wretch like me."

In the kitchen, after the dishwasher had been loaded and turned on and all that remained were the dirty pots and pans and a few leftover serving pieces, Gloria said, "I'll wash and you dry, or I'll dry and you wash. Whichever you prefer."

"I'll wash," Kristin said, pulling on a pair of yellow rubber gloves Vico had laid on the counter and getting busy with a scouring pad.

From the living room, they could hear the sound of instruments being tuned. Cal hadn't particularly wanted to bring his guitar along, but when you were at Dave's stage, he'd told her this morning, you needed to play with somebody else whenever you got a chance.

"My husband can't believe his good fortune," Gloria said as Kristin passed her a clean pot. "He says Cal's not just a great player but a great teacher too."

"Well, according to him, Dave's progressing by leaps and bounds."

"He lives with that thing in his hands now. For forty years he's said he can't carry on a conversation while watching a football game. But he can certainly watch while he plays the mandolin."

"Cal's never been able to do anything else when he plays. He usually closes his eyes."

"Maybe he's trying to see the notes."

"Seeing them wouldn't do him any good. He can't read music."

"That's amazing. So he's just a natural musician?"

"He'd object to that term."

"Why?"

"I'm not sure."

"You never asked?"

"No, I never did," Kristin said, handing her a sparkling gravy boat. "I guess I always felt like the music was just for him. He used to play once a week with a bunch of other people at a little country store—this was close to Sacramento—and they'd all smile while they played, nodding at one another like they were sending special signals or whatever, but he never did. He just sat there with his eyes shut. When it was time for him to take a solo, he seemed to sense it."

Gloria wiped the dish dry and stood it on the counter next to the pot. "How did he learn to play?"

"I'm not sure. He never told me."

"There's a lot you don't know about your husband."

The assessment was inarguable, the reasons hard to explain. For one thing, she could tell at once he was a private person, that he wouldn't willingly surrender large chunks of information about himself or his past; for another, she was afraid to learn too much. The more you thought you knew, the worse it might hurt if it proved untrue.

"I guess that's right," she told Gloria. "Maybe I'm short on curiosity."

"Well, curiosity can be good, or it can be bad. There's no such thing as a standard marriage. What works for one doesn't work for another."

"It looks as if yours works well for you."

"More or less."

"But not completely?"

Gloria laughed. "I live in Cedar Park, Massachusetts. Not in heaven."

"Was your marriage ever in trouble?"

"Maybe once. But that was a long time ago."

"What made it last?"

"It wasn't just love. I could easily love somebody and still leave him. People do that all the time. It was mostly that I'd gotten so used to having him around. And honestly? He's a really great guy. He doted on our kids, he still dotes on me and we never have to call a plumber. He can work miracles with toilets and garbage disposals."

"Cal can do pretty much anything around a house, including building one from the ground up."

"It looks to me like you've got a great situation. A man that can take care of a house, serenade you on the guitar and who's madly in love with you."

The statement shocked her so badly she couldn't disguise her surprise. "What makes you say that?"

Gloria was wiping down the huge turkey platter. "I have eyes," she said. "And since I'm sixty-three, I usually know what I'm looking at. Don't you?"

"I'm not sure."

"Well, trust me then, because I am. And you know what? Good men don't come along all that often. When you've got one, it's best to keep him close by. There are too many women looking for something they can't find."

They finished the dishes, leaving all of them neatly stacked on the counter, then poured themselves two more glasses of wine and went into the living room.

Another ballgame was on, but Vico had turned the sound off so Dave and Cal could play. Kristin knew most of the tunes, though not always by name. They slowed them down to a crawl, so Dave wouldn't be forced into making mistakes. Every now and then Cal voiced encouragement. "That's it, go on and reach for that D, you can hit it." Then Dave laid the mandolin on the rug, and while Cal played chords and runs on the guitar the retired policeman sang "I Saw the Light." He had a pretty voice, high and clear, if a little too nasal for her taste.

She sat there and listened for a few more minutes and decided not to drink the wine in her glass. She'd already had too much. Back in the kitchen, she'd come close to telling the wife of her husband's new friend that while she didn't know he was in love with her, she knew she wasn't in love with him and that her marriage might be about to end. And that would've been cowardly. At least Philip had the decency to tell her to her face.

It was after seven, and they'd been gone several hours, so she could easily say she needed to look in on Suzy. "I'm going to check on the dog," she said. "I'll be back in a little while."

"Why don't you bring one of the big guy's mandolins?" Dave asked. "I'd love to hear him bear down on that F-5."

She glanced at Cal. "Want me to?"

"Might as well," he said without looking at her. "It's in the gray fiberglass case."

Outside, she checked to see if Matt's car was in the driveway, but it wasn't. Probably still at his boss's place. She unlocked her door and, as she'd suspected, Suzy dashed down the hallway and into the kitchen, where she stood panting at the back door. When Kristin opened it, she bounded down the steps into a distant corner.

The night was clear and cold. She'd left her coat over at Vico's, so she pulled her wrap around her shoulders, waiting patiently on the steps. Lately, she'd noticed that Suzy was having trouble negotiating stairs, and if winter was as harsh as the forecasters were predicting she'd have a rough time. She'd never even seen snow before, and it was hard to imagine how she'd handle icy steps and the salt on the streets and sidewalks.

Kristin let her back inside and then picked up her cell, which had been lying on the windowsill, and without pondering she called Matt, entered in her list of contacts as *S. Connulty.* She didn't know what to say if he answered, and for that reason she mostly hoped he wouldn't. She thought she might tell him she couldn't do this anymore. If he asked why, she thought she'd serve up a single word in reply: *Guilt.* He probably wouldn't ask, though. He'd probably try to talk her out of making any decision until they could see each other, and most likely she'd agree. And then the decision wouldn't get made.

She was relieved when the call went to voice mail. "I hope you're having a nice time at your boss's," she said. "I came home to let Suzy out, and now I have to go back. I couldn't risk writing to you about it last night, but I spoke yesterday to one of my plagiarists and things are even more complicated than I thought. I believe I'm going to have to try to help her. I wish we could talk over the weekend, but I know you'll be with your daughters. . . . Well, have a good time, okay?" Before ending the call she added, "By the way, Matt . . . I love you."

She was standing in front of the kitchen window when she said it, her eyes trained on the China Bear saltshaker she'd purchased at a Chapel Hill flea market twenty-five years ago. It always sat on the windowsill, as amusement for when she was washing dishes. If the saltshaker hadn't been there, she might have looked out the window, and if she had she couldn't have failed to see her husband standing at the sink in Vico's kitchen, looking right at her.

cal drove into downtown montvale the following Monday and bought several cans of paint. When he got back home, he pulled most of the living room furniture into the dining room, spread an old speckled tarp on the floor and went to work priming the walls. He meant to have the ground floor looking good before Christmas. He had half a mind to buy a tree this year, though he'd resented having to in California. They'd only done it because she always gave an end-of-semester party for other administrators, and while none of them, according to her, was the least bit religious, they would've considered it odd if she didn't have a Christmas tree. Even the Jewish provost had one.

Why Cal wanted a tree this year was a mystery to him, and maybe it was nothing more than living in a place with wintery weather. In the valley you could swim on Christmas Day if you wanted to, and most years he did, since he'd usually drunk far too much the night before, and the water in the pool was always bracing.

He worked through the day, stopping only to eat lunch and play the mandolin for a little while. In the afternoon, he went though his CDs and found *David Grisman's Acoustic Christmas,* set the Bose to repeat and listened to the disc all the way through three or four times. When he'd finished priming the walls and taken a shower, he pulled out one of the Martins and tried playing "Auld Lang Syne," doing his best to replicate Mike Marshall's cross-picked guitar break. Easier said than done. But he thought Dave would probably enjoy learning to play a holiday tune on the mandolin, and it would be nice to accompany him on guitar.

He drank a couple of beers, popped a slab of Trader Joe's frozen lasagna in the microwave and ate it with a little salad. After that, he washed the dishes and looked at the clock. Seven forty. He let Suzy out for a few minutes, then called her back inside, put on a heavy jacket and a pair of gloves and a wool cap and left the house.

In the days when he was working with his late friend Ernesto at the construction company in Modesto, he'd seen guys overlook all kinds of problems. A tile man would lay a crooked row in the shower of somebody's two-million-dollar home, then walk off and leave it. A carpenter would sister-up a floor joist with the nails on the wrong side. They simply didn't want to see those flaws and hoped no one else would either, but sooner or later someone always did.

His wife had been walking home from the train station late at night, even though it was already cold out, and if she wanted him to come get her—to drive up to Bradbury or down East Border to the station—all she had to do was ask. He didn't suggest it because from the outset their marriage had been based on the assumption that neither of them would intrude on the other's privacy. There were boundaries, and they respected them. If she came home late, she came home late. If she wanted to walk, she walked. If he'd changed his last name, well, he'd changed his last name. If he wanted to stay up all night and sleep in a different room, he did. That they retained some rights for themselves didn't mean they couldn't trust each other. As the last year had proven, there wasn't much in the world you could bank on, but he'd always banked on that.

The other night, when he stood in Vico's kitchen drinking a glass of water and saw her mouthing those unmistakable words, he knew there was something he couldn't overlook much longer. What he didn't know, and was scared to imagine, was what he'd do when forced to place a label on it.

The Cedar Park station had just two sets of tracks, each with a covered platform and three or four benches. There was also a small parking lot that could accommodate forty or fifty vehicles. Most of the spaces were unoccupied when he got there. He took a seat on the southbound side, choosing a bench at the north end of the platform. He could stay out of the light there while keeping an eye on both the platform and the lot.

Around eight thirty it started to rain, and the night felt even colder. A southbound train should be arriving at eight fifty-three; that was the one she usually took, assuming she'd been telling him the truth. He hoped she was on it now. Then he could stop thinking about whatever was wrong until at least this time tomorrow.

The train pulled in, only about two minutes late, rainwater streaming off the cars. As they passed, he watched the windows but didn't see her. The train was nearly empty anyway. How many people would be riding toward Boston at this time of night? Almost everyone would be going in the opposite direction, heading home after working late in the city.

The conductor stepped down and scanned the platform, his gaze briefly meeting Cal's. No one else got off. Eventually, he waved toward the front of the train and climbed aboard, and a moment later the undercarriage creaked into motion.

Cal continued to sit there. A northbound train pulled in a few minutes later, and ten or twelve people got off. The ones who didn't immediately find their cars in the lot opened their umbrellas and slogged away on foot.

About nine fifteen a car turned in, either a Honda or a Toyota. The driver headed for the end of the lot, not far from where Cal was sitting, finally turning into an open space. When he saw the dented rear bumper, Cal recognized the car. He watched as two heads came together in the front seat for a long kiss. And when the passenger door opened, his wife climbed out under her umbrella.

the next morning the rain turned to snow, the flakes big amorphous butterflies that melted the instant they fluttered to earth. After taking a peek out, Matt padded downstairs in his bathrobe and slippers, turned the heat up and put on a pot of coffee. Then he unlocked the front door and stepped onto the porch to pick up the *Globe*. He thought he'd spend half an hour with the paper, read a couple more chapters of *Kristin Lavransdatter*, then devote a few minutes to the little exercise he'd begun on Sunday night after Nowicki drove away with the girls. It probably wouldn't amount to much, but you never knew. Nobody, he'd decided, could deny you the right to hope except yourself.

The paper lay on the top step, rolled up in a yellow plastic bag, and he was just pulling it out when he realized that something in his immediate environment wasn't quite right. He stood there for a moment trying to figure out what had changed. Then it hit him. The view across his driveway to the next-door neighbor's house was unobstructed.

He dropped the paper and bounded down the steps, intending to make sure that in his brandy-addled state last night, he hadn't driven in farther than usual. His haste might have accounted for what happened next: his left foot slid out from under him, and he sprawled onto the walkway, clipping the back of his head on the bottom step.

Stunned, he lay there for a moment before it dawned on him that he had nothing on beneath his bathrobe, so he pulled it closed and struggled upright.

He hobbled across the mushy yard, the slush seeping into his slippers. The driveway, as he'd feared, was empty. Had he left the car unlocked? Maybe so, but nobody ever stole anything on Essex Street. As far as he knew, he was the only thief who'd ever lived here, and he'd committed his crimes elsewhere.

Frankie sent Dushay to pick him up, and on the way to work Matt got a primer on hot-wiring a car. "In some ways it used to be easier," Dushay said. "In others it was harder. There's always trade-offs. See, if the car was made before '86, you could do everything that needed doing through the engine bay. You had a carburetor, one ignition coil, a distributor. Piece of cake, right? Yeah, as long as you knew what you were up to. But what if you didn't? Where'd you turn for instruction? I mean, you can't walk into the station and say, 'Excuse me, Sergeant, I'm an aspiring car thief, and I wondered if you could tell me how the people you've apprehended went about their business.'

"But these days, virtually every vehicle uses electronic chips, transponder verification, real sophisticated technology. But the good news—if you're a car thief, anyways—is you can find fucking *training* videos online. The shit's on YouTube. Can you believe that?"

Matt wasn't in the mood for Dushay's wit and wisdom. When he'd checked his cell, there was a message from Kristin, left around seven thirty, with train-type noises in the background. "Since your car's gone," she said, "I thought you must've driven out for breakfast or something." He heard her take a couple of deep breaths, like she was on the verge of hyperventilating. "Listen, Matt, Cal's acting strange. He was gone last night when I got home, and when he came back he was soaked to the bone and barely spoke to me. He left again sometime later, and when I got up this morning he was sitting on the couch drinking whiskey from a coffee cup. The place is a mess—paint cans everywhere, some of the furniture in the wrong room. Please call me as soon as you can. It's probably nothing, he's always been moody and has trouble sleeping, and he often starts jobs and quits for a while. But I don't know. . . . I'm just a little unnerved." He'd already tried her twice unsuccessfully. The last time he left a message begging her to phone him back soon.

The lunch queue was already forming when they got to Zizza's, so they both tied their aprons on and went to work. Matt set his cell to vibrate. If he received a call, he was going to pretend it was the cops, step into the back room and take it. The stolen car didn't worry him nearly as much as the message from Kristin. The automobile was insured. The relationship wasn't.

She didn't phone him until close to two that afternoon, and by then he really had gotten a call from the cops telling him the car had been found half submerged in Pleasant Pond. Whoever stole it drove it through the parking lot at Cellucci's Funeral Home, down the bank and into the water. It had been towed to a salvage yard in Wakefield. His insurance agent warned it might be totaled.

When she called he'd just begun serving a customer, so he motioned for Dushay to help and hurried into the back room. "Hey," he said.

"Hi, Matt." She sounded shaky. Not a good sign.

"What's the matter?"

"Where were you this morning?"

The accusatory note was impossible to miss. To his mind, that *was* a good sign, proof she'd staked her claim. "I was at home."

"But your car was gone."

"It got stolen."

"You're joking."

"I wish. It's been found, though. Somebody ran it into Pleasant Pond."

"What time?"

"I don't know. I was probably asleep."

"Did they catch whoever did it?"

"No, and they're not going to try. The cop I spoke to said that unless they find a body inside or a good-sized stash, they don't even bother to check for fingerprints."

"I wonder if Cal didn't steal it," she said.

That was a possibility he hadn't considered. He figured if her husband ever found out about them, he'd beat him to death and be done with it. Or he'd pack up and disappear. Kristin wouldn't be the one who left the marriage. That was just a fact, and facts had to be accepted. "I assumed it was just some kids," he told her.

"Why would a kid steal your car in the middle of the night and drive it into a pond?"

"Why would a fifty-year-old man?"

"Because if you don't have a car, you and I can't do what we do. Can we?"

He'd already thought about that. "I'm going to rent one. My boss'll take me to pick it up as soon as we close."

"Matt," she said. Nothing more.

Here it comes, he thought, and the truth announced itself in his knees. Just at that moment Frankie stepped into the back room and whispered, "Cops?"

Matt nodded.

"They catch the thief?"

He shook his head.

Frankie studied him for a moment, as if he were considering saying something else. Finally, he left.

"Yes?" Matt said.

"I think we need to be careful."

He went over and stood beside the big reach-in freezer that hadn't worked for twenty years, turning his back to the room so that neither Frankie nor Dushay could see his face if they came in unannounced. "I thought we were being careful."

"If we were, we never would've done what we did."

At Tufts, he'd taken only one creative writing class, because criticism always seemed to rob him of whatever determination he'd mustered. But he recalled that the novelist who taught the course said tense is much more than a time marker; it's a metaphysical signpost that tells the reader if he's in the Land of Is or the Land of Was.

"Are we in the Land of Was?" he asked her now.

"Are we where?"

"Are we in the Land of Was?"

"Oz?" she said.

He saw himself then as he would have looked to anyone who stepped into the room: he'd been sent to stand in the corner, punished for unruly behavior, like a schoolboy who'd gotten caught scrawling on the walls of bathroom stalls or sticking gum on the seat of someone else's desk. He'd been bad. If this were happening to someone else, he would have found it funny. "Yes," he said, "Oz."

"I hope not," she said.

They agreed to hold off meeting for a couple of days, during which time she'd keep an eye on Cal to see if his behavior changed, though where a change in his behavior might lead went unaddressed. He knew she had plenty on her mind. She was planning to see the provost the following day about those plagiarism charges.

He'd arranged to pick up a rental at the Enterprise office in Reading, but he'd run off this morning without his wallet. So after they cleaned up at the deli, Frankie drove him home to get it. As they pulled out he asked if he had any idea who'd stolen his car.

"I'm sure it was kids," Matt said. "We used to do shit, remember?"

"I don't remember us doing any shit like that."

"Well, we broke into Penny Hill's and drank beer and smoked weed."

"We didn't break in. You had that key."

"Yeah, but I stole it."

"That's right. At one time, you saw no problem with certain types of crime. I forgot."

If you'd known Frankie as long as Matt had, you could always tell when he adopted the judicial mode, the right side of his mouth curling up in a sneer as it was doing now. "True," he said. "But that was a while back."

"What about these days? You got a big problem with theft?"

"I don't like having my car swiped."

"What about other forms of larceny?"

The conversation was causing Matt discomfort. Had Dushay ripped off the cash register? And had he, Matt, fallen under suspicion instead? That would make sense, he guessed. Except that it didn't. "What are you getting at?" he asked.

His old friend shook his head. "MD, MD."

"Frankie Z, Frankie Z. You're about to piss me off. If you got something to say, why not say it?"

"All right," Frankie said, thumping the steering wheel with his finger. "The other day, Andrea goes into the hardware to stock up on ice melt and your ex is all aflutter wanting to know if I've said anything about you having a new woman in your life. Says the girls are convinced you've got one, which jibes with what she heard from a friend, who told her she'd seen you having drinks with a blonde at that place up in North Reading that used to be Mister Mike's. And that got me to thinking. I realized you've had a bounce in your step lately, MD. A bounce in your step, and a smile on your face, and you get a shitload of text messages and voice mails at work.

"And all of that points in one direction: feminine companionship. So I asked myself what type of female could come into

MD's life that he wouldn't want to tell his buddy about. Want to know what conclusion I reached?" he asked, turning into Matt's empty driveway.

One of the saddest things that could happen to you, it had always seemed to him, was being questioned about something good in your life when you knew, or at least suspected, it was already over. When he was still at the bookstore, he'd made the mistake of telling a few writers that he was working on a novel himself, so the next time they came to do a reading and he took them out to dinner, the kindest among them made a point of asking how his own work was coming. He'd lied to Richard Russo, Andre Dubus III, Tom Perrotta—he couldn't even recall how many others. He pretended the manuscript kept growing and growing, that he had a big unwieldy mess on his hands. They must have known he wasn't telling the truth, and when they heard he'd been robbing the store they probably weren't that surprised. "Okay," he said. "Go ahead and tell me what conclusion you reached."

Frankie put the car in park and cut the engine. "I didn't reach one."

"Sure you did."

"No, I didn't. I didn't reach one when I heard about the bookstore business, either. You want to know why?"

As if on cue, Cal Stevens appeared in the sideview mirror. The dog was plodding along with him. He stopped and stared at the car, and his eyes had that hollowed-out look. Matt waited to see if he would drop the leash and make a move. If he did, Matt decided, he wouldn't resist. Whatever was going to happen could happen. He just hoped Frankie would have the good sense to stay out of it, to run around the corner of the house, whip out his cell and call the cops.

That, of course, was the exact opposite of what would have occurred if Cal had stepped over to the car, jerked open the passenger-side door and begun pummeling Matt. Frankie would've come to his aid, high blood pressure and all, and then he would've been beaten to a pulp as well. But Cal didn't advance on the car, just turned his gaze back to the sidewalk ahead, and he and the dog walked on.

Frankie hadn't even noticed his presence. "I didn't reach any conclusion," he said, "because I don't believe anything I hear about you till you're the one I hear it from. There's a word for somebody who takes that kind of position. You know what it is?"

Before they went inside, Matt would sit there in the car and spill the whole story, knowing that *who, what, when* and *where* could only go so far. It wouldn't explain how he'd felt when he first held her on her basement stairs, when he saw the slump in her shoulders on the platform in Andover, when she stood in the garden outside Penny Hill's house that cold October night and wrapped herself in her own embrace. *Who, what, when* and *where* couldn't help but sound sordid. But that wouldn't matter, either to him or to Frankie.

"The word for somebody who takes that kind of position," Frankie said, "is 'friend.' It's a word everybody knows. But not everybody knows what it means."

While Matt went upstairs to get his wallet, Frankie took a leak in the downstairs bathroom. He hadn't been inside the house for a good while, but at one time he'd known it as well as his own, having spent many nights in Matt's bedroom, the two of them haggling over baseball cards or playing video games. Every now and then Matt would get going on something he'd just read, trying to interest Frankie, but that was a nonstarter. He couldn't even get him hooked on a sports book like *Late Innings.*

It wasn't that Frankie couldn't read, as some of his teachers thought. It was just simply that he didn't want to. There were stories in people's backyards and bedrooms, in alleys and under bridges, in ball parks and coliseums, in the brush-and-broom shop at Walpole, on the loading dock at Boston Sand and Gravel, even in the lunch queue at Zizza's Deli. He'd rather live his own story or help others live theirs than waste time reading one.

Day-to-day living didn't excite Matt enough, though, and never had. He'd let his nose ruin his own life, and now it looked like his prick would ruin somebody else's. Sometimes it was hard to keep loving him. But for Frankie, quitting would have been even harder.

He flushed the toilet, washed his hands, then stepped out of the bathroom. Matt hadn't come down yet, and Frankie could hear him upstairs talking to somebody. "MD," he hollered, "you on the phone with your married girlfriend?"

"Shut up! I'm speaking to somebody at the salvage yard."

"No prob. Just checking."

While he waited, he wandered into the little room off the hallway where Matt's mother used to read and listen to awful music—Beethoven, Mozart, shit like that—and write reports for the *Montvale Sun* detailing the activities of her women's club. The desk she'd used was still there, and it had Matt's laptop on it along with a printer and a small stack of pages lying next to the Dell. Idly, he glanced at the one on top.

He met her in the Boston Common on a September afternoon. It was just past four, and he'd locked the door at his bookstore for the last time. The shelves had been removed hours earlier, sold to a used-furniture outlet in Malden. The books had been gone for almost a week. A number were already for sale at the Brattle Book Shop, just a few blocks away. He'd taken a couple hundred home. He'd never had many books in his apartment, since it seemed unnecessary. Mostly what he did at work all day, especially the last few years, as fewer and fewer customers walked through the door, was read. At home he mostly drank. His wife had left him a while back and taken his daughters, and they were all living with another man.

On an ordinary day, he might not have noticed her sitting there on a bench near the Frog Pond. When he walked by she was blowing her nose. An open paperback lay in her lap, and the cover looked familiar. Since the book was upside down, he had to turn his head sideways.

Embers, *by Sándor Márai.*

Her blond hair was short and thin, and she wore business attire. Someone who worked in finance, he figured. The financial types liked to lounge in the Common or the Public Garden and use their BlackBerrys to plan ruin for everyone else. You wouldn't expect to see them reading a book like that.

His scrutiny didn't escape her notice. "Have you read it?" she asked. "Or only heard about it?"

Frankie stood there for a moment, then sadly shook his head. He wouldn't have turned to the next page if you paid him.

on the day before thanksgiving, when Kristin had sat down with Gwendolyn Conley in the booth in Whole Foods, she knew she was making a mistake. It wasn't the place to have the conversation, especially with the holiday coming, but it was where they'd run into each other. "Gwendolyn," she'd begun.

"Actually," Conley said, "I prefer to be called Gwen."

"Gwen," she said, "fine. I need to talk to you about the article you published last year."

"What about it?"

She didn't even try to strike the proper tone. "What in the name of God were you thinking?" she asked. "The article's full of passages stolen from other writers. Did you assume no one would notice?"

Right there in Whole Foods, she saw the life drain out of the younger woman. Her stomach growled so loudly she clamped her hand over her belly, as if fierce pressure would suppress the rumbling. "I don't understand how that could've happened. I did the research. I gave it to . . ."

"You gave it to whom?" Kristin asked, though she already knew the answer. What had happened instantly became clear to her.

Conley swallowed hard while continuing to press on her stomach. "Would you like some of my coffee?"

"No, thank you. I've already had too much. You gave your research, I'm guessing, to Robert Dilson-Alvarez, and he promised to shape it into a publishable article. Am I right about that?"

The younger woman stood up. Kristin thought she was going to leave, and if that had happened she would have been relieved. Instead, Conley stepped over to the trash receptacle and dropped her paper cup inside. When she sat back down, she said, "Look, I'm not the greatest teacher in the world, but I'm a good researcher. I work hard. It's just that I can't write very well. I'm struggling to raise my kids without a partner, I can't afford to lose my job, and Robert's a really fine writer. So yes, I gave it to him. I suggested we put both of our names on it, but he said the administration's trying to make it as hard to get tenure as they possibly can and probably would insist the article didn't count unless it was single-authored. So that's how we left it. Maybe it was wrong, but I *did* the research."

"Did you then read the article?"

"Of course."

"And you didn't realize some of the passages were lifted directly, without attribution?"

"I remember thinking that a couple things sounded familiar, but Robert's usually meticulous in everything he does, so I didn't question him. I'm sure that for whatever reason he just was in a hurry and omitted a quotation mark or two. It happens. You know that as well as I do. Or at least I assume you do, since you used to do research yourself."

"Yes, I did. I was never very good at it, though, and I think you're mistaken about how good Robert is."

"He's good enough to publish a book."

"So he didn't tell you that he plagiarized his book too, as well as at least one of his published articles?"

The silence that followed might have lasted for only thirty or forty seconds, but to Kristin it seemed much longer. It seemed about as long as her own silence after Philip informed her he'd accepted a position at Ann Arbor and would be leaving with his thesis student at the end of the semester. It was the kind of silence that lingers long after words break it. "You and Robert are lovers, aren't you, Gwen?" she asked.

"We were."

"But not any longer?"

"I told him I couldn't keep doing that to Krisztina."

"Krisztina?"

"Robert's wife. She's Hungarian. She used to be my best friend." She ran her tongue over her bottom lip. "Obviously, I don't even know how to be my own friend."

Conley was slightly built. Her shoulder-length hair had a few streaks of gray, and she wasn't wearing any makeup. Despite being dressed in a nice skirt and blouse, she had the look of a woman who'd been discarded. And it was this, rather than the chill Kristin had felt upon hearing the name of Dilson-Alvarez's wife, that made her move over to take a seat beside Conley and put an arm around her shoulders. "Gwen," she said, "let's try to figure out what to do next."

A week later, the day after Matt's car got stolen, she and Donna were walking across the quad to a meeting in the office of Norm Vance, the dean of liberal arts. It was snowing heavily this morning—three or four inches were on the ground when she woke, probably five or six now—and she could already see that she needed a better pair of boots. At one time in her life snow was hardly unusual, but her years in California had left her ill-equipped to deal with it. "You probably don't mind the snow, do you?" she asked Donna.

"I certainly don't love it."

She glanced at her assistant's face and saw the special frown reserved for encounters with senior administrators, whom she liked even less than the faculty.

Several times over the last few days, Kristin had wondered how Donna would react if she casually mentioned that on the holiday she'd met a neighbor named Vico who used to live in Gloucester. She never would've done so, because acting on this prurient interest would violate the other woman's privacy. So she almost dropped her briefcase when Donna said, "I got a call Monday from Vic Cignetti. I understand he talked turkey at Thanksgiving."

"Oh."

"Oh? Is that all you can say?"

"I don't know what else to say. I'm a little embarrassed, I guess."

"For yourself? Or for me?"

"For both of us."

"Well, don't be. All right? That's why I brought it up. He told me what he'd done, then started to apologize, worried that he'd hurt my career or whatever, but I cut him off. 'First of all,' I said, 'what career? I'm a secretary. I'll never be anything but a secretary, and before long I'll retire and quit being even that. Second,' I said, 'it will just make me more interesting to my boss. She'll see me as something other than a dried-up old witch.'"

"I don't see you as a witch, Donna."

"You just see me as dried up."

"Not that, either."

"Well, I am. More or less." She laughed. "Though every now and then there'll be a little shower."

They were both still chuckling when they walked into Norm Vance's office, where Joanne Bedard glared at them as if they were giggling at a funeral.

"The reason I asked for this meeting," Kristin began as the four of them sat around the conference table, "is that a couple of weeks ago one of the department chairs told me about an envelope that showed up in his mailbox. It contained photocopies of two articles written by professors in his department. It also contained photocopies of several pages from articles published by other authors, and these had a number of highlighted passages that were incorporated word for word in the articles supposedly written by his faculty members. The passages were used without attribution." She nodded at Donna. "Could you give the dean and the provost the packets we prepared?"

Donna set a manila envelope in front of each of them, but neither administrator touched the material. The dean was watching the provost, to see what she would do, and she was looking at the envelope as if it were filled with anthrax.

Finally, Bedard looked up at Kristin. "This is coming from the history department, isn't it?"

"Yes."

"That's a horrible department," she said, turning to the dean. "Wouldn't you say that's the least accomplished, most troublesome faculty in your entire college?"

As if she'd just slipped a quarter in him and pulled a lever, Vance said, "I'm sorry to say that I'm in total agreement."

"They're mean-spirited and jealous, and this isn't the first time someone in that department's tried to slander a colleague. People over there have sent hate mail to one another, left threatening messages on answering machines, you name it. They're just a bunch of malcontents." She shoved the manila envelope across the table at Donna.

Donna didn't hesitate and just pushed it right back, stunning Kristin and the dean as badly as Bedard. "You'd better take a look inside," she said. "You're also dealing with a plagiarized book, and there's a statement in there from a publisher to that effect."

If the provost could've acted, her broad, peasant features would have rendered her a perfect political commissar in any number of films about the old Soviet Bloc. With undisguised spite she gazed over her granny lenses and said, "We don't need you at this meeting. I don't know why Dr. Stevens thought it was appropriate to include you."

Kristin had wanted her here because, based on what the history chair had said, Joanne Bedard was likely to dismiss any charges she brought. She wanted a witness, and Donna had seen more than enough. "If you wouldn't mind," Kristin told her, "go on back to the office and finish that spreadsheet we were working on. I'll see you in a little while."

"Perfect," Donna said, then stood up and briefly touched Kristin on the shoulder. When she left, the door closed emphatically.

For a while, no one spoke. Then the provost said, "All right. I'll take a look at what's in here. And if it's not exactly as you say, I'm heading straight to President Randall's office, and anybody who took part in this inquisition, yourself included, will pay a bitter price. People in that department have been jealous of Robert Dilson-Alvarez since the day he got here. They don't have his degrees, they don't have his intelligence, they don't have his charisma."

She was still undoing the clasp when Kristin asked, "What makes you so sure this concerns Dilson-Alvarez? I never mentioned his name."

Bedard didn't answer, just ripped open the envelope. Noticing that the other person at the table still hadn't touched his, she snapped, "Open that. You're the dean, after all."

Kristin sat there with her arms crossed as they paged through the evidence. Outside, the snow was coming down even harder, swirling in the wind. The forecast was for between twelve and eighteen inches. It would be a great night to sit in front of a fire with Matt and drink a bottle of wine, but that wasn't going to happen. She would ask Cal to build a fire, wanting to sit down beside him and ask why he'd suddenly grown so silent. She had files on Dilson-Alvarez and Conley, and she'd begun to suspect Cal had one on her. She might as well find out how much of the truth it contained.

After the provost spent four or five minutes looking through the pages, her hand began to pull at a few locks of hair in her pageboy. The dean was bald, so all he could do was probe his G. Gordon Liddy mustache with his index finger. Neither of them said a word. Once or twice Kristin saw him glancing at Bedard, as if he hoped she would think of some means of making this all go away.

The last two items were Blatchford's e-mailed statement and a letter from Kristin that provided an account of her conversation with Gwendolyn Conley, noting that she'd asked Dilson-Alvarez to list himself as coauthor of her article, which he'd declined to do. Kristin's letter also stated that Conley told her Dilson-Alvarez refused to return her original research materials, so under the pressure of deadlines she hadn't had the opportunity to compare the text of the article against the sources; while this didn't excuse the unattributed passages, it was in Kristin's opinion a mitigating factor. "Refused," she knew, was too strong a word. What Conley actually said was "Robert never gave it back."

At any other institution where she'd studied or worked, both faculty members would have been fired summarily. But North Shore State wasn't Case Western, UNC or the University of California. Their standards were all but nonexistent, and there were plenty of incompetent, unscrupulous people on campus, including the two sitting at the table. Gwen had two children from a broken marriage, and she'd been misled by a devious, possibly sociopathic man she was inexplicably in love with, so Kristin hoped the administration would slap her on the wrist and let her keep her job. She'd told Gwen she would do everything she could to secure that outcome. As for Dilson-Alvarez, she hoped he'd be gone before the end of the semester—ideally, in shame, though that's something he probably never felt.

Once she'd gone through all the pages, Bedard said, "Well, this doesn't look good."

"No, it doesn't," Vance agreed.

"I'm very disappointed," the provost added, "in those two."

The dean shook his head. "It's regrettable. It really and truly is. Some people . . ."

Bedard pulled her glasses off and laid them on the table. Word had recently begun to circulate that she was contemplating retirement. She'd been divorced for close to twenty years, according to Donna, and as far as anybody knew she hadn't had a single companion in all that time. Supposedly there were grandchildren, a son or daughter in another state, given the pictures propped on her desk. Maybe she'd move wherever they were. But how she would fill her days without an office to go to was hard to imagine, just as Kristin couldn't imagine how she would spend her time when she was needed nowhere at all.

"Kristin," the provost said, "I see you spoke to Professor Conley. Did you talk to Dr. Dilson-Alvarez?"

"No."

"May I ask why?"

She'd anticipated this question but not that she would answer it honestly. The words just came to her, like the notes Cal played in his solos. The difference was that she didn't have to close her eyes to make them flow. "Because," she said, "Robert Dilson-Alvarez is the kind of man who can explain almost anything away if you give him the chance, and I refuse to cooperate. He plagiarized a book and used it to get hired here. It's listed on the vita he included with his tenure application. He plagiarized parts of an article that he published in a respected journal, which is about to print a retraction that will hardly cast a positive light on this institution. Those are the facts. They're irrefutable. What happened in the writing of Gwen Conley's article is open to conjecture, I suppose, though it's clear enough to me that he hoodwinked her just as he'd hoodwinked the university. If you or the dean would like to question Dilson-Alvarez, that's up to you. My job is finished. I've done what I was supposed to."

She stood and lifted her coat and scarf off the back of the chair, picked up her briefcase and left without saying good-bye.

cal sat in a rocker on the front porch, drinking Booker's from a coffee cup and watching the snow pile up. The wind was blowing it in all over him now, salting his hair and sugaring his eyebrows, the flakes on his pants and sweater beginning to melt from his body heat. Whenever anybody drove down the street, they invariably slowed and stared. The guy driving the snowplow actually stopped and shook his head.

Matt Drinnan had left for work maybe half an hour earlier in his rental car. Before climbing into it, he'd looked down the street and seen Cal sitting there. For a second or two they stared at each other, and Cal raised his cup as if proposing a toast. His neighbor wasted no time driving off.

Cal had been thinking that in a little while, he'd grab a crowbar, go on down the street and bust into Drinnan's house through the back door. He had no idea what he'd discover. He thought maybe he'd check out his computer, if it was turned on, and see if he'd cleared the history or had any digital photos stored there. Maybe his landline, too, assuming he had one, in case anything interesting showed up on his message machine or caller ID. Prowl through his dresser, go through the clothes hamper.

Despite being covered in snow, he was warm and not just from the whiskey. The heat had been building inside him for days. He was seeing stuff he didn't need to see. The other night he saw Ernesto crumple to the hardpan, his body afire. And his father dead on the floor of his cell, the concrete washed red. Then a man stretched out in a dry creek bed with blood seeping from a wound in his head.

He had another slug of Booker's, set the cup in the snow

and rose from the rocker. He walked over, pulled open the storm door and grasped the knob on the wooden door, but it had locked behind him. "Goddamn it to fuck," he said, and reached down to move the sliding washer on the little bar to prop the storm door open. Then he backed up a couple of feet and threw his shoulder against the front door, the lock splintering through the jamb. The door swept inward and knocked over the coat rack. Suzy came running, barking and panting. When she saw it was him, she looked confused.

"Easy girl," he said, patting her head. "You know I'd never hurt you. When I leave here, I'm taking you with me." He knelt to give her a hug and let her slobber on his face, then she lumbered back into the kitchen and lay down on her pillow as if nothing had ever gone wrong. Dogs have it made.

He opened the basement door and flipped on the wall switch, went down the narrow stairs and, stepping over to his workbench, grabbed the crowbar, the tempered steel gleaming in the fluorescent light. Strictly speaking, he guessed he didn't really need it, since he'd just broken into his own house with no tools. But he wanted to use it. Certain kinds of damage only steel can do.

He was halfway up the stairs when he heard sounds from the front porch, someone stamping boots on the mat, a tentative tapping. He wouldn't have cared, but given the fucking door, any fool would've assumed somebody had broken into his house. If he stayed where he was, whoever it was—most likely Vico, the worrywart—might go call the cops. And cops were the last people he wanted to see right now.

He stepped into the hallway, forgetting he was brandishing a crowbar, covered in rapidly melting snow, reeking of whiskey and probably looking like a madman.

Dave's wife stood at the door, snowflakes speckling her red woolen cap and the shoulders of her dark down coat. Gloria looked from his face to the crowbar and the gouged door jamb. Cal watched her trying to add it all up and make it come out even.

"I didn't know your phone number," she said.

He was still standing about halfway down the hall, and she was outside on the porch. The storm door rocked in the wind, slamming against the clapboard, and snow was blowing in behind her, starting to accumulate on the floor. It occurred to him that he needed to invite her inside, so he did.

She stepped over the threshold. "I just had a doctor's appointment," she told him.

"I hope you're all right."

"It was routine. But my doctor's in Montvale, and since I was nearby I wanted to ask you a question."

"All right. Go ahead."

"Maybe we ought to close the door, though? At least one of them?"

"I'll close 'em both." He propped the crowbar against the wall and then, when he passed by, saw her glance into the living room, where the walls were still unpainted and the furniture in disarray. He slipped the washer over and pulled the storm door closed, then shut the other one.

She was standing there with her back to him, looking down the hallway into the kitchen, where Suzy was stretched out watching her. "I'd like to buy Dave a better mandolin," she said, turning toward him. "So I wanted to check with you and see if . . . Cal? Are you okay? Something's wrong, isn't it?"

He towered over her, at least a foot taller and wreathed in whiskey fumes, and any woman in her position would've had a right to be afraid. After all, she'd met him only the other day and must have learned from her husband or the Cedar Park paper, if not both, that back in October he'd beaten a guy to within an inch of his life. Yet he knew, as surely as he'd ever known anything, that if he didn't put some distance between them in the next few seconds, she would pull off her hat and gloves and drape her coat over the pineapple post and then, without any sign from him that he needed or welcomed closer contact, wrap her arms around him and invite him to tell her what was wrong. So he held his breath and waited.

"her name," Gloria told Dave that night in the alcove off their bedroom, "was Jacinta."

They were sitting on the love seat, and a candle was lit on the small wicker table in front of them. The storm had knocked the power out in their section of Cedar Park. Inside, the temperature was only about fifty degrees, but they'd wrapped themselves in wool blankets. Dave, who was sipping Irish whiskey laced with sugar and lemon juice, wore wool socks. His feet were almost always freezing, and she worried about his circulation. So far his blood pressure was no worse than borderline, but both of his brothers had already suffered strokes.

"He had a class with her his senior year in high school," she said. "It was a big school in Bakersfield, a couple thousand students. He told me that these days the student body's probably about fifty percent Hispanic, but back then it was more like twenty-five or thirty. The Latinas were excluded from student government, and they never got elected cheerleader or class favorite or most likely to succeed. He explained all of this to me patiently, as though he thought I might be disinclined to believe it. 'Imagine that,' I finally said, hoping to make him lighten up, 'Latinas being discriminated against.' He thought I was serious. 'It happened,' he tells me. 'It really did.'

"Her family had bought a house that his father's company built. He didn't know this when he first got interested in her, and she didn't know whose son he was, and by the time they figured it out neither one of them cared. When they started going together he kept it from his father, who he said was the worst man he ever knew, and he never told him anything that mattered. And she kept it from her whole family."

"Why'd she do that?" Dave asked, pulling her closer until her head rested on his left shoulder.

"Because they were having problems with their house, and it was ruining their lives. Her people were second generation. Both her parents had decent jobs that kept them out of the fields, and they'd sunk everything they'd saved into the place. I don't know what all the problems were—bad plumbing or ventilation or something like that, and the foundation was shifting and the walls were cracking. Her dad was angry all the time, and her mother was too, and apparently she blamed her husband for buying the house. They were fighting a lot, almost always about the same thing.

"Finally the girl's father went to see a lawyer, and it turned out lots of people had been filing lawsuits but nobody ever won because the company had all the judges in their pocket. So that just made her dad even angrier. And along about this time, some friend of his spotted Cal with his daughter at a pizza place and realized whose son he was.

"So after hearing this, Jacinta's father went home and confronted her, calling her a *puta,* and then his wife got into it, telling him that since he'd given away everything they had to Cal's father, maybe their daughter thought she had no choice but to try to get it back. So he slapped his wife, which he'd never done before, and then his daughter came after him with a steam iron, and when he tried to wrestle it away, the iron hit her in the face and broke her nose. The next time Cal saw her, she looked like she'd gone a couple rounds with Teofilo Stevenson."

She stopped then and asked if she could have a drop of Dave's whiskey. He expressed surprise, because she'd always claimed that even the smell of it turned her stomach, but he handed the glass to her anyway, and she took a sip. It tasted about as bad as she'd expected, maybe a little worse, but at least it warmed her up. She could see why someone might drink it, especially if he'd been sitting outside in the snow like Cal had before she came over. He'd confessed that to her, along with so much else, and then he got choked up and asked if she would hold him again, just for a moment or two. According to the digital display on the DVR, she'd held him nearly ten minutes, occasionally patting his back, and the whole time she'd felt as if she had a giant child in her arms. That was one part she'd never tell Dave. Another part was that Cal said she reminded him of Jacinta. The third thing she hoped she wouldn't have to tell him was that Cal had discovered Kristin was having an affair with a neighbor and he was afraid—that was the word he used—he might go down the street to the guy's house and do what he'd already done twice in his life, and that this time the result might be even worse.

"The girl's father managed a truck stop out on the edge of Bakersfield, not far from the new subdivision where they'd bought the house. He used to drive his pickup to work, but lately, according to the girl, he often walked. She didn't know why, and Cal didn't tell her that all the land between the subdivision and the truck stop belonged to his father and had NO TRESPASSING signs everywhere.

"Her father usually went in around seven in the morning and worked until lunch, came back home and took a nap, then went back in around four in the afternoon and stayed until nine or ten. The truck stop never closed, and his hours weren't always that regular, but he had to have his siesta and, when he got back up, immediately headed for work. That was one thing you could count on.

"This tract of land was bisected by a creek. For most of the year it was bone-dry, but in the spring runoff from the Sierras sometimes turned it into a river. Cal's father was planning to build luxury homes on either side of it, thinking people would pay premium prices for the pleasure of saying they lived on a riverbank for a few weeks of the year. You couldn't get from Jacinta's subdivision to the truck stop without crossing the creek bed. It was deep enough that until you were in it you couldn't see the bottom, which was littered with refuse. Old tires, paint cans, anything that washed down from the foothills and got stranded there when the water ran out.

"Cal said he didn't tell Jacinta what he intended to do because he knew she'd tell him not to, and he didn't really know what his intentions were anyway. Looking back, he thinks he just hoped to tell her father who he was, explain that he knew better than anybody that his father was a ruthless asshole and that the one thing he'd always promised himself was that he'd die before he turned into that kind of man himself. Then he'd ask her father not to lay a hand on his wife or daughter anymore. He'd make the request in a completely reasonable fashion, because he knew his girlfriend's father was a decent man who worked hard for his family and deserved respect. He was actually thinking he might one day be his father-in-law and the grandfather of his children.

"He said he doesn't even think he was angry when he stepped down into the creek bed to wait. He had on a pair of shorts and some hiking boots and a T-shirt, and he'd brought a canteen with him, because this was midsummer and it was over a hundred that afternoon. He got there about three and sat down near the bottom of the bank, where he spotted a couple of huge rats scurrying around looking for something to eat.

"He said he waited and waited, just sitting there in that baking heat. He was about to give up when her father appeared, a little guy in his late thirties who wore khaki workclothes and a Peterbilt cap. He had his head down, so he didn't see Cal until he stood up and said, 'Excuse me, *Señor* Garza.'

"He said he'd thought a lot about how to address him. He'd taken Spanish in junior high, but he wasn't certain about degrees of formality. He was pretty sure *Hola, Señor Garza* would be unduly informal, and he thought *Disculpame, por favor, Señor Garza* might be the wrong idiom altogether, so he decided to split the difference, using English *and* Spanish, and he's always thought that was what enraged the man—the notion that Cal might see him as half one thing, half another.

"It was clear Garza knew who he was. For one thing, there couldn't be that many six-and-half-foot teenagers walking around Bakersfield at any given time, and anyway Cal had his father's features. So his girlfriend's father looked at him for a moment, then called him a motherfucker and told him that if he ever found out he'd so much as gotten near his daughter again, he'd kill him and piss on his corpse.

"Cal said something happened inside him then. He began to think in a completely rational manner about doing irrational things. The first was to take a couple steps toward the other man. It was late afternoon and the sun was behind him, and he wanted Garza to become aware of the shadow he cast on his face. He said that was the strangest thing when he thought back on it—that he was aware he was casting a shadow. He let Garza feel it for a few seconds, then told him that if he ever laid a hand on his daughter again, he would kill him. And just to make the experience a little more humiliating, he said that after killing him he'd call his father and tell him he needed help disposing of his remains, because his dad was great when it came to getting rid of a nuisance."

Beside her, Dave shifted and took a big swallow of whiskey. "Jesus Christ," he said. "I don't know if I want to hear the rest of this."

"You probably don't. But I'm afraid you have no choice."

At first, Cal had told her, Garza didn't react. His face got a little darker, maybe, but he didn't say anything and didn't do anything, so Cal thought the encounter was over. He was already starting to despise himself for what he'd said, but at the same time he was sorry that nothing more was going to happen. He'd never had a girlfriend before, and he was really in love with Jacinta, and now here was this guy who'd hit his wife and broken his daughter's nose telling him he didn't have the right to see her. They stood there looking at each other for a moment, and then Cal shrugged and turned to climb away, and that was when Garza made his move.

Cal's knees buckled, and he pitched onto the creek bank. It was quite a kick, given the man's size. He rolled over just as his girlfriend's father brought his arm forward. Garza had found a stone as big as a shot put and intended to crush his skull. He took the blow on his left forearm. Within seconds he'd gotten out from under the other man, turned him onto his back and straddled him.

He hadn't played sports, wasn't particularly athletic and had never been in a fight. But it seemed to come naturally. To get started, he slapped Garza a few times. Slapping another man's face, he'd heard his father say, was worse than hitting him with your fists. Garza cursed him, calling him names in Spanish, some of which Cal knew and others he didn't. He began to pound away at him then, knocking a few teeth out, breaking his nose, busting his own knuckles. He didn't know how long the beating lasted, but he kept it up long after Garza had quit cussing. It was only when he saw the pink Pepto-Bismol-like froth coating his lips that he decided it was time to stop.

He lifted his girlfriend's father to his feet, whirled him around and threw him on the ground. He intended that to be his final statement—to show he could toss him aside like a piece of garbage—but Garza must have landed on a bottle or a jar, because he heard a crunching sound. When he turned him over, there was a gash in his forehead and glass shards embedded near his right eye.

The lesson to be learned from what had happened—as his father told him later on, after Cal declined to ask what it might be—was simple: if you mean to administer a beating, take care when choosing your spot.

He hadn't taken care because he didn't plan on beating the

guy up. But he had anyway, and in the aftermath he realized that his position was almost as bad as Garza's: he couldn't leave him there. He had to get him away from the creek bed for fear that if his wounds weren't treated he might die or go blind.

He'd borrowed his mom's Mercedes, and it was parked at the truck stop. He could think of only one thing to do, so he hoisted the man's body over his shoulder, Garza groaning once or twice as he stumbled across the parched ground. Fortunately, the Mercedes was in a corner of the lot, where a semi blocked it from view, and he deposited his load into the backseat.

The closest hospital was about four miles away. Originally founded by nuns in the twenties, it had recently moved north and was one of the reasons his father started building in that direction. People want to live close to medical care, he said. What Cal didn't know was that about two years ago his father had wangled an appointment to the board of trustees. That accrued to Cal's good fortune on a day when not much else had.

"He pulls up to the emergency entrance and there's a wheel-chair just sitting by the door, so he runs over, grabs it and rolls it back to the car. Garza's still lying there, his face and torso covered in blood. Cal pulls him upright and shoves him into the chair. He rolls him inside and leaves him by the admissions window, then turns and starts to leave. 'Hey,' he hears someone holler, 'wait a minute,' but he's already out the door. He jumps into his mother's car, and as he peels away he looks in the rear-view mirror and sees an orderly and a security guard run out of the emergency entrance. The orderly's mouth is moving, and the guard's writing something on a pad, so he knows they've got the number off the license plate."

She paused. During his days on the force, her husband almost never told her what had happened on his shift unless she asked, and even then she suspected she got an edited version. In thirty-five years he'd been involved in a handful of gun battles, and in one of them an officer was shot, but he didn't mention it until after she saw it on WBZ. "The reason I'm telling you all of this," she said, "is so you won't be taken by surprise if he tells you himself. The thing is, he considers you his friend. And if ever a man needed friends, this one does."

Dave sighed and shook his head. "So what happened next?" he asked. "I hope you're not going to tell me his old man had this Garza bumped off?"

"No, he didn't have him killed. He bought him." She explained that because Cal was scared and couldn't see any way around it, he went home and told his father what he'd done. His dad sat there for a minute, stone-faced, and Cal thought he was going to jump up and hit him or tell him to get out of his house and never come back. But instead he burst out laughing and slapped his knee and, for the first and only time in all their years together, enveloped his son in a bear hug. " 'Well, at least I know your mother's not a whore,' he said. 'For eighteen years I've wondered if it was really possible you sprang from my loins. Now I've got my answer.' He started making phone calls, and within a few days the whole thing was settled. Garza lost his sight in that eye and had blurred vision in the other for a long time—maybe forever, as far as Cal knows—but his hospital bills were covered, nobody filed a police report, and Jacinta's family got a new house in a better subdivision."

"What happened between him and the girl?"

"That was part of the arrangement. He had to promise not to see her again, but she didn't want anything to do with him anyway. She wrote him a letter telling him she would hate him as long as she lived, that as bad a man as his father might be, he was even worse."

"He told you all this?" Dave said. "That's amazing. I knew he was keeping some secrets, but I put him down as the kind of guy who'd take 'em with him to the grave."

They heard a rumbling noise when the furnace started up,

and through the window they saw lights flash back on in the house across the street.

Gloria was disappointed. She would've preferred the night remain dark. "He told me," she said, "because I asked him what was wrong. Apparently, nobody else ever cared enough to inquire."

kristin hadn't left work until six fifteen, by which time there were just a few flurries. The roads were mostly clear or at least passable, and the bus deposited her in Andover only a few minutes behind schedule. Still, she missed her train and had to sit on the platform and wait for the next one. Around seven thirty, the LED sign informed her that the seven thirty-five would be delayed half an hour. At eight o'clock, it said it would arrive in ten minutes, and at eight ten it said it would arrive at eight thirty-five.

She hadn't heard from Cal, so who knew what he thought she was up to. Once or twice she started to call and explain, but other, more serious explanations might need to be offered later, and she decided it was best to get through all of that at once and then see what remained of their marriage. To her surprise, she didn't hear from Matt either. She'd sent him a text around four that afternoon, but he didn't write back.

Sitting alone on the platform, hugging the down coat to her body, she recalled how her mother looked when she went home for Thanksgiving the year she met Phil. Her mother was often in her bathrobe and, in Kristin's recollections, even when she was talking on the phone to one friend or another, the hand that wasn't holding the receiver always seemed to be pulling the robe tightly to her body, as if she were freezing, though the house Kristin grew up in stayed warm no matter how cold it got outside. This was the period when her mother was reaching the decision to let it all go, to forgive both her father for his betrayal and Sarah Connulty for her part in it. In their last years, after Kristin's father died, the two women once again became inseparable. When her mother called to tell her she'd found Mrs. Connulty facedown in the snow, Kristin attempted to soothe her by remarking that it was wonderful they'd repaired their friendship. To which her mother replied, "That wasn't ever really in question." Only then did Kristin understand that her mother had to forgive her father in order to forgive her friend, for whom she must have felt a deeper, more satisfying love than she ever had for him.

By the time the train finally pulled in, it was eight forty-three. Nobody else was waiting. The other would-be passengers, a woman in her early thirties and an ill-shaven guy wearing a Bruins cap, had already given up. She called somebody to come get her, and he finally walked off into the night.

On the short ride to Cedar Park, she worried about making it up the hill into Montvale. Articles in both local papers had questioned whether enough money had been allocated for snow removal, pointing out that the *Farmers' Almanac* was predicting an especially tough winter. And according to the *Globe,* the *Almanac* almost never got it wrong. She hoped she, too, wouldn't end up half buried in white powder.

When the train reached her stop, the parking lot was almost empty, and the few cars that remained were scarcely identifiable. They looked like giant snowdrifts. Over in the corner nearest the street, one vehicle waited with its lights on, smoke billowing from its exhaust pipe. It had backed into the spot, so she couldn't tell what make or model it was but hoped that perhaps Matt was waiting for her in his rental, despite her request that he steer clear of her for at least a few days. Then she wouldn't have to walk home. And maybe, if only for a moment, they could embrace. She'd gotten scared after her meeting with Joanne Bedard and Norm Vance. By refusing to talk to Dilson-Alvarez, she'd been negligent, letting feelings and personalities influence her decision. In her job that was the cardinal sin. And if it made her feel more fully human, it also left her wondering if she hadn't just handed the provost a blank pink slip on which she could write the name Kristin Stevens.

As she neared the street and saw the familiar circle and arrow on the grille of the car belching smoke, she realized it was her own Volvo. Cal opened the door and climbed out. He was wearing a heavy flannel shirt, one with lots of padding sewn into the lining. Above his forehead, as though purposely aligned with his nose, was a ridiculous-looking streak of cream-colored paint. She didn't know it yet, but he'd spent the better part of the day painting the living room and priming the walls in the dining room and den. By the weekend the house would look like new. It would no longer seem like a set of walls they'd tried to fit themselves into because they had nowhere else to go.

"Hi," he said in the same bashful tone she'd first heard at the crossroads grocery, "could I interest you in a lift?"

There in the parking lot at the Cedar Park station, on a night when an early season storm dumped between eighteen and twenty-eight inches of heavy, wet snow over New England, at the beginning of a long hard winter that would throw every municipality in eastern Massachusetts even further into the red, her affair with Matt Drinnan came to an end. It would be a couple days before she knew it, and a couple more before she said it, and on a Saturday night in February, when Cal and Dave went to Framingham for an annual bluegrass festival honoring some long-dead friend of Dave's, she and Matt would meet for dinner, and afterward he'd suggest they visit Penny Hill Park one last time. Saying no would almost kill her. She knew that when she returned home and went into the bathroom to wash off her makeup, she'd see the face of a woman for whom life held no more surprises.

"A lift," she told her husband in front of the idling Volvo, "is exactly what I could use." He'd driven a car into a pond for her. If need be, he'd drive one off a cliff.

on the final day of exams, after most students had already left for the break, Donna stepped into Kristin's office and placed a Christmas tin on her desk. "It's just some homemade fudge," she said. "But I think it's pretty good. Charlie says so, anyway."

"Thank you. I should've brought you something, but I forgot. You'll have to forgive me."

Rather than leave, her assistant asked, "Mind if I sit down?"

She did mind, but she said of course not and gestured at a chair. Donna knew she had a meeting with the provost in half an hour, and she also knew Kristin was concerned. The university's general counsel would be there; the presence of a lawyer meant someone was in trouble, and Kristin couldn't rule out the possibility that in this case it might be her. For the first time since becoming an administrator, she'd behaved unprofessionally. She should have interviewed Dilson-Alvarez. He was a liar, certainly, but deserved the chance to lie to her.

"Your eyes are a little red," Donna observed.

She cried in the office so she wouldn't cry at home. This past Saturday, on a trip into Boston for Christmas shopping, she and Cal got off at the wrong subway stop and had to cross the Common in freezing rain to reach Newbury. She saw an elderly black man sitting under a tree, one hand holding up an umbrella with broken spokes, the other squeezing a 7-Eleven cup. Jangling the coins he'd collected, he forecast the weather. "Thirty-four degrees, ladies and gentlemen, a compact low-pressure cell tending ever eastward. Gusty winds arriving 'round about midnight as the rain is transmogrified into frozen particulates. Roads may ice up and bridges become treacherous, the power may go off and darkness descend. But everybody must remember that the spring will come again. Winter's got a shelf life just like everything else." She dropped a five into the cup and held her tears until Monday.

"I've been having some allergies," she told Donna. She opened her desk drawer, pulled out the Visine that she'd picked up yesterday at CVS and squirted a drop into each eye, then capped the small bottle and put it away.

"It's good you've got that," Donna said. "You wouldn't want the provost to think she'd gotten under your skin and made you cry."

"No, I wouldn't."

"Especially since I don't think there's anything that woman could do to make you cry."

"No, there really isn't."

"If she could, she would."

"I'm sure."

"But she can't."

"That's right."

"So it must've been something else. Because you've definitely suffered some water loss, Kristin. And I think it left through your eyes."

She'd parked on the street across from the deli one evening last week, a few minutes before it closed. Matt and the owner finally stepped out of the door together. The other man locked it, and they chatted a moment, then his boss slapped him on the back and walked away. When Matt headed toward the municipal parking lot, she put her car in gear.

He was fussing with his key ring when she pulled in behind his rental. He stopped and stood watching her, his coat collar up. She got out of the Volvo but left the motor idling. Later, when she realized she hadn't shut the car off, it bothered her. She hoped he would understand why she hadn't—that she didn't want to give herself a chance to settle in, not even in a public parking lot on a cold December evening.

She leaned against him. "Hold me for a minute," she said, and he did. "You smell like liverwurst," she told him. He didn't say a word, just clung to her, and she knew he was preparing to let her go for good. So without wasting any time, she said what she had to say, offering up all the predictable clichés: that she couldn't go on deceiving her husband any longer, that he was a good man who didn't deserve to be lied to, that the last few weeks had meant more to her than Matt would probably ever know, that he was a fine person too and she hoped he'd find the happiness he deserved with someone else. He turned loose of her then and said something that made little or no sense. "There's a lot I don't know about you," he told her. "But I'm going to figure it out. Everything you never got around to telling me? I'll be down the street imagining it. You'll see the light on in my window, and you'll know that's what I'm up to. I'll be imagining you. In fact, I've already started."

She knew Donna was trying to be her friend. Yet even in the absence of any other candidates, she couldn't share her secrets. She wasn't a storyteller and never had been. "I'm all right," she said. "It's been a year of upheaval. First I lost my job, then we had to move. It's taken some getting used to. And I feel a little handicapped because there's so much traffic here, and I can't drive very well."

Donna wasn't buying it for a minute, but she didn't dispute her right to offer it for sale. "Well, if you ever need to talk, I'm around to listen. And I keep my mouth shut."

"I know you do."

"Because let's face it," the older woman said. "Given everything I've done, a person has to."

"There's a history here," Joanne Bedard stated, tapping the stack of manila folders that lay on the table in her private conference room. "But since all three of us know what that history is, I don't think we need to delve too deeply into it, even though the people whose careers are at stake happen to be historians. We're here to bring things to a speedy conclusion, because what we have to keep in mind—first, last and always—is the good of the institution."

There were three files in the stack, each with a tab on it. The top one said *Plagiarism Investigation*. The next one said *Gwendolyn Conley*, and the one below it said *Robert Dilson-Alvarez*.

The provost turned to the school's attorney, a woman about Kristin's age with whom so far she'd had few dealings. "Could I ask you to go ahead and summarize your findings and the actions we'll be taking?"

The general counsel hadn't said more than a few sentences before Kristin reached a couple of conclusions. The first was that while she herself was not a lawyer, her demeanor, in most of the dealings she'd had with faculty down through the years, was remarkably similar to this woman's. They used the same measured tone, so that no word or phrase appeared to mean more than any other, and they were careful, when reading from prepared materials, to establish eye contact at regular intervals. The second conclusion was that the general counsel had never entertained the possibility she might one day have to worry about her own inappropriate actions. Things like that didn't happen to people like her. They happened to the less thoughtful or the impassioned, to those with an inborn penchant for shady conduct.

"None of what we've discovered about Professor Conley or Professor Dilson-Alvarez can play a role in the tenure and promotion process," the attorney said. "The material that the chair of the department brought to your attention was not in either professor's file, and therefore we can't retroactively call it to the attention of the departmental committee. And since the departmental committee didn't have access to this information, neither the school committee nor the university-wide committee can have access to it. Strictly speaking, neither Dean Vance nor Provost Bedard should know about it either, and since you brought it to their attention, both professors could accuse you of attempting to bias the administration against their candidacies. But the dean and the provost have both assured President Randall and me that they won't let it influence their decisions, no matter how they might feel personally about the faculty members in question."

She went on to explain that even though the information Kristin had collected couldn't be used to determine tenure or promotion, the university had found both professors guilty of multiple lapses in judgment. To begin with, the article submitted under Gwendolyn Conley's name should have listed Robert Dilson-Alvarez as coauthor. And both Conley and Dilson-Alvarez should have thoroughly checked their quotations. Their scholarly practices left "mush" to be desired, she said, then corrected herself—"I meant *much*"—and both of them would have to submit letters of apology to the journals that had published their work, as well as to the authors whose words, in their negligence, they had misappropriated.

The charge that Dilson-Alvarez had plagiarized his book was without merit. The book had never actually been published, so the rights of the Finnish author and his publisher had not been violated. The person who perhaps should have taken action against him—Julian Blatchford—had chosen not to, due to perfectly realistic concerns: pursuing a lawsuit would have been costly, and even if the publishing house prevailed it was unlikely to recoup its losses, because Dilson-Alvarez was not wealthy. He had, of course, listed the book on his vita when he applied for his current position. But the university's guidelines specified that only publications during the probationary period could be considered in the tenure decision. One could argue, if one wanted to, that North Shore State had not exercised due diligence when hiring Dilson-Alvarez, but any attempt to terminate him for an offense committed seven years ago would be traumatic for the institution, since he would certainly ask the faculty union to contest the effort.

"Where that leaves us," the attorney continued, "is that we sent letters to both professors, giving them three days to dispute our findings, which they chose not to do. Those letters are now part of their files. In Professor Conley's case, we noted that she failed to acknowledge her coauthor and that she also failed to acknowledge the work of other scholars in preparing her paper for publication. She's been warned that any future offenses of this nature, if they're discovered, could lead to sanctions that might include termination. The letter we've placed in Professor Dilson-Alvarez's file notes that he should have listed himself as coauthor of Conley's article, and that when preparing both that article and his own for publication, he did not adhere to the school's scholarly standards. He's been informed that he can no longer list the book 'To Shoot Down a European': Frantz Fanon's Theory of Therapeutic Violence on his vita, and it has been removed from his faculty page on the department's website. He also received a warning about future offenses, with wording similar to that in the letter we issued to Professor Conley."

She closed the folder she'd been reading from and popped the latches on her briefcase. When she opened it, Kristin saw that it contained several other files, and the tab on the top one said Kristin Stevens. "Did either of you have any questions?" she asked.

"I don't," the provost said. "What about you, Kristin?"

She understood that the general counsel was going to be excused the moment she made it plain she would not raise a fuss about the manner in which the university had chosen to deal with Conley and Dilson-Alvarez. And that if she did raise one, the attorney would stay. "No," she said, "I think you've covered it."

The lawyer gathered all her files and placed them in the briefcase. The lid came down, and the latch snapped shut. "Happy holidays," she said. "I'm off to another meeting. One of the custodians has been running a Ponzi scheme from plant ops."

When the door closed behind her, Bedard said, "She was ready to place a letter in your file too."

"I see," Kristin said. "What was that letter going to say?"

"That for whatever reason, you'd allowed your personal feelings to cloud your judgment and that this cloudiness, or whatever word she would've used, had led to the denial of due process for Robert. The language would have been mild but vaguely threatening, so if you made too much of a stink the school could distance itself from you, as well as the other two. But you know that perfectly well. You've played the game a long time, and you probably always played it well until now. I'm surprised you got emotionally involved. I was beginning to think you didn't have any emotions."

Perhaps because her build was so robust, it had been easy up until now to forget that Joanne Bedard was nearly seventy. But this morning she looked her age. Her face was drawn, her complexion pale. Though never elegantly dressed, she usually took care with her clothing, yet today she wore a pin-striped jacket that clashed with her magenta-and-white polka-dot blouse. There was a coffee stain on one of her lapels.

"It's odd that you say so," Kristin replied. "I never thought you had any either."

"Not even after you saw how I let Robert make a fool of me?"

"He strikes me as the kind of man who could make a fool out of any number of women."

"But not you."

"Not me," Kristin said. "Because I refused to talk to him. Otherwise maybe he could have."

The provost laid her hands on the table. "The thing is, Robert reminds me of my husband."

"He reminds me of my ex-husband too," Kristin said, then

immediately regretted it. The less this woman knew about her, the better.

"I didn't say ex-husband," Bedard snapped. "I said husband."

"I'm sorry. I heard you were divorced."

"You hear all kinds of things around a college campus. You hear things at the doctor's office; you hear things at the grocery; you hear them on the street. Most of them aren't true. My husband died before I ever came here. In South Dakota. He was quite a few years older. Still, he had some traits in common with Robert. He looked a good bit like him, for one thing, and he was really bright, and he knew how to talk to women. Robert has the same skill set. That's why it always puzzled me that people here disliked him so much. Of course, they saw a different person from the one who went to a great deal of trouble to cultivate me." She locked her fingers together. "I've submitted my resignation. Effective the end of the spring semester."

"I'm sorry," Kristin said.

"No, you're not. But that's all right. You know as well as I do that in a position like mine or yours, you'll never make a lot of friends around campus. People are rarely sad to see us go. Do you think there was much mourning when you left your previous school?"

"I don't think there was any at all."

"Well, that's just par for the course. The thing is, we both add up to much more than the sum of our mistakes, no matter how many we might've made. We're more than the name plates on our doors. I play the piano. Did you know that? I make my own wine. I sew. I cook. I *bake* things. I have a lot of great neighbors in Swampscott. I have friends in Minnesota where I grew up. I have friends in South Dakota. I have a lovely daughter and a wonderful son-in-law and three beautiful grandchildren in Cape Girardeau, Missouri. I'm sure that away from school you lead a full life too. Right?"

Her earlier remark about how one heard lots of things

around campus made Kristin wonder if perhaps her recent indiscretions had really gone unnoticed. The many afternoons she and Matt had stopped for martinis in North Reading, the times he'd picked her up at the Andover station or let her out in Cedar Park: who was to say that no one who worked with her had ever glimpsed her in the company of the wrong man? What if someone had hacked her e-mail and passed on certain tidbits?

On the other hand, why should it matter? Whatever Cal knew would not be acted on again. It had led to the drowning of an old car that was already headed for the junk heap. She would never tell a soul what had taken place in the dark at Penny Hill Park, and idle speculation, if it existed, would fade over time. Unless she granted herself access to her memories, it would be as if the last few months had never happened.

"My life away from school is just fine," she said.

Provost Bedard stood up and straightened her jacket. "Then we both have plenty to be grateful for," she said.

That evening she left work early, taking the bus to Andover and climbing aboard the 5:25 for the first time since September. Another snowstorm was bearing down on them, but Cal would be waiting for her at the Cedar Park station tonight and every night from now until she retired or one of them died and left the other alone.

As the train passed southward through Wilmington, North Reading and Wakefield, she remembered playing with Patty Connulty on the banks of the Susquehanna, how her Airedale George loved fetching a slobber-soaked Frisbee. She recalled the day Mrs. Connulty scraped ice off her windshield while tears froze on her cheeks, and the evening her father held her aloft and told her there were people in this world who hated family bliss, as well as how her mother clutched her robe with one hand, the phone with the other, preparing to let it all go.

She saw Philip sitting on a bench in an Ole Miss hoodie, Cal holding a dying oriole in his hand, Matt standing at the bottom of the basement stairs, looking up at her while water lapped at his boots. Surrendering to these memories, she leaned against the window and closed her eyes, her mind rich with images that burned like embers.

acknowledgments

As always, Ewa and Lena Yarbrough and Antonina Parris-Yarbrough made the writing much easier with their love and advice. My debt to them is immeasurable. I'm also grateful to my friends and colleagues at Emerson College, especially Maria Flook, Pablo Medina, Pamela Painter, Ladette Randolph, John Skoyles, John Trimbur and Jerald Walker. Sloan Harris remains the best agent any writer could ever have, and I am grateful to him and Kristyn Keene for their continued support. Thanks also to Ruthie Reisner at Knopf and to Wyatt Prunty and the rest of my colleagues at the Sewanee Writers' Conference. Lastly, very special thanks to Gary Fisketjon, my friend and editor, who continues to amaze me even after all these years.

A NOTE ABOUT THE AUTHOR

Born in Indianola, Mississippi, Steve Yarbrough is the author of five previous novels and three collections of stories. A PEN/Faulkner finalist, he has received the Mississippi Authors Award, the California Book Award, the Richard Wright Award, and an award from the Mississippi Institute of Arts and Letters. He teaches at Emerson College and lives with his wife in Stoneham, Massachusetts.

A NOTE ON THE TYPE

This book was set in Adobe Garamond. Designed for the Adobe Corporation by Robert Slimbach, the fonts are based on types first cut by Claude Garamond (c. 1480–1561). Garamond was a pupil of Geoffroy Tory and is believed to have followed the Venetian models, although he introduced a number of important differences, and it is to him that we owe the letter we now know as "old style."

Typeset by Scribe, Philadelphia, Pennsylvania
Printed and bound by RR Donnelley, Harrisonburg, Virginia
Designed by Robert C. Olsson